BILLY FIXIT

An Unlikely Friendship

Zach Sheridan

Billy Fixit An Unlikely Friendship, 1st Edition.

Rev. 12, 12-16-25

ISBN 978-1-7383943-6-4

Contents

Chapter 1: A New Road

At ten years old, you don't worry much because you haven't yet learned to think for yourself. That was the reason for my lack of interest when my father told me we were moving to the quaint, South Central Ontario town of Grand Valley. However, I suspected by his anxious tone, perhaps my own lacklustre reaction might be an underestimation of the changes about to come to our lives.

In my earlier years, we lived in the modern satellite community of Bramalea, 50 kilometres northwest from downtown Toronto. Before that, we lived in the heart of Toronto, but the inner-city constraints and, in the words of my father, *failings,* drove us to the highly touted *latest and greatest* version of suburbia, the first of its kind in Canada. However, it didn't take long for the familiar smell and feel of the city to spread outwards and begin to overtake our community in Bramalea. That led to the day my father announced we were moving.

It was a crisp October day in 1990 when we piled into the Jeep Cherokee on the Saturday of the following weekend: my father, my mother, my 13-year-old brother, Andy, and I, for what my father said would be a short trip. He must have said that for my benefit, hoping the words would keep me quiet. Unfortunately, he was wrong. With the typical impatience of a ten-year-old, I remained quiet for the first 15 minutes, but after that, I couldn't hold back my excitement any longer, blurting out, "Are we there yet!"

I asked a few more times with my mother each time calmly giving the obligatory, "soon," as the reply.

I glanced at Andy, sitting beside me and noticed he was frowning, something I didn't see him do often. I watched for a few seconds seeing the frown was persistent, and he was cracking the knuckles on his hand, a sure sign he wasn't happy. I realized he wasn't frustrated or angry at the drive; he was worried.

At such a young age, I didn't have anything to worry about. I was a *kid,* and that meant I didn't need to worry about anything because I didn't have responsibilities. My mother and father looked after my needs. They carried the responsibilities, leaving me without a care in the world, whether that be in Toronto, Bramalea or anywhere else we moved. If anything, this new country town sounded like the beginning of a great, new adventure.

For Andy, it was different. Recently, he began to shower and wash his hair every day. He worried if his clothes didn't match, and as the days came when pimples erupted on his face, he panicked, using cream to hide them just like a girl would. It reminded me it was around then when his concern for things he never used to care about began; when girls became part of his young life. As I watched him in the back of the Jeep, I figured that's what was worrying him. Those girls who he used to make fun of, who now called him on the phone or came by the house to call on him, wouldn't be around in Grand Valley.

It seemed like we had been driving through the countryside forever when we entered a town, and it was large, not quite a big city, but I still considered it a city nonetheless. I asked if this was our new home, but my father glanced in the mirror and shook his head. After ten minutes, we left Orangeville and were back in the middle of no where, continuing through the colourful countryside.

By now, my impatience was piquing, and even Andy began to fidget. Finally, a few miles later, just ahead in the distance, we spied two buildings. Once we came closer, they were revealed as a small country store with three gas pumps out front, and behind it, a farm house covered in white wood siding. The buildings alone were not important, but their location put them at a crossroads, and beside the country station was a green traffic sign. On it were the words, *Grand Valley*, with an arrow pointing north.

I leaned forward, my hands gripping the top edges of the two front bucket seats. Things didn't look much different as we passed two more old, two-story farm houses set back in fields of tilled soil, the black earth having been prepared for the next growing season. The vision would indeed have been bleak if it wasn't for the many trees growing along the farm's borders and the forests in the background, those trees holding a mix of bright fall colours: red, light green and orange. The beauty distracted me, helping me suffer through my restlessness.

It didn't take long before my father slowed the car just before the road swept left and angled downward. For a moment, I glanced at my mother as she whispered, "This is Grand Valley."

When I returned my keen gaze through the windshield, on the other side of the road in front of us, was my first recollection of Grand Valley, forever to be engrained in my memory. There stood a large chalet, reminiscent of similar ones you would see in Switzerland, set beside a mountain stream meandering through the rolling foothills at the base of a towering, snow-covered peak. The chalet was white stucco with brown trim, including intricately carved barge boards. But the most eye-catching feature was the two-sided fireplace at the corner of the house nearest the road, consisting of round stones in a myriad of colours, puzzled together from the base of the wall to a yard above the roof line.

I glanced towards Andy as I bounced on the seat cushion. "Look—an *Edelweiss house!*"

My brother just shook his head, but I was not to be deterred, insisting the description was accurate. I continued to repeat the assertion over and over in a scratchy, irritating tone, one only possible from a younger sibling. Months later, once we settled in the town and I found a few friends, I mentioned the Edelweiss house to them, and they knew exactly what I was talking about. At ten-years-old, it was always a victory when I was right. In any case, it was the first house I saw in Grand Valley, and it was a good memory, but it was not that way forever.

I recollect back to that day and my formative years that followed. Those years didn't come up often in idle conversation, but once in my early adult life, while out for a drink with my work colleagues, in a moment of awkward silence, one of them asked me, "Where are you from?"

Since I was fresh out of college, I did not find the probing question odd. I gave them the name, "Grand Valley," and thought that would be the end of it. However, the same person, seeing we were two drinks in, and we had exhausted any substantive conversation, asked a follow up. "What is your best and worst memories growing up there?"

Although my colleague's effort at a cerebral question in a second-rate bar was commendable, I thought it frivolous. This was reinforced by the blank stares from my fellow workers who had never heard of my home town. It wasn't a surprise. Even in the population at large, few had heard the town's name, but even those who had would not be able to place it on a map, and most certainly they would never have visited the rural town.

I was new to the accounting firm, and I had the sense my colleagues were looking for a tidbit they could salivate on—something with some meat on the bone. Even though they expected a juicy response, I suspect they thought my answer would be simple. But two drinks in, *simple* was not in my vocabulary. Therefore, rubbing my chin, giving them the illusion the question was a difficult, thought-provoking one, I told them, "I will start with my worst memory of Grand Valley since it readily comes to mind."

So, I began a lengthy ramble. "One day, when I was 13, we heard the *whomp, whomp,* of a helicopter's rotor blades breaking the air overhead. By then, we knew a helicopter only came close to Grand Valley when a bad car accident occurred nearby. At the top of the hill, on the south side of town, there was a small power plant with a paved parking lot large enough for the aircraft to land. Predictably, after a lengthy pause when we knew the patient was being loaded, we heard the rotors speeding up. Then, the sound drifted off into the distance as the helicopter flew south, most likely to a hospital in Toronto.

News travels fast in a small town, and such was the case the following day. We heard a small delivery truck had been travelling south up the sweeping road leading out of town. Four motorcycles were travelling north along the same curve. However, these weren't real bikers; rather, they were likely *Bay Street Bankers* who cosplayed the biker persona on weekends. Not shaving for a few days and donning knock-off black leather outfits, allowed them the stress relief they needed from their 9-to-5 jobs. No one really knew if that was the reality. Perhaps it wasn't inexperience that caused the accident; maybe they just weren't as focused as they should have been.

Ultimately, it didn't matter. For whatever reason, one of the motor cycles sideswiped the delivery truck in front of the chalet. The bike was knocked on its side, and the two riders skidded across the pavement into the low concrete barriers put in place to protect the Edelweiss house. The man lifted his visor and rose to a sitting position once he realized he was uninjured. His girlfriend, beside him on her back, also lifted herself up on her elbows. He was about to ask how she was when he saw the blood. It ran in a blotchy line from her to a point 25 metres back, in front of the chalet.

Just like that, the wonderful vision of my Edelweiss house, the first wonderful memory of my new home, turned into my worst memory. My mind's eye vision of the chalet that could have been on a Swiss picture postcard was now corrupted by the horrifying vision of a bloody stump of a foot in a black leather biker boot sitting on the white line in the middle of the road."

At that point, my overly detailed response to my friend's frivolous question had them staring at me, wide eyed, their beer glasses hanging from their fingers and their jaws hanging slack. In that instance, I taught my friends a lesson; don't ask questions you don't want the answers to.

For a few moments, a quiet tension hung over us. My curious colleague broke it, clearing her throat before asking, "What about your best memory of Grand Valley?"

As for the best memory of the quaint town, where I spent my teenage years growing up, I had many—so many it was impossible to narrow it down to even a few. In any case, my coworkers knew *feel-good* stories were never as interesting as the gory, bad-news accountings, and I just provided them with an awesome one. Consequently, my answer, although it might have seemed like I didn't even try to think about a thoughtful response, was honest.

I raised my half-finished glass of beer and told them, "The good memories I have about Grand Valley are absolutely everything else."

Chapter 2: Kim's Coffee Shop

That October day when my father first drove our family to Grand Valley was memorable because the trees were well into their colour changing cycle. There were many maple trees in the area, some turning light brown while others turned red like the colour in the heart of a cluster of burning coals. There were also oak trees that changed colour later than most other trees, leaving their leaves just beginning the process of losing their deep green colour. Intermingled amongst these were the evergreen trees: an abundance of spruce, pine and cedar.

I was awed by the size of these towering trees as they reached for the billowing clouds, quite a few being well over a hundred years old. We didn't see those in Bramalea since, when the cookie-cutter subdivisions were built, the trees and everything else had been leveled in preparation for construction.

We slowed as we entered the town, and my father rolled down the window. The fresh scent of the autumn season, cut grass with a hint of manure from the surrounding fields, added a sharp snap to the welcoming sight of the kaleidoscope of trees. My excitement grew as we came off the final curve, seeing Main Street lined on each side by a row of linked buildings. It reminded me of western towns I had seen in old movies, except there were no tumbleweeds or cowboy hats, and the buildings were different colours of dark brick instead of weathered wood planks. Nevertheless, in my imagination, I saw myself wearing a badge as all the townsfolk called me, "Sheriff Kovacs."

There were only about ten shops on either side. We were by them in the blink of an eye before my father turned to the right, sending us into a subdivision of older houses. Two turns later, we were driving down a long, straight road, the asphalt a spiderweb of cracks filled with jet-black tar. Near the far end of the road, my father slowed, then stopped in front of a red brick house on the north side of the street.

He said, "This is where we're going to be living."

To my brother's protests I scooted over, climbing on top of his legs, pressing my nose against the glass. Right beside the car was a *For Sale* sign, and taped over it, on an angle, was a decal reading, *Sold*. My face lifted, allowing a better view of the house. It was an older, large, red-brick farmhouse except, many years ago, someone had infused the design with a Victorian flair. The window frames and all other trim were bright white, as were the three steps leading up to the half wrap around porch extending across the entire front of the house and down one side. I could tell the house had a huge back yard, because when I looked down the wide driveway, far behind the house, I saw a large, two-story garage.

Andy had stopped his whining since he was also preoccupied inspecting our new home. I glanced at him, seeing the lines of worry had left his face. *Maybe I was wrong about his concern for the young, suburban girls he would have to leave behind.*

He seemed in a trance as he stared out the window when I slapped him on the shoulder. "The house is awesome, don't ya think!"

His mouth twisted into a frown as he dragged me off his legs, throwing me to the other side of the back seat. Both Andy and I were tall for our age, but I was catching up to him quicker than he liked. I knew there would come a day when he'd try and manhandle me like that, and I'd smack him good. For now, I settled for calling him an ass, after which my mother scolded both of us into silence.

It was well past lunch time. My youthful attention span was such that my thoughts were—*okay, I've seen it—now, I'm hungry*. Pushing my face between the front seats, I told my parents as much. We drove back down to Main Street and the downtown core where we stopped at a coffee and sandwich shop. We piled out of the car and entered the long, narrow room with a barnboard covered counter at the far end. On a blackboard behind a middle-aged woman, written in white chalk, were the culinary options.

I was having a difficult time reading the scrawl, but I did decipher the word, *bacon*. I started bouncing while pulling on my mother's sleeve, imploring her to order me a bacon sandwich, one of my favourite things in the whole world. Andy, with less exuberance, requested the same before my mother told us to find a table in the small eating area between the counter and the wall-to-wall front windows.

As the woman was waiting for the bacon to cook, she glanced at my father with a raised brow and offered, "I haven't seen you in town before, have I?"

My father had a square-jawed face that usually carried a stern appearance, but he made his best effort to smile as he replied, "We recently bought a house on Grant Street."

"Really? Which one?"

"Number 54."

The lady's eyes lit up. "The Morrison house. That's a great place! Welcome to The Valley!"

My mother added, "Wow! I'm surprised you know the house and who lives there."

By now the woman was putting together the sandwiches. She looked up over the rim of her glasses and chuckled. "This is a small town—around 1,500 people according to my last count. We don't see many new people, so everyone knows everyone else." She shrugged. "That's just the way it is here." As she handed over the sandwiches and cold cans of cola, she added, "My name is Kim. Just drop in any time, and let us know if there is anything you need help with." She bobbled her head. "You know, new town and new friends to make."

My mom liked to talk more than my dad. In fact, a lot more. She took it upon herself to introduce all of us and thanked Kim for her kindness.

As I ate my sandwich, even at ten-years-old, I was getting a great vibe about our new little town. Kim was forthcoming and friendly, even though there really was no need. After all, my dad had already paid and put two loonies in the tip jar on the counter. She was being nice for no reason other than she had a genuinely nice personality. The house had looked great, and I noticed, as we parked the car in front of the coffee shop, there were quite a few kids around my age hanging around on the sidewalk. Many were on their bikes, but the most critical detail was, there were no parents with them. They were running wild and free! It was a good omen the move was going to be great!

Chapter 3: The Dudes

My great expectations of Grand Valley waned somewhat after we moved in. After all, it was February, and in South Central Ontario that meant we were at the height of the extreme cold season felt on the escarpment.

The escarpment, correctly named the Niagara Escarpment, is a raised landmass that runs from Fort Erie, around Lake Ontario, then north across Ontario until it reaches Lake Huron. From that point, it carries on until it reaches Sault St. Marie, a place some would consider the end of the known world. Close to the middle of the province, it passes along the west side of Grand Valley, leaving a depression on the leeward side that the town is nestled in. Slight, natural rises on the other three sides of the town provide some protection from the winter winds tending to rip across the frozen farmlands surrounding the hollow.

It was still bitterly cold in February with much more snowfall than what we had ever seen in Bramalea. The fluffy snowflakes fell more often, and the berms of salt, ice and snow bordering the roads were higher than I'd seen before. Being young, I received fewer shovelling duties than Andy, but I was still expected to go out and help my father as best I could. However, I knew, if I strategically whined at the correct moments, like when my father was heaving an exceptionally heavy load of wet snow, he would get sick of it and order me back into the house. At ten, I had no worries, but I certainly had priorities and shovelling wasn't one of them.

However, that wasn't what had my new home expectations faltering. It was the fact the kids I saw about when we first came in October, didn't spend much time outside in the cold. I was enrolled in the local school, eventually making a couple of friends, but I found here, just as it was in any new school, it was tough to fit in with a new crowd. It didn't help that I was on the shy side when meeting new people, often playing the, "who's-going-to-say-hi-first," game.

On the positive side, we had great neighbours. In no time, my father became friends with Kurt living next door, and Ryan and Jim living across the road. They immediately showed us how things were different in a rural town. In early February, no sooner had our moving truck backed into the driveway and we started moving boxes, when two men we didn't know started bringing boxes into the house. That was Jim and Kurt. Without even asking, they knew the neighbourly thing to do was to pitch in, even though it was icy cold. It left me scratching my head since this would have never happened in suburbia.

With the extra help, along with the fact my father was organized to the point of being obsessive compulsive, the truck was emptied in an impressive two hours. When it came to moving or packing, my father took charge. In this instance he told my mom, "Don't label the boxes with their contents. Just write which room the box is going into on the box." I didn't think it made much sense until I saw the truck emptied so quickly.

Late in the afternoon, we received another instance of kindness. Maureen, a woman who lived five houses down from us, came over and asked if we wanted to have dinner at her house.

My mother replied, "No, we just arrived, and we don't want to inconvenience anyone."

Maureen added, "I have a big roast in the oven, and it's much too large for my husband and I, so it's not a problem."

My dad was in the living room, sprawled out on an armchair, half asleep. My mom saw this, then turned back to Maureen. "Honestly, we are all just exhausted. I appreciate the invite, but we will be fine for tonight."

Once Maureen left, my mom told my dad she was going to get a pizza for dinner. She glanced at me and said, "Want to come?"

Sure," I replied, but I moaned, "We had a chance for roast beef, and we're getting pizza—really?"

"If you would have helped more, then you would be too tired for roast at Maureen's house, just as we are." With that, she gave my shoulder a gentle nudge and said, "Get your coat on."

The pizza place in Grand Valley was in an odd building being only half the width of Kim's Coffee Shop. It was no wider than a wide hallway, and at the end was Ralph. As weird as the narrow building was, even stranger was buying pizza from a place called "Ralph's Pizza." At least in Bramalea, the pizza places had the right names: Mario's, Vesuvio's and Sicilian, to name a few. Fortunately, Ralph's pizza did not disappoint, tasting especially good on our first night in our new home.

Things improved greatly in early April when the snow, although not completely melted, receded significantly. It was enough that one weekend my father asked Andy and I to come out to the garage with him. At that time, my dad was a tradesman toolmaker, working in Brampton at the American Motors Jeep plant. He was good with his hands and liked making things. So it wasn't unusual that he owned a few machines: a lathe, a bending press and a small milling machine. He also had a cutoff saw and needed some help moving it. So, between the three of us, we were able to drag it to the location my dad preferred. The double wide garage was now set up with half for his little metal shop, and the other half was set up as his man cave, with a woodstove, an old couch, a scratched-up coffee table and, of course, a beer fridge.

This was typical of a rural garage. It was used as a workshop, a man cave, or, in a worst case, storage, but it was never used for vehicles unless it was for dirt bikes or four wheelers. These were a few of the unwritten rules in a country town that quickly became evident to me.

I was about to ask my dad if there was anything else when I saw an old, dust-covered bike leaning against the wood stud wall beside the fridge. I pointed and said, "What's that, Dad?"

We both walked over, and my dad pulled the dirty bike out. He explained, "I was cleaning out the loft above the garage. There was junk up there from the last family and I suspect even from the family before. This bike was up there behind some boxes of junk."

The bike was different from any I had seen before. It had a long black seat and the handle bars were long, stretching upward a good foot. I rubbed one hand on the dusty front bar in front of the seat, revealing a bright red colour under the thick layer of dust and grime.

My dad explained, "This bike is at least 15 years old, although it looks like it's been sitting up there without ever having been used. That seat is called a banana seat and those are monkey bars." He added, "They don't make bikes like this any more."

There were hand brakes for both wheels, and there was a gear shifter on the centre bar just in front of the banana seat. I could tell by the numbers on the bezel it had three speeds. I looked at my dad, eyes wide. "Can I have it?"

Andy pipped in, "The chain is rusted, and I guarantee you those gears are seized up."

My dad added, "I was going to get you and Andy a new bike, maybe a ten speed for Andy and one of those BMX dirt bikes for you. Wouldn't you prefer that, Joe?"

The corners of my lips curled down, pulling my eyes open wide. My words came slow, high pitched and fragile. "You always said you could fix anything mechanical. I like this bike." I cracked a hopeful smile. "No one will have a bike like this, Dad."

Two weeks later, Andy had just left to ride around the block on his new ten speed. My shoulders sagged until my father said he had something for me. He led me out to the garage, and when he opened the bay door, there, leaning on a new kick stand was the red bike. I jumped a foot in the air as I whooped out a yell. "It looks brand new!"

My dad made a new chain for it. The gears just needed some lube after which they worked fine, and both hand brakes had been replaced. The red paint was perfect, and on the angled bar from under the seat to the front vertical bar, the word *Chopper* was printed in bright, yellow letters made to look like flames. I did a quick walk around and saw the only flaw was two of the letters had the yellow decals partly peeled off. It didn't matter. I told my dad the bike was perfect.

I think that brought a wider smile to his face than mine. He ruffled my hair and said, "Well, go on. Try it out."

He didn't need to ask me twice. I hopped on and away I went. I rode up and down our street ten times before I figured out the three gears. Third gear was used for going super fast, but would be impossible when riding up a hill. That's what first gear was for, and that was a good thing because there was an abundance of hills in Grand Valley. That left second gear, which was used most of the time, for cruising and looking cool.

The next day I rode my bike to school, and from that day on, I rode it there and back every day. I never went anywhere without my Chopper. Later that week, when I came out of school, a group of boys were admiring my bike. When I came up to it, they left except for two of them. Nik was in my class, the same age I was, but I didn't know him well because he kept to himself, a trait I also practiced. Chris was a year older and a year ahead. I had seen him around, but I didn't know him at all.

I said, "hi," then bent down to unlock my bike.

Nik whispered something to Chris, then said to me, "Cool bike. You bring that from the big city?"

I threw one leg over the banana seat and sat on the bike. "Naw. It was in the garage when we moved in, and my dad fixed it up."

"Lucky you," Chris said. He pulled on a pair of mirror-faced sunglasses, which was odd since it wasn't sunny out, and said, "We'll see ya round."

The next day was Saturday, and in the morning, I was sitting in a chair on our front porch, thinking about what trouble I could get into. By now, I'd ridden my bike all over town. I knew every road and every crack and pothole on them. At the same time I was planning my day, I was feeding Phoebus a couple of treats.

Phoebus was a big, mostly lethargic yellow lab who belonged to Kurt next door. In reality he was a neighbourhood dog, free to wander up and down Grant Street. By wandering, I mean plodding. I don't ever recall seeing Phoebus run; maybe a slow gait in an emergency, but plodding was his normal speed. He would visit anyone who was outside, looking for a nuzzle on his head or a scratch on his back. When I came out the front door earlier that morning, Phoebus was fast asleep on the chair I was now sitting in.

His ears perked up when he first saw me, but I turned and went back inside. When I returned, he had assumed a formal sitting position beside the chair. He was not new to this process, so I sat down and he lifted a paw. I took it, gave it a shake, and then held out one of the treats I had brought out with me. We didn't have a dog, but since many who lived on Grant Street did, we kept a stash of dog treats. However, Phoebus managed to be the primary recipient. I had found him to be a clever dog, and the neighbourhood rumour was he had a knack for pulling down on screen door handles to gain entry into people's homes. As the story goes, once a neighbour came in from the backyard to find his roast, which had been resting on the kitchen counter, gone. When he looked out the front screen door, Phoebus was half way through devouring it.

My daydreaming was interrupted by the creaky sound of a screen door. A second later, I saw my neighbour, Kurt, walking across his lawn in his housecoat and slippers, coffee cup in hand. He glanced over, waved and yelled, "How's it going, Kid?"

I waved back and watched as he continued across the road towards Jim's house. Oddly, Jim's front door was on the side of his house, at the top of three stairs. As I had seen before, Kurt just walked in—no hello—no knock—just straight in. No more than a minute later, he was coming back, and when he came close enough, I could see the steam coming off his hot coffee. My dad had seen this camaraderie amongst Jim, Kurt and Ryan as well. Although he became good friends with them, and they were very much a foursome, he made it clear, they were never going to just walk into his house.

When I heard Kurt's screen door crack as it closed behind him, I turned to the opposite direction where I saw two kids riding down the street. When they came closer, I saw it was Nik Luzkin and Chris Eckland, once again wearing their fancy sunglasses. They were riding BMX dirt bikes, and I was a bit surprised when they turned up my driveway.

Not getting off their bikes, Nik said, "Let's go for a ride."

Since I still hadn't made many friends outside of seeing other kids at school, I was quick to accept. I opened the front screen door and yelled in to my mom, telling her I was going riding. My Chopper was in the driveway, so I hopped on before the three of us rode west towards the main drag.

However, when we hit the Main Street intersection, Chris led us across the intersection, continuing up Amaranth Street. I stood up on the pedals, pedaling hard to catch up beside Nik and Chris. "Where we going?"

Chris turned his face to me and replied, "First, my house, then we have something to do."

We turned right on Emma Street until we reached a white aluminum sided house. I'd been by it before, thinking it must be the biggest house in Grand Valley. I was surprised to see three other kid's bikes parked beside the garage, and we dropped our bikes beside theirs after which Chris led us to the back of the yard where a massive maple tree stood. At first, I didn't see it, but when we were beside the thick, gnarled trunk, I looked up and saw a tree fort. Nik scurried up a suspended ladder, and Chris pointed, indicating I should go next. Chris was the last to climb up.

The fort was big with old lawn chair cushions strewn about on the plywood flooring. There were three other young boys waiting for us, and oddly, each of them also had sunglasses, albeit, they were pushed up on their heads. One wore similar mirrored glasses to Chris's, and the second boy had similar glasses with brown frames while the last boy had black wrap-around, futuristic sunglasses.

Chris pointed to each boy as he said, "Mitch, Chet, Ronnie—this is Joe."

I nodded and said, "hi," back to them.

Once Nik and Chris sat down, I followed their lead, dropping onto a cushion, a little perplexed about what was happening.

Chris quickly removed my confusion. "This is my gang. We're *The Dudes*."

My eyebrows curled in. One of the reasons my dad said we left Bramalea was because he was seeing elements of gangs there.

Chris, seeing the look on my face, waved his hand. "Not that kind of gang. We're just good friends. We're tight, and we ride together. We take an oath swearing to that, and if anyone in the gang needs help, the rest of us show up."

Tilting my head, I asked, "So you're not criminals?"

They all burst out laughing, and when it subsided, Nik clarified, "Hell, no! We just ride around and have fun." He looked at each of the other three boys, then towards Chris as he gave a nod with his chin.

"You want to join our gang?" Chris suggested.

I didn't have many other friends in Grand Valley, so it didn't take me long to tell them I would.

For a few seconds, it became awkward as there was a prolonged silence. I thought, *maybe they didn't expect me to agree so quickly.*

Chris finally said, "Okay, I think you'll be a good fit, but you need to go through an initiation."

That was a big word for me, and I didn't know what it meant, and I told them so.

Chris dumbed it down. "You have to do something to prove you really want to be one of the Dudes."

I must have still had a confused look on my face since Nik added, "You have to do something to prove you're not a wimp!"

Leaning back on my hands, trying to look casual, I replied, "When, and what do I have to do?"

Chris rose to his feet, and the other Dudes followed suit. "Now, and we're going to show you."

By the time I was on my feet, Chris, Chet, Ronnie and Mitch were already down the ladder. They let me go next with Nik being last down on the grass.

It felt pretty cool, six of us riding in a pack as we biked down Main Street with Chris leading the way. The only thing making it odd was I was the only one not wearing sunglasses, what I was quickly learning was symbolic of the Dudes.

After the downtown buildings, Main Street turned into Water Street as it snaked away, following the curves of the Grand River. At that point, there was a small bridge that crossed the river to the subdivision on the southeast side.

Chris stopped us there and pushed his sunglasses up onto his head. "That's Brooklin over there. The Dudes aren't welcome there because that's where the other Grand Valley bike gang is."

"Another...gang?" I sputtered.

"Yeah. The Boys of Brooklin, or we just call them, *The Boys.*"

I was scratching my head, wondering, *what had I gotten myself into?*

Chris pulled his bike alongside mine and put his hand on my shoulder. "Brooklin is an old part of town, as old as the areas you and I live in. You're going to ride over the bridge and keep going straight. About 150 yards down, on your right, you'll see a little park alongside the river. You'll also see two picnic tables there, and that's where the Boys of Brooklin usually hang out."

"What then?"

Nik answered, "You just ride back, and meet us here. Simple really."

I was thinking I could do "simple" as long as I didn't run into the other gang, and I didn't do anything stupid.

Chris must have been reading my mind because that's when he added a *stupid* thing I had to do. "When you get down there, you'll probably see some of the Boys at a picnic table. You're going to yell at them, 'I'm a Dude and the Boys of Brooklin suck!'"

"You're crazy!" I yelled.

Mitch asked, "Are you a chicken?"

With a snarl, I said, "No. I'll do it. But you guys better not take off on me."

Nik stated in an assuring tone, "I'm going to follow you half way down since I want to make sure I hear you say the words to them."

I took a few moments to think about it. When I woke up that morning, I didn't think my day would involve getting beat up by a gang of boys. However, I was confident my bike was faster than the BMX varieties the boys in town tended to have. As long as the road on the other side of the bridge wasn't rough, and it didn't have huge potholes all over it, I should make it out alive.

I turned to Nik, and with my lips stretched wide and barely open. I grumbled, "Let's go."

Nik led me across the bridge, and after 50 yards we stopped. Nik pointed ahead and to the right. In the distance I saw the edge of a clearing where the road curled to the left. Nik whispered, "The picnic tables are just behind those trees. The Boys will be there. Just yell at them and ride like heck. I'll be waiting for you here."

I nodded and started down through the bowels of Brooklin. My gaze glanced left and right, looking out for the Boys who might jump me just for being on their turf. I did feel some relief from my anxiety when I noticed the houses in this area were old, but elegant, with manicured gardens and well cared for lawns. However, as I rode closer to the parkette, the brightly coloured flowers didn't keep the tension I felt from returning. I rode faster, and when I reached the little parkette, I saw the two picnic tables, and beside them were three boys. Two were on their bikes, and one was sitting on the table, his bike on its side on the grass.

One of the boys noticed me and pushed the second boy in the shoulder. Now, all three were watching me as I went through their home turf. I made a *U* turn, and on my way back, I stopped next to the little park, thirty yards from the Boys. I was shaking and so was my voice when I yelled out, "I'm a Dude, and the Boys Suck!" For good measure, I added, "You assholes!"

The original look of irritation when they first saw me, now changed to all-out, red-faced, eye-bulging anger. The Boys were after me in a second, but I had a good head start. It didn't take me long to have the bike *kickin it* in third gear. I was racing along while keeping a constant distance to the three boys chasing behind me who were yelling obscenities.

Nik saw the same thing at the same time I did. Another young boy just burst out of his house ahead of me. He must have heard my foul yell, and was now racing for his bike as he saw his friends chasing me; he was on his bike in a flash. Nik, not expecting the surprise, hightailed it out of there, speeding for the bridge while the new boy was barreling out of his long driveway. It was going to be close, but I veered to the left, just out of range as the rider cut across just behind me. He swept around in a wide curve, joining the other three riders, all now in a line chasing me. Pedaling for my life on my Chopper, I made it to the bridge and over the rise. The Dudes were waiting for me when I pressed the handbrakes, skidding to a stop beside them.

A few seconds later, the four Boys flew over the rise, but surprised by the Dudes waiting there in superior numbers, they pressed their own brakes and screeched to a collective stop. It was then that I noticed they all had blue bandanas tied to their handlebars. The tallest Brooklin Boy put his hand across his brow to shield his eyes from the sun. "Nice one," he said to Chris through a sly grin.

"How's it going, Mike?" Chris replied.

"We're good. It was close." He then looked squarely at me. "Nice bike and nice riding, but don't let us catch you over here on our turf again." He didn't wait for a reply as he turned his bike and rode back to his side of the bridge, followed by the rest of his gang.

Once the Boys were gone, all the Dudes had a good laugh. Nik slapped his thigh, "You should have heard him yell! That was almost as good as the look on his scared shitless face when he was riding towards me!"

Wiping the sweat from my brow, I wasn't as amused.

Chris slapped me on the back. "Don't listen to them. You did great!" He had a small, black plastic bag hanging off his handlebar. Pulling it free, he reached in, retrieving a pair of black wrap-around sunglasses, just like the futuristic ones Mitch had on. With a proud grin, he handed them to me. "You're now officially a Dude!"

Chapter 4: Billy Fixit

The next few weeks were great. The Dudes were my new friends, especially Chris and Nik. With Chris being a year older, I looked up to him. He was decisive without being overbearing, coming from a family having deep roots in Grand Valley. In fact, he was a sixth generation Eckland, his great, great, great grandfather being one of the original founders in 1866. That was unusual, but not altogether rare. Many people who moved to The Valley fell in love with country life, general lower prices of everything and friendlier people, so they never left. For others, there was a normal phenomenon whereby their children might fall to the call of a bigger city and increased opportunity. Simplified, it was a matter of whether people could be satisfied at some point in their life, or were they forever looking for the next big job with an even bigger expense account. Chris's parents had made the decision, long ago, that they were more than satisfied with the benefits of small-town life.

My parents moved to Grand Valley, at least in part, for those same reasons; less crime and lower prices, especially lower house prices being at the forefront of their logic. It still remained to be seen how long those benefits would outweigh the detriments. How long would it take before my dad became sick of the one-hour drive to work and back every day? How many times would he have to double back to Orangeville, a 20-minute drive each way, because he forgot one of the five items he had on his pick-up list? I hoped he worked through those negative aspects because, so far, I was loving it in my new country town.

Even Andy was coming around to the benefits of our move. The suburban girls he initially pined over, were long forgotten when a few new Valley girls all but threw themselves at him; the new boy in town. Although the stereotype of small-town country girls is for them to be reserved, dainty and shy, after the first 20 phone calls they made to Andy at our house, my assumptions were squashed. More so, they were obliterated when I made the mistake of answering the phone to their aggressive, "I won't take no for an answer" attitude, when I told them he was not available.

However, the best result of our move was I could now say I had my first best friend; that was Nik. We made an odd-looking pair with my dirty-blonde hair which always turned lighter in the summer, along with my sky-blue eyes. Nik, on the other hand, had jet black hair, similar to my brother Andy's, and he had dark, piercing eyes that were quite a contrast to his pale skin. Most kids, myself included, would start to tan after a short time in the sun, so by the end of June, we would all be as dark as a golden-brown coconut, but not Nik. His skin always remained lily white, or straight to pink if he was in the sun for too long without a long-sleeved shirt and protective cream.

My father also thought the two of us were an odd pair, one he did not altogether appreciate. My father, Steve Kovacs, was born in Hungary and came to Canada in 1957 after the Hungarian Revolution. He was only five when my grandparents escaped the oppression of the Russians with him in hand.

Therein was the problem. Nik's last name was *Luzkin*—a typical Russian surname. Even though Nik's grandparents were born in Russia, they escaped to Poland when they were young. Nik's parents were born there, and Nik was born in Canada after they emigrated. None of that mattered to my father. He had heard too many stories of the communists in Hungary to not think of Nik Luzkin as a Russian. But my father, and I don't say this just because he is my father, is a very decent man. He never showed a temper, never raised a hand to anyone, although he was a typical blue-collar worker with big hands and a quiet, confident demeanour. It was an appearance that, by just looking at him, would have people wary and wondering if that quiet personality ever erupted, they would not want to be on the receiving end. In that manner, my father was proactive to his conflicts. Nevertheless, any bigotry he had about people tended to fade once he got to know them better. So it took him a little time to accept Nik and I were friends. He was polite and friendly with Nik, but still a little aloof while keeping a close eye on our growing relationship.

There was a day in the middle of June when Nik and I were on the front porch of our house. Nik was petting Phoebus who had come over to say hello, and we were about to make our plans for the day. I heard the phone ring in the kitchen, and thought about just ignoring it. Andy was out, and I wasn't about to start playing "20 questions" with one of his girlfriends. Thankfully, the ringing ended, but no sooner had it stopped when it began ringing again.

I went inside and picked the receiver off the hook attached to the phone hanging on the wall. It was my mother. First, she gave me heck for not answering the phone the first time, then she asked me for some help. She was at work and forgot her lunch in the fridge, so she asked if I could ride it over to her. A few minutes later Nik and I were on our bikes, riding over to the Royal Bank located at the far end of the downtown block.

My mother didn't have any intentions or need to work when we moved to The Valley. My father made good money, and he always had overtime if we needed something extra, but when my mother set up our bank accounts at the Royal Bank, she got to chatting with the teller. It seemed that way everywhere you went in Grand Valley; everyone was friendly and chatty.

Before long, my mom was telling the bank employee how she had worked at a bank in Bramalea before she moved to town. Next thing you knew, she was introduced to the bank manager who explained they were short handed since it was hard to find people with bank experience to work in a small somewhat isolated town. He offered her a job on the spot, and after some negotiations, she agreed to help out on Fridays and Saturdays, the days the manager was having trouble covering.

When we arrived at the bank, Nik leaned his bike against the wall while I pushed down the kickstand of mine, after which I leaned down and locked the Chopper. Nik just rolled his eyes since he told me many times no one steals anything in Grand Valley, but still, I never took the chance. My bike was my pride and joy, and I locked it every time it wasn't under me, even when I parked it in our garage.

Once inside the bank, my mom caught sight of the two of us and scooted out from behind the counter. When she was beside us, she leaned down and whispered the kind of grating whisper only a mother could manage. "Take off your sunglasses," she hissed. "You two look like hoodlums about to rob the place."

I handed her the bag holding her lunch, then pushed my futuristic, wrap-around glasses up on my head. "How's that?"

"I have to get back to work." She had her purse with her and unclipped the clasp before fumbling her fingers inside it. I was getting excited because I could see she was looking for change, but she wasn't being successful. My eyes grew wide, matching my dimpled smile. *Yes,* I thought as she handed me a five-dollar bill.

"You two go get a bagel for lunch at the coffee shop," she said. Then, she leaned down and kissed me on the cheek. With an evil grin, she turned and gave Nik a similar kiss.

As Nik was wiping his cheek, I whined, "Lay off the Russian kid!"

We sprinted out the door the way ten-year-olds would, and a minute later we were sitting on our bikes. We both lowered our sunglasses to their previous position. After all, it was June, and the sun was directly overhead, beating down on us.

Nik asked, "We going for bagels?"

"Hell, no." I nodded towards one of the shops on the other side of Main Street. Nik knew I was pointing towards *W.T. O'Neil's Variety*. There were actually two variety stores in Grand Valley almost side by side; W.T. O'Neil's and a Mac's Milk just three shops to the north, but the Mac's Milk was a cookie-cutter, generic store, whereas O'Neil's had distinctive stuff you couldn't get anywhere else.

We parked our bikes and went in. As we always did, first, we said hello to Mr. O'Neil.

Glancing down through his wire-rimmed glasses, he asked, "Candy?"

We both nodded our heads up and down, and in response he handed us a plastic baggy. This was the great thing about the candy at Mr. O'Neil's place. You could buy it in bulk. Just off to his right, he had 20 square, glass bins with wood lids. Each was filled with a different kind of candy, both hard and soft varieties being available. There were candy scoops Mr. O'Neil insisted customers use, even though our adolescent instinct was to just stick our grabby hands in.

Nik turned back to Mr. O'Neil and said, "We're going to look around a bit, first."

Mr. O'Neil just shrugged, giving it no further thought.

We also knew Mr. O'Neil didn't like us running in his store, so we walked—that fast-walking shuffle we could do as kids that was just as fast as if we *were* running. We knew exactly where we were going. At the back of the store, there was a toy section. There were toy cars of different sizes, little bags of toy soldiers, little airplanes packaged with sling shots and bags of marbles. We spent some time there, picking up different items, inspecting the contents of the bags. For a brief moment we thought, we had enough money to buy a small toy or two, but we came in for candy, so we returned our focus there.

From the very back corner of the store, Nik headed down the aisle, straight towards the front of the store. As kids would do, I headed to the next aisle over, so I could do my fast shuffle and beat him back to the candy section. However, when I turned the corner, with my eyes looking at my feet, I smashed full on into something. I toppled over onto my back, and when I looked up, I saw a mountain of a man standing over me. There was a fluorescent light behind him, making his shadowy figure look like a huge bear in overalls.

I leaned up on my elbow to get a better look. He was an older man, with shoulder-length, scraggly, grey hair, and the same-coloured beard and moustache. On top of his head was a faded, green baseball cap struggling to keep the hair in, and as my gaze lowered, I saw he was wearing black denim overalls over a white t-shirt. The bottom cuffs of the overalls were worn, with strings of white hanging over the faded, brown work boots sporting scuffs and cuts over the toes.

Before I could get up, he reached down and grabbed my arm with his wrinkled fingers. I noticed they were stronger than they looked as he helped me to my feet.

"Thanks, Mister," I whispered.

Now that I was on my feet, he didn't look as imposing a figure. He was about the same height as my dad, but thinner. His face and arms were dark brown from an overabundance of time in the sun. His eyes were blue, darker than mine, but a nice blue nevertheless, and there was a network of wrinkles on his face. Some would say, from that, he looked old, but my first impression was, he looked wise.

"You need to be careful, Son," he said.

I just nodded as he leaned down and picked up my sunglasses that had flown off my face. He cracked a smile. "Might be better to wait till you're outside before you put these back on."

I nodded again. "Yes, Sir."

"Best you get going and not keep your friend waiting."

I looked past the old man and saw Nik's face peeking around the stand at the far end of the aisle. I gave the man a hasty thank you and made my way to Nik.

Once around the corner, Nik looked at me wide-eyed, "You okay?"

I waved his concern away. "Sure."

Not satisfied, he grabbed my arm and began squeezing it up and down. "You sure? He grabbed you hard."

I pulled my arm away and pointed to the candy bins. "Don't be a goof. He helped me up is all." That sweet tooth reminder had Nik forgetting all about the collision. We shifted the last few feet to the candy bins where I held the bag, and both of us pointed to different containers. When we both agreed, Nik would use the candy scoop to put a small amount of candy in the bag. That was the great thing about the candies there. You could just fill up your bag with a mix of whatever you wanted, Mr. O'Neil would weigh it…*eazy peazy.*

We had been there before, so we estimated $5 worth, but when it was weighed Mr. O'Neil said, "$5.25."

I already had the $5 bill held out towards him, and when he said the price, I hesitated, pulling it back. Looking at Nik, he didn't have a cent on him, so he just shrugged.

Seeing our predicament, Mr. O'Neil said, "Good thing for you I'm having a sale on candy today. 25 cents off candy over $5."

I had a silly, wide grin on my face as I traded him my $5 bill for the treasure bag of candy. We left the store, making our way back to the other side of Main Street where we had our preferred bench. We took our time eating one piece of candy at a time until my stomach started to hurt. I closed up the bag and finally asked the question that hadn't left my mind. "Do you know the old guy in the store?"

He replied. "That's Billy. You want to keep away from him. You saw the way he bowled you over."

I pushed the sunglasses up on my head and left them there even though the sun had me squinting. "He didn't. I ran into him. It was my fault."

Leaning towards me, Nik's voice rose. "I saw the way he grabbed you!"

"He was just helping me up." Nik seemed upset Billy didn't hurt me. After he slouched back onto the wooden slats of the bench, I asked, "Does Billy have a last name?"

Nik shrugged. "Probably, but no one knows it. Everyone just knows him as *Billy Fixit.*"

"Why?"

"Cause that's what he does—he fixes stuff," Nik clarified.

We sat there for a bit longer, and Nik explained to me more about Billy and what he did in Grand Valley. He explained it well for a ten-year-old, and over the next few weeks I saw and heard more that described Billy Fixit. I asked Chris Eckland about Billy when I saw him, and he explained it even better, both because he was older and his family had lived in Grand Valley for generations.

Most people thought Billy was born in Grand Valley because they had seen him there for as far back as they could remember. But Chris's dad told Chris, who told me, Billy showed up when Chris's father was ten, and that was 30 years ago. When he arrived, he just hung around, but eventually started looking for odd jobs. And the oddest thing about those odd jobs was, when he was done, and the person tried to pay Billy, he refused payment. Billy would just say he was just helping out. This became a pattern where Billy would keep busy with small jobs, prioritizing work for people who were older or had physical reasons they couldn't do the work themselves. After that, he helped people who just didn't have time, but for those who were lazy, or were trying to take advantage of free help, they weren't on Billy's radar.

People in Grand Valley were friendly, and they were thankful to Billy for helping the citizens of the town. At the same time, most of these people had too much pride to take charity. So it didn't take long before Billy couldn't walk down a street in Grand Valley without getting multiple invites to lunch or dinner. Sometimes, if someone saw Billy walking down the street on a hot day, they would run a cold drink out to him—just because.

Soon, the businesses fell in line. If Billy ever needed a doctor or a dentist, he could just walk in and get his ailment looked after for no charge. The doctor and dentist knew if they ever needed help fixing a sign, or picking up some chairs, or painting a room, or fixing a leaky faucet, they could just call Billy, and he would take care of it. After a couple of years, everyone knew about the symbiotic relationship Billy had with the town; the townsfolk looked after Billy and Billy looked after the town. They were bartering their friendliness.

No one knew Billy's last name. When they asked him, he avoided the question, and would say, "It's just Billy." With that said, the story of Billy Fixit began.

Still, because Billy was working on most days, his hands were usually a little black, and often his clothes were stained since he was almost always on his way to or from a job. That led the kids in Grand Valley to stay clear of him, creating their own urban legend of a child eating man who roamed the streets of Grand Valley after midnight. It was that fanciful and colourful description Nik was providing between bites of candy when Nik pointed. "There he is."

I followed the direction of his finger to the hardware store. Billy had just exited and was walking around the corner of the building with a bag of supplies. When Billy returned, we saw the wheel of a larger bicycle, then the older man sitting on the seat. Finally, to my shock, two side-by-side wheels became visible. Billy was sitting on a three-wheeler with a large plastic container attached to the back.

Nik explained, "Billy walks whenever he can. He has that bike so he can get to a job when he needs only a few tools. He also has an old, black van for jobs that are further away, or if he needs to take lots of tools or supplies."

I turned to Nik with my nose scrunched above a scowl. "Nik, I think you're full of shit, and you're pulling my leg about Billy being dangerous. He looks just fine to me."

Billy was riding his bike along the shops on the west side of Main Street. He lifted his hand in a friendly wave to a man sitting on another bench across the road in front of Mac's Milk.

Bouncing on the bench, Nik screeched, "Did you see that? He waved at *The Worm!*"

I shook my head. What the heck is *The Worm?*"

Nik leaned forward and cranked his neck until his eyes found mine. He looked serious. "There's three people you don't want to mess with in town: Billy, that man on the bench we call the Worm, and there's another guy you'll see soon enough, who we call *The Tongue.*"

I couldn't say anything in response because, how do you respond to something like that? Instead, I just kept listening.

Pointing to the man across the way on the bench, he said, "Look at him."

I did. I watched him carefully, and now saw he was shaking all over. His legs were shaking one way and his shoulders back and forth in a different rhythm, and his head was moving to a whole different beat. "What's wrong with him?"

"My dad told me he had some kind of accident when he was younger and his muscles are all messed up," Nik explained. "Everyone is scared of him, so keep yourself clear."

I was only ten and knew very little about handicaps, accidents and muscle issues, but it didn't sound like whatever happened was his fault, and it didn't mean he was some kind of monster. I thought that to myself, but at the same time, it's the kind of story that scares someone who is young. It was likely I would take Nik's advice. "What about, The Tongue?"

"We don't see him around town as often, but when he is, you'll know. He's an older guy, older than Billy. He's fat and usually has his belly hanging out from under his shirt. He has crazy, white hair, going in every direction."

"Like a bum?" I asked.

"I'm just telling you what he looks like so you'll know." He leaned closer to me, his voice barely above a whisper. "His tongue is cut in half, right down the middle. He can move each side of it in different directions like a snake."

I abruptly pulled back, bawling my fingers into fists and rubbing my eyes.

I couldn't unsee what Nik had described! I pulled one hand down while opening one eye. "You're pulling my leg?"

Nik made it worse. "He can't talk at all. He just makes weird sounds. When girls walk by, he sticks out his dancing tongue, waggling it at them, and to make it worse, he pretends he's licking them. When they run away, he laughs, but even that doesn't sound normal."

My hands moved up, supporting my forehead as I leaned over. "Why are you telling me this shit? I'm going to have nightmares forever."

Nik found that hilarious, holding his gut as he couldn't stop laughing.

When I looked up, I saw Billy in the distance, his bike just a speck as he was riding up Water Street. I didn't care about the Worm and the Tongue. I didn't believe the mean words Nik said about Billy. He'd helped me up when he didn't have to. When our gaze met for a moment, I saw the same mix of strength and kindness I saw when I looked at my father. For that, I'd give Billy the benefit of the doubt.

Chapter 5: The Hungarian Connection

My mother just finished scolding me. She finally had enough of my impatience. Since I woke up, I had been fidgety, running around the house, first in one room, then another, but now in her kitchen. She had a good grip of my shoulder as she leaned over me, such that even if I twisted my face away, her scratchy words were unavoidable.

When she let me go and rose up, I rubbed my shoulder making sure, even though it didn't hurt, she got the message it did. I groaned, "Sorry, Mom, but you know I get excited when *Apu* and *Anyu* come to visit."

Apu and Anyu were endearing Hungarian terms for *Father* and *Mother*. As a result, it was a term my father, and later, my mother, used. Somewhere along the way, hearing them called by those names, Andy and I just naturally did the same. At one point, as we got older, my mom corrected us. However, the term for *Grandmother* and *Grandfather*, in Hungarian, was much longer and complicated. Therefore, my father, being the born Hungarian in our household, vetoed my mother's correction and allowed us to continue using Apu and Anyu.

They lived in the heart of Toronto in an old, three-story, brown brick house on a side street just off world-famous Bloor Street. The outside had an old-world, stately elegance, but it was the inside I was in awe of every time we visited them. There was an abundance of honey-brown oak: the entire front entry, the opulent, square-paneled wainscotting in the welcoming living room, and the three-story staircase that made subtle creaking sounds complimenting the *Rat Pack* music Anyu played constantly. Therefore, I knew the sounds of Dean Martin, Frank Sinatra and Vic Damone at a young age when I was too innocent to know better.

I realized not keeping my knowledge of the golden oldies secret was an error. Once, when I didn't know Nik was nearby, he caught me doing a little dance while I was singing "Mac The Knife." I begged him not to tell the Dudes, but his silence was only bought with a British chocolate bar, the kind only sold at O'Neil's Variety.

I loved going to my grandparent's house, but they also looked forward to their regular visits to our new country home. Although we were a longer drive, they came more often than when we lived in the suburban sprawl of Bramalea.

Once I twisted free of my mother, I flew out the front door, continuing my aimless running, burning off my abundance of adolescent energy. I was playing catch, throwing a ball against the side of the garage when I heard the crackle of tires on pavement as their car pulled into the driveway. I was a thin lad with gangly stick-legs, but they could move rapidly when I needed them to. Consequently, I was beside the car before they had pulled their suitcase from the rear seat area. Throwing my arms around Apu first with a little too much exuberance, it forced him to shuffle back a step. Before he could tussle my hair, I was away from him, running towards Anyu. She was short and heavy-set with a face as round as a warm apple pie. I slowed my pace just before I gave her a huge hug. She returned the embrace while placing a kiss on the top of my head. She said, "How is my little Joszef?"

Anyu and Apu were the only people who got away with calling me by my proper birth name. Andy, who they called Andras, and I, let them get away with tons of stuff. They were kind to us—sure because they are our grandparents, but my brother and I felt there was much more to it. And the added bonus was, they always brought food with them! My mom used to get mad at them for that ritual, but eventually she accepted this was a Hungarian custom she was not going to be successful in changing.

So, since my Anyu had no intention of releasing me anytime soon, I watched my grandfather on the other side of the car. He retrieved a large, brown bag from the rear seat area, placing it on the roof of the car. There was a red, white and green emblem printed on the bag. I recognized it as the emblem of the Toronto Hungarian Market. Inside it, I knew would be different salamis and cheeses, the kind you could only get from a market true to its ethnic roots. Next, he put a large cake box on the roof.

I looked up at Anyu with one eye closed, the other squinting against the sunshine. Speculatively, I asked, "Dobos Torte?"

She rolled her eyes dramatically before returning her gaze back to me. "Of course, Hungarian Dobos Torte! You don't think we would bring you Boston Cream, or German Black Forest, do you? Bah!"

She was correct. Dobos Torte was the absolute best authentic Hungarian cake. There had to be 15 layers of cake, then cream, then cake, then more cream—the layers were endless! And the top was covered with thin wedges of candied caramel; my mouth was drooling as I thought about it!

By that time, the rest of my family was on the driveway greeting my grandparents. They formed a tight group, shuffling onto the grass halfway to the porch, where they stopped and started to chat. I never understood this part of the ritual. Why not just go inside? No, they would chit-chat there for ten minutes, then make their way to the porch, where they would likely stop again for another ten minutes. And my dad was more jubilant than any of us because, for the next two days, he could have conversations in Hungarian. He was so excited, jabbering in Hungarian, a language I only knew a few words of, that he forgot he was holding the front door open the entire time.

Things changed when Apu and Anyu came to visit. It was clear, at these times, my dad was in charge. From the upstairs linen closet, he would retrieve the Hungarian collection. A white silk table cloth, embroidered with red and blue flowers at the ends of embroidered, green stems, was placed on the dining room table. A smaller rectangular, matching cloth was placed on the living room coffee table, and similar embroidered doilies were placed on the two end tables, under the lamps.

Since my father also grew up in Apu's Toronto house, he had a sentimental spot for older music, preferring Andy Williams or Al Martino. When all of us finally made it into the house, I was thinking life couldn't be better. Salami, cake, Apu, Anyu and "Spanish Eyes" playing on the record player—life was grand!

Things also changed in the kitchen when my grandparents came to visit. My father took over the cooking. Today, the cabbage rolls were already simmering in a large pot on the stove—yes, on the stove, not in the oven. My father taught me early on, the cabbage rolls made in other ethnic households, baked in the oven with tomato sauce, were insulting. He told me, cabbage rolls were always eaten with sour cream and rye bread. His eyes would narrow, a sign of foreboding, as he warned me if he ever saw me eating cabbage rolls with tomato sauce, or white bread, there would be a reckoning of huge proportions.

Sour cream was a staple in a Hungarian home. It was one of the basics a Hungarian could not do without, and we Hungarians put it on almost everything. That's why it made sense, every time my Apu came to visit, one of the first things he did was open the fridge and inspect its contents. Pickles—*check*. Butter, not margarine—*check*. Horse radish—*check*. And of course, he would grin ear to ear when he saw the container of sour cream. If he ever saw the half-sized containers, he would just shake his head in disbelief, and that incredulity grew if he saw the low-fat, *less-than-5%* varieties.

Once it came to dinner time, I loved the cabbage rolls along with the smoked sausage cooked with it. My apu would glance over to me from time to time, lowering a disapproving eyebrow when he saw I was setting aside the cabbage and only eating the meat-rice filling. I knew what he was thinking at that time because he told me often enough. *You are young, and you will do better as you grow.* He was right. I was 18 years old when I came to the realization the cabbage was awesome as well.

After dinner finished with a liberal slice of cake, we watched a movie in the evening. We watched a lot of DVDs in those days since Grand Valley didn't have cable. An antenna tower was attached to the side of the house, controlled by a clunky control box inside. There was a round knob, and when you turned it, you could hear the grinding noise of the aerial antenna rotating to receive the required signal for a given channel. I didn't like that aspect of Grand Valley life so much, but it was a sacrifice I readily made for the freedom and friends I found in The Valley.

My grandparents always stayed overnight since it was such a long drive back to Toronto. That led to another favorite event, and that was breakfast; not just any breakfast, but a Hungarian breakfast. That meant my mother and father prepared three massive trays of food. On one was a variety of cheese and salami that had been brought from Toronto, along with hardboiled eggs my mother had made. Another platter was covered in sliced tomatoes, sweet and hot peppers, cucumbers and green onions. The last platter was overflowing with bread-rolls and rye bread.

As long as the weather behaved, it was mandatory for us to eat at a table on our back patio. It didn't matter that we were constantly swatting at flies, or that, on hot mornings, we were sweating while we ate. It was all part of the required Hungarian ritual. An added bonus was, with our best pleading and support from Apu and Anyu, my mother let Andy and I have a piece of Dobos Torte cake. Cake after breakfast! Life couldn't get much better than that!

It was noon when Apu indicated it was time to go since it was a long drive home, and if they didn't leave soon, they would hit rush hour traffic in Toronto. It took a while to pack their stuff, but once that was done, they were on the front porch beginning their ritualistic goodbyes. After ten minutes, I was getting impatient, so I walked down to the garage and collected my bike. When I arrived back at the front yard, my parents and grandparents had moved the goodbyes from the porch to the grass beside the car. I heard Apu say, "goodbye," for what should have been the final time, but as he opened the car door, Anyu brought up another, "oh, I almost forgot," and that was the beginning of another wordy delay. Finally, they managed to get in the car, and they left.

It was unusual for me to be home for two days straight, so I was itching to go cruising. In addition, because I was home for so long, I had eaten so much food, I felt sluggish, and that's saying something for a ten-year-old!

With a wave to my parents, I was on my way, biking west up Grant Street. At the intersection, I was about to turn left when I heard a shrill whistle behind me. I made a little loop and looked back down my street. Four houses away, on the left, I saw Billy Fixit with his hand waving over his head. He was wearing black overalls, but the green ballcap was replaced with a light-blue one. I raised my arms out to the side and lifted my shoulders— the international symbol for, *what's up?*

This time, it was clear he was waving me towards him. I wasn't sure I wanted to go back, instantly recalling Nik's words that he was some kind of a child-eating monster, but that thought was replaced by my memory of his honest eyes. There was something there that told me the fairy tales the kids of Grand Valley told about him weren't true.

I pedaled back to where he was, and once there, he looked me up and down, saying, "Nice bike. Don't see any of those around anymore."

"Thanks."

"I was hoping you could help me for five minutes," he said. "Just need an extra set of hands."

"Sure," I replied just before I followed him up the driveway of Ms. Frances Stevens house.

Although I had seen Ms. Stevens around town, I had never met her. When we moved into our new house, over the following two weeks, every neighbour from our street came over at one point or the other. They brought casseroles, pies, macaroni salads and welcome baskets. Most of these neighbours my mom invited in for tea or coffee, and I was introduced to some of them. However, Ms. Stevens visited on a day I was out riding.

Her house looked as nice as ours, and at least as big, just her house was long and narrow, made of brown brick. The front door was set half way back along the side, right behind a long wood porch. A feature I liked, one not seen often in Grand Valley, was a brown brick quarter-wall with thick stone copings on top of it, holding back the raised front lawn down the length of the driveway.

Billy led me up the steps cut into the short wall, then onto the front porch where he explained, "One of the wood boards is rotten, so I'm replacing it." He pointed to the twisted, eight-foot-long board he had already removed.

The board was cracked and looked soft. I'd seen that kind of rot before, but the odd smell coming to me was not of rot. "What's that smell?"

Billy pointed to the other eight-foot board leaning against the brick wall.

"You're probably smelling that board. It's made of cedar."

"Why are you using a smelly board?"

Billy had a deep voice, consistent with his chuckle. "That's a good smell, Son." Then, his eyebrows lowered as he realized they hadn't been introduced. "I'm Billy. What's your name?"

I didn't tell him I knew who he was. Raising my eyebrows, I pretended it was the first time I heard the name. "I'm Joe. I live up the street at number 54."

He leaned over, held out his hand, and shook mine. "Nice to meet you, Joe."

He saw me scrunch my nose again, and it brought Billy back to the cedar board. He said, "That old, rotten board is made of spruce. Now, there aren't any trees that are bad trees, but spruce is, let's say, a weak tree. Bugs and ants like to eat it, and water seeps into it really easy." He saw I was paying close attention, so he continued. "Cedar is a much better tree. It has natural chemicals in it that keeps the water from seeping in, and bugs don't like it much either. So cedar lasts much longer than spruce, or most other woods."

I wore my sunglasses so often, I forgot they were sitting on the top of my head. I wouldn't have noticed except when I scratched my head, my fingers hit them. One eye closed, I squinted at Billy, "So, if I ever make anything for outside, I should use cedar."

Billy had a crack of a smile on his face between his beard and moustache, "That's right, as long as you can afford it. Cedar lasts longer, but it costs you more as well."

Happy to have learned something new, I asked, "You said you needed help."

"Right," Billy answered. He picked up the cedar board, placing it on the railing where the old spruce board had been removed. He called me over and pointed down, "See that pencil line there. Hold this end against it while I screw in the other end."

I nodded, then he walked to the other end of the board. He had an electric drill at the end of a long extension cord. After adjusting his end, he then peered up at me, "You on the line?"

I checked it again. "Yup."

He drilled down making a small hole before he changed the drill bit to a screw driver bit, then drove in a long screw. After striding back to my end, he saw the wood was still exactly on the line. "Good work," he said.

He did the same process at my end, drilling a hole, followed by securing a screw. He stretched back, then looked down at his work.

"Anything else, Billy?" It sounded weird to me, calling an adult by their first name. My parents taught me to always be polite and use, *Mister Somebody*, or *Miss Somebody* else. However, I didn't know Billy's last name, and I wasn't about to call him, Mr. Fixit.

"Ah, no. If you're in a hurry to get somewhere, we're done, but if you want to put in a couple of screws for me, you can stay."

My eyes turned into big white balls. "You'll let me use the drill?"

"Sure, but I'll need to help you."

Since the two screws were already in, the wood couldn't move around. There were four more screws to install, and for each, Billy let me hold the drill with my finger on the trigger. He held one hand over mine, and the other at the front of the housing. He told me to pull the trigger, and to not release it until he told me to. For the first hole, when the drill started, it scared the heck out of me, and the drill stopped when my finger came off the trigger. He didn't admonish me, rather, his deep voice gave me encouraging words, and the second effort was perfect. After that, the other three screw holes were *eazy…peazy*.

Billy changed the drill so it held the screw driver bit. "This part is harder, so we need to be even more careful. His smile was a bit bigger this time as he winked at me. He held the drill with me, his grip tighter this time. The screws went in, and the bit only came off the screw head twice. Billy told me that was really good for my first time.

I was now holding the drill by my side, when I said, "My dad's a toolmaker and is good with tools. He tries to teach me stuff sometimes."

He ruffled my hair and said, "That explains it."

Just then, the front door opened, and Ms. Frances Stevens walked out. She took one look at me, holding a drill that looked almost as big as I was, then her gaze snapped towards Billy. "What in God's name are you doing? He's just a boy." She took quick steps towards me and relieved me of the drill, handing it back to Billy. Her eyes locked on him and narrowed to slits as her foot tapped a brisk rhythm on the porch board.

Billy gave her a barely perceptible sheepish grin, but his blue eyes brightened. It was like he was laughing inside.

She turned away, mumbling, "Men." Then, she looked down at me. "Speaking of men, who might you be?"
"Joe." I pointed up the street. "I live up at number 54."

Her brow furrowed, but for only a few seconds before she said, "You're June's younger boy!"

"Yes, Ma'am," I replied.

I noticed Ms. Stevens was pretty. It didn't seem to matter when she was angry with Billy, or irritated, or giving me a hello, she was nice to look at. She looked like she was the same age as Billy, her long, grey hair pulled back neatly so that it draped down her back, and she had a nice smile to boot.

"You two look like you're done for the day. How about a piece of cake and some lemonade?"

Billy said yes, but I couldn't eat cake again. "Thank you, Ma'am. Lemonade would be nice, but I am still full from breakfast."

She put her hands on her hips, twisting her face into a grimace. "I'm going to have to talk to your mother. A boy your age refusing cake! That's just not right." She gave Billy a playful wink before scurrying inside.

Billy and I sat on two of the chairs on the wood porch. I was learning Billy wasn't a big talker, at least until you mentioned something he was interested in. The quiet was killing me so, I asked him, "When I bumped into you at the store, what were you doing there?" I asked him because, honestly, I couldn't think of a thing in that store an older man like Billy would want or need.

"That's where I get my comics," he replied. "There was a new issue of *The Submariner* Jake O'Neil was holding for me."

I turned sideways, staring at him. "Aren't you too old for comics?"

He tilted his head. "I don't think so. How about you? Do you like comics?"

I scratched my head. "I don't really know. I 've only ever read one or two, and not lately."

He smirked. "Aren't you a little young to *not* be reading comics, or at least know if you'd like them?"

It took me a few seconds to figure out he was pulling my leg and making a joke. "Why do you like reading?"

"I don't just read comics. I read lots of books as well. Always have."

To me, at that moment, his face changed some, or maybe it was just my perception based on what he said. It wasn't any longer the face of a man who worked all day with his hands. It was the face of someone who had much more to him, and it made me curious.

"When you get older, you'll see life isn't an easy thing. There are lots of things to worry about."

"I don't worry at all," I chirped.

"Sure, because your parents do your worrying for you. The last ten years or so haven't been easy for a lot of people around here." He saw I was getting confused, so he slowed down the explanation and kept it simple. "You see, almost all adults have to deal with the banks. There are times when that goes smoothly; other times, it doesn't. Lately, those times have been bad. Some people lost their jobs, some lost their cars, some even lost their homes."

"What does any of the complicated stuff have to do with reading?"

Billy took a moment to think about the complex details. In the early '80s, interest rates went sky high, as high as 21 per cent across Canada. For many people, it made more sense to walk away from their house, rather than renegotiate a mortgage. People weren't buying houses, so the prices of houses, across the board, plummeted. Again, people's houses weren't worth as much as what their mortgage was.

That started to turn around in the mid '80s until 1990, when interest rates lowered to ten per cent. It was better, but there were still many people who had great financial losses. Grand Valley, wasn't immune to these consequences. Although, being a smaller town, those consequences were not as wide spread, but the townsfolk certainly weren't as happy as they were in previous eras. Simply put, many had lost hope.

Those were Billy's thoughts as he tried to give me a simple answer about the reading connection, one I still did not understand. After a long sigh, he said, "When someone reads a book, and if it's a really good book, it makes you feel like you're right in the story as one of the characters. It's the same when you read a comic. You're right in there with the hero, saving people and putting criminals in jail. During that time, you forget about your bank problems, or about many other issues going on in life."

"Does that mean you read because you have issues you're trying to forget?"

For a moment, Billy's entire face sagged. He didn't answer. It was a good thing I wasn't old enough to understand the reflex response. It was also a good thing that, at that moment, Ms. Stevens came out with a tray supporting a piece of cake and three large lemonades.

Since my attention span at ten was severely limited, I lost any thought of reading—who, what or why—and bounced on the chair until Ms. Stevens handed me the cold glass of lemonade. I didn't say too much else as I sipped on the straw, making a scrunched face every time I got a bit too much lemon. When I heard the gurgle revealing the glass was empty, I rose and thanked Ms. Stevens for the drink.

Billy interjected, "I'll be here again tomorrow. Frances has a few fence boards needing replaced. Want to help out?"

I'd been at Ms. Stevens house for over an hour, and I couldn't say I didn't enjoy it. I learned how to use a drill. I found out Billy was smart. My mind was deliberating the decision when Ms. Stevens interrupted my thoughts. The sly grin on her face told me, even though she was looking at Billy, her words were for me. She said, "I was thinking of barbequing some chicken for lunch tomorrow along with some of my potato salad. What do you think?"

Billy was about to answer, when I asked, "Do you barbecue with gas, or the old way?"

"You mean on charcoal?" she asked me.

"Yeah. On charcoal." I always liked the charcoal method. My dad did as well. When she verified it would be an old-fashioned barbecue, I promptly said, "I'll be around in the morning," as I tried to hold back my silly grin. We said our goodbyes, and Billy walked me down to my bike. My foot expertly flicked up the kickstand, then I left, looking for what kind of trouble I could get into next.

Frances and Billy remained on the porch. They sat quietly for a time, enjoying the afternoon heat that was building. The river running through the valley and the breeze that blew over the farm lands, tending to swirl once it hit the valley, left a layer of thick air lingering in the sluggish summer months. The result was a layer of humidity that often sat on the small town like a thick, wool blanket. It was something older people enjoyed, but for many younger people, it just made them sweat.

"If you're going to start work early tomorrow, why don't you sleep over," she offered. "I have my spare room you can use."

Billy straightened up in his chair and cleared his throat. "No, that wouldn't be right, you being a widow. People would talk, and that wouldn't be fair to you."

"Fred's been dead for two years now." She said the words, even though she knew, he knew the dates very well. For a long time, Billy didn't have anyone he considered a friend. He considered the people he knew as acquaintances. The exception was Frances, and long before that her husband. For even longer, Fred had been the only person he considered a good friend. That made his wife, Frances, a friend, and when Fred died, with both of them needing companionship, they became better friends and maybe even more than that.

However, every time Frances asked him to stay over, he refused. A few times, she even explained how her living alone in a big house wasn't good for her. She would suggest Billy just move in, sharing the space as good friends, not making it into anything more than that. Billy rejected her each time that topic came up. Frances always thought this was because Billy didn't want to denigrate the memory of her late husband, but she was wrong.

As Billy once again told her, he would go back to his apartment later in the afternoon, she mistakenly thought the source of Billy's hesitation was Fred. It wasn't. He shared more thoughts with Frances than anyone else, but his internal demons, Billy kept those to himself.

Chapter 6: Leaving Town

Lying in his bed with his hands under the back of his head, Eddy was keenly listening. He could hear the occasional clank of a pot or the clatter of a plate. He knew Mildred, the housemaid, was the source of those noises. Breakfast finished 30 minutes ago, and she was in the process of cleaning up. But that wasn't what he was listening for. A few minutes later, he heard it. Beyond the kitchen clatter, he heard a slight rumble. In the large garage three floors below his bedroom, a car engine had been started. He jumped to his feet, darting to the window. Gently pulling back the silk curtain, he peeked through the small crack in between the two sides of the fabric.

A white Mercedes came into view after it darted out of the garage. His mother was on her way. She would pick up Mary Kendall before driving to Duncan's Cove, a 45-minute drive from their Bedford home. Once a month, they went for their spa day by the sea, and they would not return until at least 4:00 p.m.

This was the second time that morning he had been listening for a car. Much earlier, at 6:30 a.m., he watched his father leave in the Jaguar. That meant, now, the only car remaining in the garage was the Cadillac Eldorado Brougham. He could live with that. It was big, handling like a boat, but it was luxurious. He had taken it out for a spin a few times, but usually with his father in the passenger seat to make sure Eddy kept to the speed limit. There had been a few rare occasions when Eddy took it without his knowledge, but this time it wasn't going to just be a joyride to relieve his boredom; he had a task with purpose to attend to.

When he saw the clock tick down to 9:45 a.m., he rose and descended down the sweeping, curved staircase. Two flights and a few steps later, he was in the kitchen. Henri, the butler and Mildred's husband, was sitting with her in the kitchen, drinking piping-hot coffee from a mug.

He rose, when he saw Eddy. "Young Master, Good Morning."

Eddy walked over, kissed Mildred on the cheek, then looked warmly at Henri. Both had been family servants from before Eddy was born. He had spent as much time growing up with them as with his parents—maybe more. Consequently, *Aunt* and *Uncle* were descriptions Eddy thought appropriate.

"Are you still considering your ill-advised adventure today?" Henri asked through his heavy French accent.

"Yes. I'm leaving now. Can you come and take care of the garage door for me?"

Henri glanced at his wife, shrugged, then led Eddy down the stairs to the lower level where Eddy opened the lock box secured to the wall, retrieving the keys for the Cadillac. He rolled down the window after he started the engine, and at the same time, Henri pushed the garage door open. Henri leaned down as Eddy was about to drive by him. Eddy stopped, knowing what he was going to say.

Henri put both hands on the body metal framing the window opening. "Make sure you are home by 3:00 p.m. Mildred and I will keep silent about your escapades, but if asked, we will not lie."

Eddy nodded before he pulled out, continuing down the long driveway to the main road. Their opulent house was one of 30 in a high-end, remote subdivision, 20 miles from Halifax centre. He had only a five-minute drive before turning up another driveway within the subdivision. Bart was waiting at the foot of the wide, marble stairs leading from the double, front doors. When Eddy pulled the car beside him, Bart threw a large duffle bag in the back before entering the front passenger seat area.

Eddy was 19 years old. Bart had just turned 18, and they were best friends. Driving the car in a circle, Eddy made his way around the large water fountain, then returned to the long driveway leading to the main road.

"You sure you want to do this? Six months is a long time, Bart."

Bart's lips were set in a tight line as he turned to Eddy and nodded. Bart didn't need to explain the situation again. Eddy understood the facts. Bart and his father did not get along. He could have handled his father not being attentive, or even ignoring him. He could even have handled his father being angry enough to hit him. However, what Bart's father did was berate and humiliate his son every chance he had. Nothing Bart did was good enough. It was the kind of mental beating Bart had taken for the last six years, so it didn't take him long to know, at the first opportunity, he would leave.

His mother didn't help. She should have supported him, but she was afraid of her husband and likely petrified of losing the rich lifestyle he provided. When Bart's father ripped into Bart, her reaction was always to pour herself another drink, or pop one of those anti-depressants she was fond of.

Bart turned 18 two months ago. Legally, he was free to go where he wanted now, so he made his plan with Eddy's help. Bart had told Eddy his mother had given him enough money to cover his six-month, cross Canada vacation. In reality, his mother and father knew nothing about the adventure he had planned. Many times, he had carefully watched his father open the safe in his office. This morning, after his father left for work, he opened it and retrieved enough money to cover his trip.

They were half way to Halifax Station where Bart would take a train west when Bart's daydream was interrupted by the sound of a siren from behind them. Looking in the side mirror, Eddy saw the police car with the two red lights spinning, one on either side of the siren in the middle of the roof. Bart whispered, "Pull over and just stay calm."

Eddy didn't need the advice since he was already in the process of bringing the vehicle to a stop. The police officer exited the black and white Buick and strode towards the driver's door with an air of importance. When he arrived at the open driver's window, with two thumbs stuck in his belt, he said, "Mornin, Boys."

Eddy gulped, then managed, "Morning, Officer."

"Nice car," the officer offered. "Is this the new 1958 version?"

"No, Sir. This car is a year old, so the '57 Cadillac Eldorado Brougham."

Plucking a thumb free, the officer lifted a hand to rub his chin while his gaze inspected the side of the car from front to back. "I like this in black with the silver roof. Lots of class."

"Were we speeding, Officer?" Eddy asked.

"No, not at all. But seeing two young kids driving one of the most expensive cars I've seen in the last six months, well, that tickled my curiosity. Do you own this car?"

"My father owns it."

"Maybe we should give your father a call to see if that's true," the officer said, one eyebrow raised.

"That might be difficult," Eddy replied as he glanced at his watch. "His plane would have just left for his business meeting in Fredericton."

The officer, his face tightening as he fought to maintain his composure, snapped his response. "There aren't flights scheduled from Halifax to Fredericton—ever. If people want to go there, they need to drive or take the train."

"Except if you own a private plane, and my father does."

41

For a moment, the officers eyebrows rose and he didn't breathe. Finally, he took in a deep inhale, and his eyebrows knit together. "Show me your ID, Son."

Eddy handed over his driver's license.

The officer inspected it, then brought it closer to his gaze as he mumbled, "Edgar Macneil." The name was familiar, but he couldn't put his finger on it. Then, the fog cleared. "Are you related to Roger Macneil, the owner of the Macneil Paper Company?"

"He's my father."

The officer gulped as he thought, thankfully, *he hadn't tried to reach the kid's parents.* He leaned down, looking across the car. In a raised voice, he said, "How about you, Boy. ID."

Bart reached over and handed him his driver's license.

The officer inspected it, but, this time, only for a second. "Bart Kendall. Let me guess, son of Mitch Kendall, the man who owns every ship leaving the Halifax docks, the same docks he also owns?"

"That would be correct," Bart replied.

The officer handed back their licences and thought, *this is 15 minutes of my life I'll never get back.* He wasn't going to waste any more time. "You two have a great day." He rapped his knuckles on the roof, indicating they were free to go.

Once they were again on their way to the train station, and they saw the police car make a *U* turn to head in the opposite direction, both boys starting laughing uproariously. They punched each other on the shoulder, quite proud of the way they handled the police officer.

They continued to the train station, but Eddy turned into the parking lot of the Hotel Nova Scotian, the old building connected to Halifax Station. Eddy and Bart walked in through the large rotating glass doors, then to the back of the lobby where the restaurant was located. Earlier, they had agreed they would have lunch together before Bart's cross-country trek. They asked for a seat by the window, where they both ordered sandwiches and a cold drink.

As they ate, they looked out the wall-to-wall window where, 200 yards away, a large ocean-going vessel, black with rust visible above the water line, was docked. On the dock beside it, men scurried about, and fork lifts carried heavy loads to a loading point. From there, a mesh wrap, hanging from a tall crane, captured the load and hoisted it away.

Eddy said, "It's awesome when you watch all those people working in coordination. And they all work for your dad."

Bart smirked. "Don't remind me. I'm trying to get away from the memory of my dad, at least for six months."

Through a chuckle, Eddy replied, "I bet you won't make it that long. You'll get homesick and be back here before you know it."

Bart's face took on a pale, drawn appearance, an odd look for someone so young. "You're a good friend, Eddy. If I come back early, it would be because I miss you."

Eddy had to look away for a moment, pretending he was interested in the work on the dock, when really, he was making sure his friend didn't see the moistness in his eyes.

After lunch, Bart slung the two straps over his shoulder, carrying the duffle bag as if it was a back pack. Shortly after, they walked through a corridor adjoining the hotel to the station.

"I know you're going to Quebec City, but where to after that?" Eddy asked.

"I'll spend a few days there, and check my options: maybe Toronto, maybe further west to Winnipeg."

A few moments later, when they were coming to the ticket counter, Bart asked his friend to wait for him as he went to purchase his ticket alone. Eddy was 15 yards away, so Bart spoke in a hushed tone. "One ticket, one way to Montreal." He didn't like lying to his friend, but later in the evening, once his parents realized Bart was missing, one of the first things they would do would be to search out Eddy. Bart's father could be overbearing, and he knew Eddy would spill his guts. Quebec City would be a good diversion.

Once the transaction was complete, Bart and Eddy walked towards the gate to the rail platforms. Bart put his hand on Eddy's shoulder, pulling him to a stop. "This is as far as you go. I'm going on by myself from here."

Holding his hand out to his friend, Bart shook it. Eddy was chuckling awkwardly as he said, "I'll see you in six months, maybe sooner."

"Sure." Bart pulled Eddy towards him and gave him a hug.

Eddy responded in the same manner, then in a quick motion, Bart pulled away and strode towards the gate. Bart had to be quick, so his friend didn't see the tears flowing down his cheeks. He told Eddy he would be gone for six months, but Bart, in his heart, knew he was never coming back.

Chapter 7: Is Billy Crazy?

I found, since summer had come to Grand Valley, I was waking up much earlier than I did when I lived in Bramalea. There was something about the town that had me thinking each day had a new adventure, and it was all the better it didn't involve watching TV or any other boring activity.

Today, the Dudes were scheduled to cruise Main Street. I was leaving the driveway when I heard a voice behind me. Kurt, in his housecoat, was on his way to Jim's to fill his coffee mug. I returned his hello as I stopped at the end of my driveway. Phoebus was already making his rounds and planted himself in front of me, his tail wagging frantically. As I leaned down and stroked behind his ears, hitting that spot he loved, I thought I really loved this town, it's quirks and the way everyone was like family.

I rode up Grant Street, making the corner just as Nik rode up next to me. We had agreed to meet at Chris's house, so we continued down the side street to Amaranth. I pressed my brakes at Amaranth, watching Nik make a wide circle back with his BMX bike once he realized I'd stopped.

"What's up?" he asked.

I felt silly—the kind of silly when something obvious is right in front of your face and had been for a long time, but suddenly, for the first time, you notice it. I asked, "Why aren't there tall trees on this street like there are on every other street in town?"

Nik formed a sideways smirk and replied, "Because the smaller trees haven't grown big yet."

I leaned over and slapped Nik on the side of his arm. "Don't be like that." I explained my confusion to him. "This town is over 100 years old, and there's towering trees everywhere. I didn't notice until now that, on this street, all the trees are small. What's with that?" I asked again as I pushed my wrap-around sunglasses up the bridge of my nose.

"What's with that—was the tornado."

"A tornado!" I screamed.

"It was five years ago." Nik pointed west to the corner of Amaranth and Main Street's. "It was big, and touched down there before it spun right along Amaranth as if it was following the line painted down the centre of the road."

My eyes were wide, like a car with high beams on. "Did ya see it?"

"Heck, no," Nik replied. "I was at home in the basement with my family. My dad threw a mattress on top of us, and we just waited for the noise to stop."

"What…what did it sound like?" I sputtered.

Nik clapped his hands together, and it made me jump. "It sounded like thunder, just constant. It didn't stop for at least a minute, but it felt like forever." He pointed up the street. "All the trees were pulled out of the ground. Some of them were found two roads over. Haven't you ever noticed something weird about the houses on Amaranth?"

"What about the houses?"

Again, he pointed. "Look. New house, new house, old house, new house, old house, old house, new house, new house. Everywhere you see a newer house is because the old house got wiped out by the tornado." He turned and pointed in the opposite direction. "See that patch of land covered with tall grass at the corner?"

"Yeah."

"The library used to be there. The tornado ripped the roof right off. They found most of it half a mile away in Sorenson's corn field. Important people came to inspect what was left, and they said it wasn't safe, so what was left of the library got torn down."

"How come no one ever told me about this till now?" I asked.

"People weren't happy after that. My dad told me, times were already tough for people in town, moneywise, then this whole street got wiped out. Even on the other streets nearby there was damage. On Grant, you were lucky being one street over. The windows of your house got blown out, just like most of your neighbours, and we were finding shingles all over town for weeks. It's a bad memory and people don't like to talk about it."

"I guess I shouldn't talk to anyone about it."

That's the first time I saw Nik angry; I mean really angry, not just for show. His face flushed red and his jaw tightened as he sneered, "You weren't here, so yeah, you don't have a right to talk about it." Thankfully, his skin returned to its normal lily-white skin tone almost instantly, and I could tell, even with his face half hidden by his glasses, he was sorry he said it like that.

"Two people were killed," he whispered. "Like I said, it wasn't a good time." He cracked a half-hearted smile to show me he was okay. "Let's get going."

We biked across Main Street and met with Chris, Mitch, Chet and Ronnie, who were waiting at Chris's house. When we biked back and reached Main Street, I yelled out, "Hey, Guys!"

They stopped, wondering what was up.

"I have to help with some work this morning, so, I'll find you guys after lunch."

Mitch asked, "Your dad need you to help him?"

I hesitated, but I figured they would find out soon enough. "No, I'm going over to Ms. Stevens's house. Billy is doing some work there, and I'm gonna help him."

"Crazy Billy!" Chris exclaimed.

For some reason, even though I knew very little about Billy, I felt bad the way Chris insulted him. "He's not crazy! I worked with him yesterday. He's smart, not crazy."

Chris laughed, thinking it was some kind of joke. I told him it wasn't, and they could come see for themselves if they wanted to. A small cloud of road dust kicked up as I pressed hard on my bike pedal. My Chopper flew forward, and I was across Main Street before I noticed they were following me. I guess they really were going to check if I was lying.

Two corners later, I was at Ms. Stevens's house. I waited at the bottom of the driveway until the rest of the Dudes were alongside me. They saw Billy's black van in the driveway, and they heard noises coming from behind it. A moment later, they saw Billy, in his usual black overalls and green ballcap, walking away from the van carrying two long boards.

Chris asked, "You're really gonna do it?"

A realization came to me, and it brought a grin to my face. "You guys are just chicken." As I walked my bike up the driveway, I knew they were watching, seeing if I really would. I couldn't help but add a dig. "Bawk...Bawk!" I turned my face, laughing at them. That gave them the push they needed, and off they rode.

I parked my bike and caught up to Billy. When he saw me, he leaned down, so he could look me square in the eye. "Hi Joe. I'm glad you could make it."

I shrugged and tilted my face towards the long boards leaning against the fence post. "I'm not sure how much I can help."

He lifted his hand and tussled my hair. "As long as you try your best, that's all that matters. Besides, you're good company, and that beats working alone."

That made me feel good, so I listened with interest as Billy explained the job. There was an eight-foot section of rotten fence, and he'd already pulled off the old boards, leaving the two cross braces between the posts.

I moved close to the boards, and inhaled deep. "These new boards are cedar. They're going to last a long time!"

I liked working with Billy because he took his time explaining things. He pointed to a box of nails and the hammer beside it. "We have 12 boards to nail up. I'll show you one easy trick, but before that, we need to go back to my truck for a minute."

I followed him to the back of his van where the two rear doors were pulled open. I thought the van was awesome because it had built in shelves, and everything was neatly in place. Billy opened one of the back drawers, pulling out a dark-blue ball cap with a red maple leaf stitched onto the front.

Tossing it to me, he said, "This'll keep the sun out of your eyes."

I couldn't find a word to say. I'd received lots of gifts from my parents and my family, even from a few friends, but I barely knew Billy. It felt awkward, but the hat was beautiful, so I lifted it onto my head. Finally, I found the words, "Thanks, Billy."

After he handed me a small pair of work gloves, we walked back up to the hole in the fence and set about working. Billy took his time and explained things well. He showed me a trick or two. First, he showed me how to hammer the nails into the wood just a bit, so they would stick. That way, you could hold the wood with one hand and use the hammer with the other. To someone older, it might have seemed simple, but to me at ten-years-old, it was *black magic*.

He let me try hammering a couple of nails, but the hammer was almost as big as I was, so that didn't go well. Next, he explained what a level was. He showed me the air bubble in the water trap, and explained if the bubble was in the middle, it meant it was level. He explained why that was important, but by then, I was lost. So, we left it simple; the bubble had to be in the centre of the tube, and that's all that mattered.

After that, Billy gave me an important job. He would hold the wood board and adjust it until I told him the bubble on the level was in the middle. Then, he would hammer in the nails. After six boards were done, Ms. Stevens came out with two cold drinks. Once we returned to work, it didn't take us long to put the rest of the boards up. By then, I could smell the unmistakeable scent of charcoal burning. On the back patio, Ms. Stevens had the barbecue lit up. Billy and I sat on two of the lawn chairs, fidgeting with impatience while Ms. Stevens cooked the chicken breasts and legs.

We ate outside. The chicken was cooked perfect, and there was potato and macaroni salads to go with it. Ms. Stevens asked which salad I'd like, and I told her my mom makes great potato salad, so I'd try hers.

After a few bites of the salad, she asked, "Is it like your mom's?"

I swallowed hard before replying. "Your potato salad is really good, but my mom's is a bit different. She puts bits of apple in it."

"That's a great idea putting apple in it, especially in the summer time. I'm going to have to visit your mom and find out what kind of apples she uses."

I was full and ready to depart. Before I did, Billy said he was doing some work at the hardware store on Friday afternoon. Through a grin, he told me I could help, but there wouldn't be any barbecue chicken. I told him I'd try and be there, then thanked Ms. Stevens for lunch before I left.

I spent the afternoon and the next few days with the Dudes. We rode around town and biked over to the quarry site a few times. The old quarry site had been mined out decades ago, but it left a depression filled with shallow hills just outside the northeast corner of town. There were trails going in every direction, cut through the tall grass.

One day, we were there when the Brooklin Boys showed up. By now, I had learned the rivalry between the Dudes and the Boys was friendly, but competitive; in fact, we were all friends. Main, Water and Amaranth Streets, along with the quarry, were neutral ground. Brooklin was their turf while my subdivision and Chris's subdivision belonged to the Dudes. But even there, the rival gang could visit the other gang's territory, they just had to drop their colours. For us, that meant no sunglasses, and for them, their blue bandanas had to be out of sight.

I did go to help Billy on Friday. I didn't care what the rest of the Dudes thought. I even showed them the cool hat Billy gave me, but they weren't convinced Billy wasn't crazy. Later, Nik took me aside and told me he needed to show me something about Billy on Monday morning. He would come and get me at 8:30 a.m.

On Monday, I was in the middle of a wide yawn, when I saw Nik pull into my driveway. I was ready, so we pulled out, and he led me towards Main Street.

"Where are we going?" I asked.

"To Vicki's."

There were three restaurants in Grand Valley. Vicki's was the oldest. In fact, people said it was the oldest building in town. It was a white sided one and a half story house with an extension off one side. It was on the south side of Taylor Drive, the road running along the top of the escarpment for the entire town's length.

Nik and I turned up Melody Lane, a good uphill trek that didn't give Nik or I trouble as we used the lower gears on our bikes. Vicki's was right on the corner, but Nik kept moving up Taylor Drive for another 30 yards. Beside Vicki's, on the east side of the street, houses lined the rest of Taylor Drive. On the opposite side, where we were parked, was a long, shallow berm, and ringing it were cedar bushes, lined up like soldiers at attention. It extended from Melody Lane, past us and for another 70 yards going north. Beyond that, farmers fields extended for as far as I could see.

"What are we waiting for?" I asked.

I didn't have to wait for Nik's answer. As if on cue, Billy walked out of Vicki's. He headed across the road towards High Point Apartments, located on a stubby dead end at the top of Melody Lane.

So far, this wasn't surprising since Billy lived in the apartment building. I asked, "Now what?"

"Follow me, quick!" Nik exclaimed.

He zipped past me on his bike, leaving me struggling to catch up. Riding along the bottom of the berm, he then made a sharp left, to all appearances having disappeared into the line of cedars. However, when I rode further along, I saw the line of bushes behind the berm turned 90 degrees and continued along the edge of a field of crops. He was already on his feet, having let his bike drop to the ground at the base of the rise. Once I was beside him, I dropped my bike beside his and followed him to the cedars. There was a break in the foliage where it looked like one of the cedars had died. He lay down prone, and I slid down beside him, looking through the gap.

"What the heck is that?" I asked, astonished at what I was seeing.

Nik explained the mass of concrete in front of us. "My dad told me, about 40 years ago, a crazy, rich guy who had a huge estate just up Hwy 25, built this place. He wanted to build a pool, the kind you see them swim in like they do in the Olympics, and he wanted it deep enough for the high divers as well. But he died, and it never got finished."

There was a huge rectangular, concrete hole, in the middle of the enclosed area, surrounded by the berm and cedars on three sides. The perimeter was completed on the fourth side by the back wall of High Point Apartments. There were split seams at the bottom of the pool, and the concrete deck area around the hole was also criss-crossed with cracks, but not many considering how old the facility was.

"Why'd anyone want to build a pool out here?" I asked. Even as a young boy, I could see this made no sense.

"How would I know?" Nik replied. "I told you the rich guy was crazy. My dad tells me too much money can do that to people."

His words were interrupted by the squeak from a door being opened. Billy, a bucket hanging from his hand, exited out a back door from the two-story apartment building. At the opposite end of the pool was a diving board hanging out over the hole. Billy headed straight for it, and once beside it, he leaned over, pulling a sopping sponge out of the bucket. He then proceeded to wash the surface of the diving board.

Nik mumbled, "I told you he was crazy. Every Monday morning at 9:00 a.m., he comes out here."

I had to admit. It was odd. The rest of the concrete was discoloured from dirt, and the chain link fence that surrounded the pool on this side of the berm, was covered in rust. So why clean the diving board?

"That's nothing," Nik added. "Keep watching."

I did. After Billy cleaned the board, he took a large wrench out of his pocket and checked the bolts holding the platform to the concrete deck. I scratched my head, but then I was really confused when he got up on the diving board and walked to the end of it, hanging over the pit. Bouncing on the board, it flexed a few inches, but then he bent his knees and it sprung even more. I was worried he was going to fall in when I saw his construction boots bounce a few inches off the board. I turned my head away, not wanting to see Billy splattered at the bottom of the pit.

Nik nudged me with his elbow. "Don't worry. He never jumps."

When I turned my gaze back to Billy, he was standing on the end of the board, his feet together. He was mumbling something, and he continued for a couple of minutes until he raised his hands into the air.

Nik tried to hold back his voice's volume by clenching his teeth. "He's fucking nuts!"

I was still watching Billy when Nik leaned towards me, his lips close to my ear. "I told you Billy was crazy. You need to stay away from him."

I didn't answer. I don't think Nik expected one. He just kept nattering in my ear. However, I saw something Nik didn't. Although silently mumbling while standing on a diving board over an empty pool would give rise to anyone thinking there was something mentally wrong with him, I saw Billy do something right before he climbed down from the diving board. He had made the sign of the cross in front of him. Billy wasn't mumbling. He was praying!

Chapter 8: The Day of Reckoning

Billy liked walking. If he wasn't carrying tools, then walking was what he preferred, so that's what he was doing. He was going to dinner, and as such, he'd left his overalls behind, replaced by a pair of black slacks and a white, short sleeve, button up shirt. Even though they were bought from *Mark's Work Warehouse* and many would still consider the clothes work attire, for Billy it was *high-end* work attire, smart but casual.

He walked down the hill from High Point Apartments and was now walking along Main Street. He almost ran into Susan Jameson when she rushed out from Foodland. Even though she was the one who burst in front of him, Billy gave his apologies. He lifted his hand instinctively to remove his hat before he realized it wasn't there. It wasn't needed, especially for a dinner, the thought of which, made him a bit nervous.

Susan smiled and apologized. "Oh, it was my fault. It seems I'm always in a hurry."

Billy told her he was going to Grant Street and would be walking right past her house. Therefore, he offered to carry her grocery bag, and before she could refuse, he pulled it from her grasp. Consequently, they walked side by side towards Amaranth Street.

Jacob Smith walked by and gave Billy and Susan a, "good afternoon."

Billy and Susan offered their own, "hello," in return.

It's the way it was throughout Grand Valley. Everyone knew everyone else, and in many cases, their parents knew their neighbour's parents. Walking by someone and not offering a greeting would be odd, and for many, it would be rude. Men often shook hands as they passed each other, and women would often stop and chat, making their errands around town more time consuming than they had to be.

"How is that light in your dining room working?" Billy asked. He had installed a new one two weeks before.

"It's just fine," Susan answered. She hesitated a few seconds, then added,

"I hate to be a burden, but the latch on my gate is rusted and loose. Do you think you could replace it for me?"

Billy stopped walking and pulled a little black book from his back pocket and a pen from his shirt pocket. He flipped through the pages, then looked over the top of it at Susan. "How about next Tuesday morning?"

Her brows furrowed. Susan was thinking, then she said, "That should be fine. Just tell Mike at the hardware store to put the parts on my tab."

He wrote the appointment into his book, then they continued towards her house which was the third one on Amaranth. Just before she went up her driveway, she turned to him and said, "Come early and I'll make you breakfast."

He'd been doing odd jobs around town for over 30 years, and he wasn't sure when he gave up trying to say no to free snacks and meals. The townsfolk were insistent, and some would take it as an insult if he refused; Susan was one of those people. "Breakfast sounds great. I'll be around at 8:00."

That brought a wide smile to Susan's face. Her house was one of those that survived the tornado. Still, there was substantial damage, and a tree fell on her car, destroying it. It never stopped amazing Billy, between tornados and hard economic times, such a simple thing like accepting a breakfast invitation could still bring a smile to people's faces.

Billy continued along Grant Street towards our house. Two days ago, my father had searched Billy out. He knew I had been spending time helping Billy work around town. It made sense to me, especially as I grew older, that a 50 something man spending time with a ten-year-old boy could and should be worrisome. As such, my father took it upon himself, unbeknownst to me, to invite Billy for dinner.

He was halfway down the road to my house, when a shout came from his right. Janice Keeling had come out the front door when she saw Billy. "Are you coming back this way?" she asked.

"Should be," he answered.

"Make sure you knock on my door when you do. I have some fresh baked muffins."

Billy froze, then turned towards her. "Corn meal?"

She chuckled. "Of course. I know it's your favourite."

He told her he'd be back in a couple of hours before continuing on to my house. This was life for Billy in Grand Valley. People asked him to fix stuff, which he happily did, and he couldn't get more than 20 yards down any road before someone invited him in for dinner, or offered him food or a drink. It sounded simple, but I suspect it was the type of uncomplicated life some would exchange, in a minute, from the stress of a boss-breathing-down-your-neck, nine to five job.

Billy knocked on our screen door. I ran to answer it, but my father snapped his fingers at me. I skidded to a stop as he stepped in front of me and opened the door.

Billy said, "Hello, 'Mr. Kovach.' I hope I'm not too early."

I looked at the clock on the far wall of our living room and saw Billy was five minutes early. Being on time was one of the things Billy told me was important. It took zero skill to be on time. You didn't need training or a college degree. It took a bit of effort, but mainly it took you having respect for others. He told me, when you're late, you send a message that you think your time is more important than their time.

My dad moved to shake Billy's hand, but each of his hands was carrying a bag. Billy quickly shifted one bag, shook my dad's hand, then handed one of the bags to him. My dad reached in and pulled out a bottle of wine. One eyebrow raised, my dad said, "This is a good Hungarian wine. Thank you." He asked, "Do you know something about Hungarians?"

Not sure how to answer that, Billy just provided an awkward smile and a shrug.

My dad didn't want Billy to be uncomfortable before he even got in the door. He said, "I ask because you pronounced our surname correctly, the way a Hungarian would. For myself, and my parents before me, it was impossible for Canadians to remember it was really pronounced Kovach. They just want to say it the way it looks as Kovacs."

After the brief introduction, Billy was shown in, and since this seemed to be a formal adult dinner, I held my hand out to Billy and said in a pretend, deep voice, "Nice to see you again."

Billy grinned from behind his grey whiskers and slapped my hand away. "Don't be like that." He saw me looking at the other brown bag, folded flat. He added, "That's for you for *later*."

I jumped in the air, yelling, "Ah, shucks!"

My mother was walking into the hallway from the kitchen in time to hear my yell. "Keep it down, Young Man," she scolded before she looked at Billy. "It's nice to finally meet you. Joe talks about you all the time."

"He's a fine boy," Billy offered.

"Have a seat in the living room," she replied. "Dinner will be ready shortly."

My father sat in his favorite arm chair while I sat beside Billy on the couch. My mother came in a few minutes later, after ensuring everything cooking in the kitchen was under control.

My father asked Billy, "So, tell us a bit about yourself."

And so, it began. I knew they invited Billy to interrogate him, I just didn't think it would begin so early.

Shrugging, Billy replied, "There's not much to tell. I've lived in Grand Valley for over 30 years. I help people out, and they help me make my way."

"What's your last name?" my mom asked.

Billy shifted on the cushion. I'd gotten to know Billy well, and I could tell he was uncomfortable. "People in town call me Billy Fixit. That's been my last name for as long as I've been here. Before that, I had another last name that isn't important. It's in the past, so if you use, *Fixit*, like everyone else in town does, that works."

My mom and dad glanced at each other. I could tell by the odd lowered brow looks they both had on their faces, the answer confused them. Even I thought Billy was being evasive.

My dad asked, "People around town say you can fix almost anything. Where did you pick up all these skills?"

"I'm good with my hands, and I like to read. There were lots of "how-to" books in the library. I used to read even more, but it's harder now since the library is gone," Billy answered.

My parents hoped the last question would bring some answers about Billy's upbringing, but he stayed silent after his answer. Finally, seeing the silence was awkward, Billy said, "I brought something for Joe. Would it be okay if I give it to him now?" He held up the paper bag.

I bounced on the couch, showing I agreed to the idea, and with a nod of his head, my dad agreed as well.

Billy handed me the bag, and in two seconds I had it open, pulling out the comic book. With wide eyes, I exclaimed, *"The Submariner!"* I flipped through it with Billy looking over my shoulder.

Seeing it was safe to leave Billy with me, my dad left to help my mom set the table, and likely have a "what-do-you-think-so-far" side discussion.

Once they left, Billy explained *The Submariner* was one of his favorites.

"Why?" I asked.

Leaning back in the couch, Billy was more relaxed since he wasn't being asked questions about his past. "Most comic books have a main character who is a hero, and everyone likes a hero. They help good people, and put bad people in jail."

"Okay, but that's all superheroes. Why the Submariner?"

Mumbling as he rubbed his chin, Billy thought I was overly curious and much too clever for a ten-year-old. It took a moment before he answered, "The Submariner is a good guy, but he has a mean streak, and he has a temper."

I interrupted, "How does that make him good?"

"People are complicated. Very few people are all good, or all bad. The Submariner has done some things he regrets, and he tries to make up for it by doing good deeds. I like that he understands what he's done wrong, and he tries to make up for it by helping people."

An idea popped into my head. "In the Submariner's world, does he help people by fixing stuff for them, like you do?"

Billy's face drooped, and for a moment he looked older. He pointed to the comic. "No, he's not like me. He does fix stuff, but in a different way. Read the comic later, and you'll see for yourself."

My mother yelled dinner was ready. Billy and I were on the way to the dining room when Andy sped down the stairs, two at a time; he wasn't the type to miss a meal. Once we sat down at the oak dining room table, my dad introduced Andy, but my brother was too busy eyeing the food on the large platter in the middle of the table to show more than a fleeting interest. My mom had made a dish of four different types of sausages with carrots and potatoes cooked in the oven. In a large, separate bowl was an almost overflowing portion of beef-flavoured rice.

My father had opened the wine in the kitchen, and now he poured a glass for everyone, except me. Andy was old enough, but he deemed me underage. I was thankful because, once, when no one was looking, I moved close to a glass of wine to sneak a sip. However, as soon as the acrid smell assaulted my nose, I wrenched my lips away, vowing to never touch the foul drink.

The conversation during dinner was pleasant enough. The probing questions towards Billy were kept to a minimum, until my mom came out with one much more direct.

"Billy, Joe tells me you let him use an electric drill."

Taking his napkin, Billy wiped the corners of his mouth. "That's not altogether accurate. I was holding the drill with him. It'd be more accurate to say he was controlling the trigger." He looked at my mom for a long moment, then the same towards my father. In a low tone, his voice calm and even, he added, "I'd never let Joe do anything dangerous."

My mother had a way of saying things nonchalantly, yet the words still carried an air of finality. She waved her hand and said, "Still, no more using tools."

Often enough, when I saw my father did not agree, he would interject his own opinion, and he did so now. "June, let's slow down a bit. He's getting older, and it wouldn't hurt him to learn about these things." He rose to his feet and said to Billy. "Come out on the porch with me. The kids can help June clean up."

I was picking up a couple of plates with one eye watching my dad lead Billy out onto the front porch. My mom and Andy were fully loaded with dishes as I followed them into our kitchen. There were two ways in: directly from the dining room, and the other was from the main hallway. I went back towards the dining room via the hallway where I tip-toed further down into the living room. Squatting down with my back against the wall right beside the open front window facing the porch, I made it my business to listen to what my dad and Billy were saying.

I arrived in time to hear my father say, "Some people would think it odd, an older man spending time with a ten-year-old boy."

"I understand," Billy answered. "If you want it to stop, I'll abide by your wishes."

"No, don't get me wrong. Joe likes spending time with you, and he likes that he is learning adult stuff." My dad emphasized his words. "I like that he is learning to work with his hands, but there has to be some ground rules."

"Of course."

"First, don't ever let me hear that you take him to your apartment. Second, my wife is half-right—no power tools, and no sharp tools like saws, knives or chisels."

Billy cracked an understanding smile. "I can do that, Mr. Kovach. I'd never let any harm come to Joe. Is there anything else?"

My dad heard the same thing I did as I spied on them from the other side of the fluttering curtain. Billy's voice was sincere, almost solemn. Both of us could tell Billy was speaking the truth.

Lifting a finger, my dad said, "There is one other thing."

"Sure."

"No more, Mr. Kovach. Call me Steve."

With the day of reckoning over, my first summer in Grand Valley continued without a worry. I split my time between the Dudes and Billy. He showed me how to use tools, but kept the ones my father specified as off limits from me. Often, it was a matter of handing tools to him, or at times just keeping him company. I enjoyed it, especially when, on a break, we would get a sandwich, a drink, or a piece of cake or pie.

Ms. Stevens became a closer friend to my mom. Shortly after Billy's first dinner at my house, Ms. Stevens did, in fact, come down to visit, making a point of asking what kind of apple she put in her potato salad. That led to Ms. Stevens asking my mom to join their Euchre club. They had four women and a fifth who wanted to join, but they needed a sixth to have three equal teams. My mom, thinking it was a fantastic idea, readily agreed.

That worked out better for my dad than my mom. In the summer, the euchre night was every Tuesday, and in the winter, it was shifted to Wednesday nights. At first, I didn't understand, but the first Tuesday night, once my mom left, my dad turned on the Toronto Blue Jays baseball game. They played a home game every Tuesday, just as the Toronto Maple Leafs hockey team played a home game every Wednesday during the winter. My father, and many other men in Grand Valley, could watch their favorite sports team in peace as the women enjoyed their preferred activities on what was known as Ladies Night.

There even came a time when Ms. Stevens asked my mom and dad up for dinner, and of course, Billy completed the foursome. It was good my parents got to know Billy better. It moved to the point where Billy was the go-to babysitter for me when they had a night out. Andy was old enough, but he was in that rut of irresponsibility that occurs at the beginning of one's teenage years.

In my opinion, for what it's worth at ten-years-old, I thought things were just swell.

Chapter 9: Two Rich Guys

The source of the Grand River was from the many creeks and streams criss-crossing central Ontario. Fifteen kilometres north of Grand Valley, Roger Thornhill was looking out the floor to ceiling windows located on the back of his massive timber home. He was in his great room, highlighted by a stone fireplace climbing to the ceiling of rough timber beams 25 feet above him. Coffee mug in hand, he was admiring the sunrise overtop the Grand River running along the back of his estate, 50 yards in the distance.

Roger woke up at 6 am every morning, even though it allowed only five hours of sleep a night. It took discipline, a trait he found critical to being successful, and for him, that success was measured in wealth. Money was never an issue because he had lots of it; more than he could ever manage to spend. His father left him a successful construction company, one started by his grandfather, then handed down through the generations. Roger had expanded the company further, now also successfully building complete homes at a wide range of locations across Ontario.

Checking his watch, Roger saw it was time to leave. He walked along the long hallway and down a flight of stairs to a metal door. Passing through it, he was in the five-bay garage. Four of the bays were occupied with a Porche, a Ferrari, a Bentley and a Cadillac SUV. His executive assistant had put his golf clubs in the Cadillac the night prior, so that's the vehicle he now entered.

He pushed the button on the garage door opener and drove out, then up the ramp onto the curved cobblestone driveway. Even though Roger was a workaholic, as most successful people were, he always took time out to relax and recharge. During the summer, that meant, once a week, he played golf with his best friend, John Robie.

John lived eight miles south of him, and his house was just as opulent as Roger's, although it was, arguably, a bit smaller. When he arrived there, Roger pulled in front of the heavy wrought-iron gates and pressed the button on the electronic console mounted to one of the two red brick columns. Lifting his hand towards the camera, he waved and shouted out, "it's Roger!" towards the microphone he knew was there.

Both gates drew open, and Roger drove the 100 yards to the main house. The long driveway swept around, giving him a view towards the back of John's property. It wasn't on the river, but John had a massive man-made pond—almost the size of a small lake. There was a short dock, and moored to it were two jet skis, two of the many man-toys John could afford.

John wasn't as punctual as Roger was, so Roger had to press the horn on the steering wheel to remind his friend he was waiting. John's man servant came out first, carrying John's golf bag, and John followed a moment later. He entered the front passenger seat area and greeted his friend.

People sometimes thought Roger and John were brothers since they looked similar. They were both six foot tall with lean builds, although John's lack of exercise was beginning to give him a soft look. They both were in their early '50s with Roger having grey hair while John's was still brown with grey only visible at his temples. The other noticeable difference was the thick, '70s porn star moustache adorning John's face.

John wasn't quite as wealthy as Roger since he wasn't born into money. He made his media empire from scratch, beginning as a newspaper reporter, then starting a small country newspaper. Shortly thereafter, he started a second, then bought two more newspaper offices. After that, he began buying regional television stations, and finally, he started a TV network in Toronto, quickly becoming the most popular network in Ontario.

However, the two friend's temperaments and aptitudes were different. Roger was a businessman, strongly rooted in economic fundamentals, and as such, he ran a tight ship based on logical decisions. On the other hand, John was a newspaperman, and that meant he was a salesman. In his professional dealings, he brought considerably more emotion to the table. As best friends, Roger and John were competitive, so during the summer, every Monday they went to the *Devil's Pulpit*, an exclusive, British style golf club a 40-minute drive from John's home.

Roger turned onto Highway 25 south when John said, "I feel like waffles. Let's go to Vicki's."

Usually, they had breakfast at the on-site clubhouse before their round of golf, but the Grand Valley restaurant had the absolute best waffles in the region. Roger didn't need much convincing, so when he was driving through Grand Valley, he turned right, continuing up the inclined road to Vicki's.

Vicki's didn't look like much from the outside, and for that matter, it wasn't much to look at from the inside either. There were four booths along the front window, the benches covered with red vinyl from at least a decade prior. Two of the seats had rips that were patched with grey duct tape. There were four additional large tables that could sit four people at each, and the chair seats were covered with the same red vinyl. Across the back of the main room was a long counter from where Vicki kept charge. Through the glass below the stainless-steel counter were several mouth-watering, homemade pies, some made by Vicki, some from another local baker.

Breakfast was a busy time. Roger and John were fortunate to find one of the booths empty. They just sat down when Vicki appeared beside them. Vicki wasn't slim by any means, but she was pretty with strawberry blonde hair, tied back in a short pony tail. "Coffee?" she asked.

"Sure," Roger replied. "And waffles, please."

"Same for me," John added.

Vicki scurried away, leaving the two friends to themselves.

John asked Roger, "How is that new housing development in Shelburne doing?"

"It's slow. Although the damn interest rates have come down, they're still too high. People are afraid and don't want to take risks, especially after the crazy rates we've been through."

"I don't know how people do it these days," John offered as he shook his head. "It's not like wages have gone up, yet everything's so damn expensive."

"How about you?" Roger asked. "How's the newspaper business?"

"It's going fine. It's only a dollar for a paper, and it's not like people don't have a dollar, but there's some people who don't want to buy a paper or turn on my station because all we do is report bad news: a hurricane in the Gulf of Mexico, a robbery in Toronto, people living in shelters, and many of those surviving just barely hanging on, pay check to pay check. People are losing hope."

Vicki brought two plates of waffles and the coffees. As a result, their conversation slowed, their priority shifting to the delicious breakfast. John was lifting the last forkful of waffles to his mouth, when something caught his eye across the road. He popped the piece of waffle in his mouth before pointing with the fork. "What's that about?"

Roger had just gulped down a mouthful of coffee. He looked out the window trying to follow the direction of the raised fork.

"There, look at the gap between those two cedar bushes."

Tilting his head, Roger now saw what John had noticed. "Who's that?"

Through a chuckle, John replied, "That's what I asked you."

Through the gap in the cedars, they saw a scruffy, older man standing on the end of a diving board at the old pool grounds. He was standing motionless, like a statue. It was as if he was in a trance.

Vicki came to the table with a pot of coffee. "Refills?"

Without taking his eyes off the odd scene across the road, Roger pointed to his cup. "Sure."

At the same time, John turned to Vicki. "Who is that guy across the road in the pool grounds?"

Vicki bent at the waist, peering out the plate glass window. It only took a moment before she rose back up. "Oh, it's Monday. That's Billy Fixit!"

"What's he doing in there? He's going to hurt himself," Roger said in a crisp tone.

Thinking she didn't like that tone, Vicki snapped, "Billy's just fine. What's it to ya?"

Roger didn't come into town often enough for Vicki to know him well, but everyone generally knew of Roger Thornhill and John Robie, the two rich guys who lived north of town. Roger straightened up and retorted, "What's it to me…I happen to own that property."

John knew the story well, and hoped Roger would not repeat it for Vicki's clarification. Roger's grandfather had started the company he now owned. His son, Roger's father, Barney, was a great swimmer. In fact, he was good enough to make the Canadian Olympic swim team. Roger's grandfather had more money than he knew what to do with, and he was becoming more eccentric as he gained more wealth. He didn't like that his son was spending all his time in Western Canada where the swimming and diving teams trained. Of course, he also donated heavily to the Canadian Olympic program, so carried quite a bit of influence. Wanting his son closer, at least for part of the time, he made an agreement with the Olympic officials; he would build a private complex in Grand Valley and the Olympic team would split their time between the two locations.

The Olympic officials were hesitant. The majority of the swim and diving team members were from Western Canada, but the donation Roger's grandfather offered was sizeable, and, ultimately, it was an offer they could not refuse.

The land was purchased from the town and construction began. It was progressing well when Roger's grandfather suddenly died of a heart attack. Roger's father, Barney, never liked the idea of the swimming complex in

Grand Valley. At the same time, he was receiving pressure from his Western teammates who didn't want to stay in the small town for any duration of time. Consequently, Barney, who was now responsible to run the company, stopped the project. For safety, the pool area was fenced off, and the housing complex that was almost completed, was finished and converted into the High Point Apartments.

Putting her hands on her hips, Vicki glowered at Roger. "If you own the pool grounds, how can you not know Billy? He lives there, and he's your superintendent who looks after the property, and that means he works for you."

John laughed. Roger ignored him and looked around Vicki towards the counter. He had never understood before, but now he did. He pointed. "That jar on the counter labelled, *Billy's Breakfast*— that's the same Billy." He moved his hand, pointing back out the window.

With a grin, Vicki elaborated, "There's only one Billy Fixit. As well as looking after your property, he does odd jobs around town. He's an important part of our community." Her eyes narrowed, showing some disdain. "Money isn't important to everyone, and Billy is like that. He won't take a cent from anyone, but then, in return, everyone in town looks after Billy." She pointed to the jar. "People who come here to eat appreciate him, so they leave a tip and put a little change in the *Billy Jar*. It's enough that it covers his breakfast that, on many days, he has here."

Roger paid the bill. It was his turn. He left a tip and put a couple of dollars in the Billy Jar. Once they left the restaurant, he said to John, "I'd better go over and get him off that diving board before he kills himself."

John nodded, then followed him across the road. After going through the apartment complex, they exited out a back door onto the concrete surround ringing the gaping hole that had once been destined to be a pool. Billy hadn't moved and was still on the end of the diving board. The two men moved closer, but they weren't noticed until Roger said, "Excuse me."

Billy twisted his face around, his eyes inspecting the two men up and down. "Hi."

Crossing his arms, John decided he would just watch. After all, it was Roger's property.

"You should come down from there," Roger urged.

"Why?"

Roger looked down into the hole. It was 16 feet deep to accommodate the diving platform that had never been built. "You could fall and hurt yourself."

Shuffling his feet, Billy turned his body so he faced Roger. He shrugged, showing his indifference. "I've done this once a week every month for many years, and I've never fallen in."

"It's an old diving board. It could break any time," Roger added. He pointed to the fasteners holding the base of the frame into the concrete. "I'm surprised those bolts haven't already snapped."

"I replace the bolts once a year, every May."

Roger was getting irritated, but, at the same time, he felt sympathy for the older man. He introduced himself and John, then explained he was the owner of the pool grounds. He wanted to continue talking to Billy, but would be more comfortable doing so if Billy was down on the concrete deck.

Once Billy came to a position beside the two men, John asked, "Why do you get up on the diving board?"

Billy realized no one had ever shown enough interest before to ask him that. Since he had done this every Monday for so long, for those who knew him, they just took it for granted it was part of the Billy Fixit routine. He removed the green ballcap and scratched his head. "I'm drawn here for some reason. I have this urge to dive into the water."

"But there is no water," Roger said.

His brows furrowing, Billy saw the two men were worried he would do something as stupid as jumping into the void. "I've got all my faculties, Gentlemen. I'd only dive in if there *was* water."

His gaze inspecting Billy, Roger thought the older, frail man wasn't likely to make such a dive without hurting himself, even if the pool was filled with water. "I'm going to suggest you stop this practice of contemplating a dive while up on that diving board. It's not safe."

Billy didn't reply, but then, Roger ran a multimillion-dollar company and rarely waited for such confirmations; he just expected his direction to be followed. As such, he smiled at Billy while slapping him on the shoulder. There was a finality to it, so Roger turned away from Billy with John following close behind.

Just before entering the apartment complex, John turned back to Billy and yelled, "You really would dive in if there was water in the pool?"

"I would, there's just one thing," Billy responded.

"What?"

"The board's not high enough."

As John walked away, he couldn't hold back the grin as he thought, *the old man really is crazy.*

Chapter 10: Murder in the Valley

My mother was a good singer, and she liked to sing around the house, especially in the summer when she had just about every window wide open. When I was younger, I didn't appreciate it much as it would often conflict with things I was trying to do—like sleep. However, as I grew older and moved away from home, I missed those songs. When I would hear one on the radio, it brought my mind back to those days of my youth when I had barely a care in the world, and as I have said before—no responsibilities.

One of those songs, made famous by Nat King Cole, was "Those Lazy-Hazy-Crazy Days of Summer." Even though the song was from two decades earlier, I recall my mom singing it often during that first summer our family spent in Grand Valley. It was a sign my mother was happy with the out-in-the-country lifestyle.

The song was also apropos for that July as a blanket of humidity had settled in the valley. And in that, the first week of July, a time when eastward winds usually brought some relief, they were nonexistent. Consequently, when I worked with Billy, we took extra breaks and the people of Grand Valley offered us more drinks, constantly warning us about the perils of dehydration and sunburns.

People were getting used to seeing Billy and I together, Billy on his three-wheel bike, and beside him, I'd be riding my Chopper with my sunglasses on. Outsiders might have been worried, thinking it odd, a man somewhere in his 50s with a ten-year-old boy, but the people of The Valley had known Billy for over 30 years. They knew better. When they saw Billy with his green ballcap on, me beside him with my blue coloured cap, they knew we were in our serious mode, likely on our way to *fixin* something for someone in town.

That's the way my summer was going by, spending some time with Billy, and just as much time with the Dudes. I also spent time with my family, but it was less than I had in the past. My parents didn't complain about it at all. When we moved, they were worried I'd be unhappy, but since they saw the opposite, they weren't about to interrupt that. Besides, as little time as I spent at home, Andy spent even less. He officially now had a girlfriend, a girl from Brooklin. Her family had a swimming pool, so they spent their time there, or they hung out at different friend's houses.

So it didn't come as a surprise to my parents that there was a day when I asked my mom if I could sleep over at Chris's house. When she asked for details, I clarified the plan. All of the Dudes would be sleeping over, but it would be a camp out. Chris's family had two big tents. One would be for sleeping, the other for playing. Since, by now, everyone in Grand Valley knew my mom, my mom was acquainted with Chris's mom, therefore she had no problem approving the adventure.

It was early afternoon when I pulled my backpack over my shoulders and threw a leg over my Chopper. I waved bye to my mom and rode to Chris's house, by now a route I could have followed with my eyes closed. I was one of the first visitors there, and the rest of the Dudes showed up shortly thereafter. There were also three neighbourhood girls who came over to play; of course, they weren't sleeping over; that was strictly for the boys.

Sasha was ten, and the other two girls were eleven: Cindy and Karen. They were identical twins. I couldn't tell them apart, mainly because I didn't care to. I had no interest in girls, but nevertheless we played different games that afternoon with the girls included. We played tag, or corn hole bean bag toss, and the whole time, I didn't know which girl was which.

That kept us occupied until dinner when Chris's father fired up the barbecue and made hamburgers and hotdogs. After filling our stomachs, we spent some time up in the tree house until the sun began to set. It was 8 p.m. when we climbed down the ladder, ready to play our favorite game: *kick the can.*

It was a great game to start playing at dusk. The rules were simple. One person was made *It*. That person would count to 50, and during that time, everyone else would hide. All the neighbours were fine with us using their yards, as long as we didn't go into the flower gardens, but hiding behind cars or bushes was just fine. A can, usually an old pop can, was placed on the curb beside the person who was *It*. Once everyone was hidden, *It* would have to find those who were hiding. *It* would call out their name and where they were, once they were spotted. Once caught, they had to come to jail, which was the driveway. Now, if someone still hiding made a dash to the metal container, kicking it away before *It* got there, all the kids in jail would be freed. Then, the round would begin all over again. And just so one person wasn't *It* forever, once the can was kicked three times, *It* was switched.

We had been playing for a while. Mitch was *It* and began counting. There were a couple of spruce bushes on the neighbour's yard, so I ran over and hid behind them. To my surprise, a moment later, one of the twins was there. I didn't know if it was Cindy or Karen. They both had the same straight, blonde hair, making them indistinguishable. Mitch was walking off in the opposite direction when she turned to me and whispered, "I think we're safe."

I glared at her, hoping she got the message we weren't hiding together. Instead, she smiled at me. She was pretty, but girls weren't on my radar, so the thought was fleeting. It was immediately replaced by my next thought; *she was acting weird.* Unfortunately, it became worse from there.

She leaned closer, giggled, then asked, "Have you ever kissed a girl?"

Angling away from her, my eyeballs were massive balls of white, trembling like two fried eggs sizzling in a pan. "Hell, no!" I sneered.

Crouched down, she inched closer. "Well, I've decided I want to kiss you." She giggled again.

Even though the nighttime air was cooler, my armpits began to sweat as my young mind became overwhelmed with panic. I peeked around the bushes and saw someone just kicked the can. Everyone was moving hiding spots, so I bolted. I ran across the road where the Richardson's had a large raised flower box near their front porch. I threw myself down, flat on my stomach, behind it. A moment later, I saw a shadow, then heard a thump beside me. When I rolled over, she was right there, and I still didn't know which one of the twins it was.

"You better let me kiss you," she whispered.

"You're crazy. I'm not kissing *any* girl."

Her lips slid into a smart-assed grin. "You better let me, or you'll be sorry."

"What're you gonna do?"

She leaned her face closer, forcing me to lean my head back. "If you let me kiss you, I won't tell anyone. It'll be our secret." Her lips tilted even more, her appearance becoming more sinister. "But if you don't kiss me, I'll tell all the Dudes you *did* kiss me."

With my teeth clenched tight, I hissed, "You're crazy!" At the same time, I thought, *although on one hand it was impressive, she was too young to be thinking up this type of diabolical reverse logic.*

She shifted closer. "Just one kiss and it's over. No one will know."

I thought about my options. If I didn't kiss her, she'll tell Chris I did, and he just might believe her. I decided to not let that happen. "Just one kiss, that's it."

She giggled and shifted until there wasn't even an inch between us. She put her hand on my shoulder and pursed her lips into a circle. Once again, my eyes were huge, as I saw her moist lips come towards me. Instinctively, I pulled away, but the back of my head banged against the flower box. Clenching my eyes tight, I felt her lips press against mine. I kept my lips pinched tight as she did some crazy sliding motion, allowing her lips to rub all over mine. I tried to twist away, but her hand moved from my shoulder to the side of my face; her grip was surprisingly strong. It was only a few seconds, but it seemed like forever before she pulled away. My lips burst open and I inhaled a massive gasp of air.

She just giggled. "Do you want to do it again?"

Not being able to take any more, I pushed up on my arms, jolting myself to a standing position. Immediately, I heard Mitch call out my name and my position behind the flower box. *Damn*, I thought. I ran, thinking jail was a much safer place than in the claws of the twin, whichever one she was.

I didn't think the night could get much worst, but I was wrong. After kick the can was over, Chris's dad made a bonfire and we had Smores. The twin who kissed me, the one I could only identify by her red shirt, didn't tell anyone, but she kept looking at me and giggling all night. I was glad when Chris's 15-year-old sister, Anne, came out with the promise of telling us ghost stories. She told two good stories that had us shaking, but laughing at each other at the same time.

Then, her face became drawn, her eyes narrow. "Now, I'm going to tell you a story about Grand Valley, and it's a true story." She had a flashlight, and she pointed it upward under her chin as she continued, placing patterns of red light and evil shadows across her face. "A few years ago, there was a family living in Grand Valley: a father, mother and two daughters. They were the friendly type and got along with everyone. They fit right into Valley life. The girls grew into teenagers then fine young adults, but they still lived in their parent's house.

The older girl came home one day and said she had a boyfriend, and since she was older, the parents didn't see this as a problem, so they asked her to invite him to dinner. A week later, there was a rumbling noise from the driveway, and when the parents went to investigate, on the driveway, they saw a tall, young man standing beside a Harley Davidson motorcycle. He was dressed completely in black, including a black leather jacket and black riding gloves. He had short hair and a long red beard. The daughter's boyfriend was a biker!"

By now, there was complete silence from the group as we listened intently.

"The parents were taken aback, but they tried their best to accept the boyfriend. To their surprise, he had a nice personality, and he was helpful. He began spending more time at the house, and quickly, the two unlikely partners were engaged. Eventually, with the daughter's urging, he was asked to move in and things seemed fine. The only thing the parents didn't like was, occasionally, they saw a flash of temper from the boyfriend. However, it was rare. Most of the time, he was well behaved and helped the parents around the house.

He was hard working. People remember him above the porch, re-shingling the roof. The sound of the hammer hitting each nail would echo in town." With her fist, Chris's sister slapped her thigh as she said the words, *"Bam! Bam! Bam!"*

By now, the hairs on the back of my neck were standing up, and I was thinking the sleep over might not have been the best idea.

Anne continued. "One day, the parents had been out for dinner, and when they came home, both the daughter and her fiancé were gone. It wasn't odd then, but the next morning, they were still missing. The father went outside. That's when he saw it. There were drops of blood making a trail from the porch to the driveway, to the very spot where he always parked his motorcycle." There were a few gasps, but Anne snapped, "Quiet!" Then, her voice lowered, barely above a whisper. "The police were called. They searched for the daughter and her boyfriend, but they had vanished, until two months later, when the police spotted him driving his motorcycle in Orangeville. They stopped him, but he wouldn't say a word. They searched the bike where just behind the seat, a saddle bag was draped over the frame. They opened one side and found a plastic bag, and there was something in it about the size of a cabbage." Anne paused, taking a moment to glare at each of the kids around the campfire.

"When they opened the bag, inside it, they found the daughter's head."

There were yells from every side of the firepit. The twins jumped to their feet, their screams being the loudest.

Anne raised her voice, yelling over the screams. She pointed a crooked finger at the twins. "To this day, in the middle of the night, people in Grand Valley swear they hear someone banging a hammer to a nail on their roof! It's the ghost of the biker!" She then slapped her fist on her thigh. *"Bam! Bam! Bam!"*

The twins bolted. They were running across the yard as fast as their feet could carry them.

For the rest of us kids, we just laughed nervously. Mitch said, "That's a great tale!"

Anne had turned off the flashlight, and her face returned to her more jovial appearance. "It's not a tale. It's a true story."

I blurted out, "No, it's not. We don't have murderers in Grand Valley!"

Chris interjected, "The story is true, but the biker is in prison for the rest of his life."

I scrunched my face. "I'm new here, so you're just screwing with me."

Nik added, "Joe, it's true. The family lived in Grand Valley, and so did the murderer."

Shaking my head, I asked, "If it's true, where's the house?"

Chris said, "You really don't know? No one told you?"

"What are you guys talking about? I asked.

Nik said, "It's your house. The family lived in your house."

I jolted to my feet. At first, I thought this was some kind of joke they were playing on me, but I knew, if it was, the look on my face right now would have them laughing. However, no one was laughing, and Nik was my best friend. He wouldn't do this to me, or would he? I wasn't going to wait around to find out. Turning, I ran for my bike. Ignoring the yells from behind me, I tore out of the driveway, riding back to my house as fast as my feet could spin the pedals.

Chris's mom had called my mom, so she was waiting on the porch when I rode up the driveway. It was 10 p.m., so she was worried since I had ridden home in the dark by myself. She was about to scold me, when she saw me throw my bike down, something I never did. By the time I ran to her, I was sobbing uncontrollably. She had no idea what was wrong until the words came in spurts. "They said...a murderer...someone was killed...in our house!"

She didn't say anything. She just hugged me tight since I couldn't stop sobbing. It took a few minutes, but finally I settled down. I pulled away from her and whispered, "Tell me it's not true. Tell me a murderer didn't live in our house."

My mom tilted her head and said, "Well..."

As soon as I heard that, I screamed, then the crying started all over again. If there wasn't any truth to it, her answer wouldn't have started with, 'well...'

She took me inside and sat on the couch beside me. She explained there was some truth to the story, but the version they told me was twisted. The family did live in our house, and so did the murderer, but long before the murder. The daughter and her biker boyfriend moved to Orangeville a year before the murder, and it happened in Orangeville, so there was no blood and no crime committed in our house.

It took a while for the pace of my heartbeats to settle down. Then, it was like I hit a wall, and I couldn't keep my eyes open. My mom stayed with me after I changed into my pajamas. There was a chair in my room, and she sat in it until I fell asleep.

Sometime during the night, my eyes shot open. I thought I heard banging. *Bam! Bam! Bam!* I crawled out of my bed. It took courage, but I pulled open the curtain with my finger. My window was directly above the porch, so right above the roof the biker had re-shingled. My mom told me that part of the story was true. I was looking down at the shingles he hammered in. I peeked in one direction, then the other, making sure no one was there.

After that, I pulled the blanket and pillow off my bed and walked down the hallway to the back of the house where my parent's bedroom was. Their door creaked when I opened it, and my mom's face tilted up. Sleepy eyed, she saw me walk to the couch nestled against the far wall. I threw the pillow across one end and crawled up, covering myself. My mom, rolled over, her soft eyes watching me until I fell asleep.

Chapter 11: The Wager

Exactly a week after Roger Thornhill and John Robie met Billy Fixit, they were once again on their way to their weekly round of golf. The difference, this time, was it was John's turn to drive, so he was the one behind the wheel of his Land Rover on Highway 25. To Roger's surprise, when they almost reached the far end of Grand Valley, John turned the vehicle up the hill towards Vicki's.

"We just ate here last week," Roger offered.

Keeping his eyes looking ahead, John mumbled, "I guess I can be unpredictably predictable."

Although John did enjoy the best waffles in the region, that wasn't the reason he was heading to Vicki's two weeks in a row. He'd been thinking about Billy, and an idea had formulated in his mind. If things this morning went as he expected, he would tell Roger soon enough.

The two friends sat in the same booth as the week prior. The events were like a rerun from the previous Monday. Vicki took their order, and in no time, they were stuffing forkfuls of syrup covered waffles into their mouths, chased down by swigs of coffee.

John looked towards the old pool grounds and pointed his fork in that direction. "It seems Billy is persistent."

Roger tilted his head, glancing at the seam between two of the cedar bushes. Again, it was like a rerun of the week prior with Billy, wearing black overalls and a green ballcap, frozen on the end of the diving board. Creases formed on Roger's forehead. "Damnit! I told him not to get up on that diving board again."

"Actually, no," John corrected. "You *suggested* he not get up on that diving board again." Earlier, John had used the word, "persistent," for Roger's sake, but what he was really thinking was Billy was consistent, even—committed, and that was an important characteristic for the plan formulating in John's mind.

Irritated, Roger hadn't even finished the last bite of waffles when he placed a $20 dollar bill on the table and said to his friend, "Let's go. I'm going to give that bum a piece of my mind."

John followed his friend, having to skip a few steps to catch up to Roger's angry pace as he crossed the road. He put his hand on Roger's shoulder and said, "I have an idea, so let me do the talking."

Raising an eyebrow, Roger glanced at John. He liked him; he considered John his best friend, but he also knew John was a salesman at heart. He could sell eyeglasses to a blind person, always working an angle to make a buck, and often, that meant a few bucks for Roger as well. Consequently, when they came to a spot beside the diving board, Roger did let John do the talking.

"Billy, can we have a talk for a minute?" John asked.

Billy turned, and seeing it was the same two men from the week prior, he climbed down from the diving board. "Hi Guys. What's up?"

"You are aware that Roger owns this site, so you work for him?"

"Yup."

"When we were here last week, he told you it wasn't safe for you to be up on the diving board, and he didn't want you to do that anymore."

Taking off his ballcap, Billy scratched his head. "The way I remember it, he said it *might* not be safe because the bolts were old." He pulled the cap back on, tugging on the bill. "I corrected him saying I replaced the bolts, and he didn't tell me not to get up on the diving board again. He only made a *suggestion.*"

Roger had enough of staying in the background. After all, he was standing right there. He opened his mouth, but John, seeing this, held his hand up, staying whatever words were about to explode forth. *Committed and clever— at least with his words,* John thought when he considered Billy.

"If we fixed up the pool and filled it with water, would you really dive in?" John asked.

"I'd like that, but I told you, the diving board isn't high enough."

John glanced down in the hole, then back up at Billy. "How high do you want it?"

Billy wasn't sure what was happening. He couldn't understand why they were asking him these questions. He thought, *maybe they were just entertaining themselves at his expense.* If he felt that was the intent, he would stop it right then, but he did work for Roger, so he needed to let the odd line of questions continue a bit longer. "This board is set at the Olympic height, and that's a little over nine feet to where the water line would be. I'd say if we double it to 18 feet, that would work."

Roger inspected Billy while John asked the questions. The overalls hung off his thin frame, although his arms appeared well muscled. He couldn't help but interject a question. "When was the last time you dove into a pool or a lake or a river?"

"When I was 12."

John missed a breath resulting in a cough. "You're kidding? You haven't done this since you were a boy, and now you want to dive from 18 feet?"

Billy shrugged. "That's what I said."

Roger shook his head and turned to leave, but John clenched the sleeve of Roger's shirt, turning him back to Billy. "This is important, Billy. It would cost us a bit of money to make all this happen. If we do that, what makes us think you won't back out?"

Taking a step forward, Billy stood directly in front of John. He was slightly taller than he was, so he tilted his head down, allowing John to see into his eyes. "You can ask anyone in town. They'll tell you I'm a man of my word. If I say I'm going to do something, that's what I'll do. Full stop."

John saw the truth and honesty in Billy's eyes. One corner of his lips angled up as he whispered, "I believe you will."

John turned to Roger. "You're the construction guy. If we built some bleachers, how many spectators do you think we could bring in?"

"What spectators?" Billy asked.

"It will cost us a bit of money to make this happen. We'll never make all of our money back from spectators, but it will help," John replied.

Roger had no idea what John was up to, other than his friend had seemingly gone crazy, almost as crazy as Billy. Nevertheless, he answered his question with a caveat, "*Hypothetically*, we could fit 500 people in here."

Glancing at Roger, then to Billy, John said, "Let's leave it at that for now. We'll be in touch."

A few minutes later, John and Roger were seated in the Land Rover, headed towards their golf club.

"What the fuck was that all about?" Roger asked.

Turning to his friend, John had a crooked smile and his eyes were gleaming with mischief under knitted brows. He said, "It's wager time."

"Oh, crap," Roger mumbled. "Here we go again."

Since Roger and John were both filthy rich and above middle age, they had exhausted many of the entertaining pleasures money could buy. Consequently, a few years ago, they had begun this habit of wagering on events, often outlandish events, more for the entertainment value than any monetary gain, albeit, they usually bet large sums of money.

John said, "I'll wager I can get Billy to dive in the pool from 18 feet, and I'll fill those bleachers with 500 people to watch him."

Rubbing his chin, Roger countered, "The 500 spectators have to pay $10 a ticket, and it has to be a dive, not a jump." As an afterthought, he added, "And Billy has to be successful. That means he doesn't drown, break his neck or any other bones. He has to come out of the pool in the same shape he went in."

"What do you think it will cost to fix up the pool and install some bleachers?" John asked.

After a few seconds of mental math, Roger replied, "$20,000."

"Okay, we'll split that, and how much is the wager?"

Again, Roger took a moment to think. He didn't think it would take much to get Billy to dive in, but getting 500 people to pay $10 each to watch an old man jump in a pool—in his mind that would never happen. "I'll wager $25,000."

"That's high!"

Laughing, Roger said, "It was your idea! No backing out now."

Pushing his hand out, he grinned at Roger. "I'm in." Roger shook it; the wager was on.

John thought he had the advantage, in fact, he knew it. Roger was a businessman, so he knew numbers and standards. John was a newsman and a salesman, so he understood people, and he also understood the environment they were in.

The '80s hadn't been kind to people. On the global stage, there were always wars in different regions around the world, and everyone expected a major war to break out in Iraq at any moment. A new disease called AIDs appeared in the early '80s. It had killed over 100,000 people in America and 1,000 people a year were dying from it in Canada. What made it worse, outside of being more predominant in the Gay community, was you could catch it from blood transfusions. So when you go to a hospital, a place where you are supposed to be cured of ailments, you can actually catch a mysterious disease that could kill you.

On top of that, Canada was in a shambles. The Quebec separatists were at their peak, and the economy, although recovering, was fragile. Unemployment was extremely high, not allowing the high interest rates to be reduced. That made life for many Canadians difficult at best.

John was a great salesman, and now he planned to sell them an elusive commodity—hope. If they had little hope for themselves, he would sell them hope for Billy and his cause.

Chapter 12: The Thinking Spot

The morning after the ghost stories at Chris's house, there was a sharp knock on our door. My mother answered to find Chris's mom standing on our porch with Chris's sister, Anne, who had told me the dark history of our house. Mrs. Eckland knew my mom because everyone knew everyone, so she gave her a warm greeting before grabbing her daughter by the shoulders and pushing her to a spot directly in front of the doorway.

Mrs. Eckland's voice had a deep tone, and her words came with a fast pace. "Well, Anne, do you have something to say?"

Anne had her hands in front of her, her fingers clinging to the fingers of her other hand, her knuckles white. Her voice was shaky. "Hi Mrs. Kovacs. I'm really sorry I scared Joe. Can I speak with him please?"

I was in the kitchen, listening when I heard my mom call out my name. I walked to the door, standing behind my mom, peeking around her.

"Hi, Joe," Anne said. "I wanted to tell you I'm sorry I told you the story of your house the way I did. Parts of it were true, but I made up other parts to make it scary. I really am sorry."

I shifted my head even further to the side and replied, "Okay, thanks." That's all I could manage verbally. However, I knew she was off my Christmas card list.

The apology seemed good enough for my mom and Mrs. Eckland. My mom asked if they wanted to come in for a cup of tea or coffee. I saw the relief on Anne's face when her mom declined. The encounter was embarrassing enough, so the sooner it was over, the better.

Anne's apology didn't help me much since I couldn't get the thought of the biker carrying a head around on his motorcycle from my mind. I couldn't sleep in my room since my thoughts always went to the biker, hammering in shingles on the roof only a few feet away. For the next few nights, I continued to sneak into my parent's room, but I knew that wouldn't last. I was surprised when Andy agreed to a solution offered by my father; Andy agreed to switch rooms. His was at the back of the house, next to my parent's room, but more importantly, as far from the roof of the front porch as was possible. Problem solved.

I think Andy felt sorry for me that week because when it came to Friday morning, he asked if I wanted to play road hockey with he and his friends. Now, he hadn't asked me to do anything with his friends before, and that wasn't because I was too small. I had taken a growth spurt during the summer, and as a result, I was only two inches shorter than he was. However, as I grew, I didn't pack on any significant weight, so I was still as skinny as a rake. In any case, he thought I could get along fine with his older friends.

It might sound odd to some that we'd play road hockey in the summer, but in Canada, we played hockey year-round. In the winter, there were leagues and games at the local rink, and every small town seemed to have an ice rink to support an insatiable need to play the best game ever invented. But we would also play road hockey year-round. Winter or summer, the preferred object in the game was a tennis ball, something that would hurt if it caught you on an unprotected area of skin. That was more of an issue in the winter when the ball hitting you was like being hit by a chunk of ice.

These risks were ones we took and, in fact, welcomed as Canadians always ready to partake in our national pastime. As such, Andy and I retrieved hockey sticks from our garage and biked over to the public school where I met Andy's friends. One net was set in front of the school's brick wall. The other was placed against the wall of the portable, 30 yards away.

Mike, one of Andy's friends had an idea. "Hey Andy, why don't we get your brother to play goal?"

"I don't want to play goal," was my instant reply.

Andy tried to convince me. "We have enough kids for six on each team and a sub. Because you're new, you'll be a sub, but if you go in goal, you'll play the whole game."

Andy and his friends were older, and I recalled how the tennis ball could hurt. My brother understood what I was thinking. To ease my fears, he pointed to a pile of homemade pads. "You won't feel a thing after we dress you up in those."

I glared at him, suspecting now, when he asked me to play, I was wrong in thinking he was just being kind. He knew they needed a goalie, and that's why I received the invite.

Grinning, Andy said, "You're not scared, are ya?"

At that point, I had no choice since all his friends were watching me, wondering if I was a chicken. I'd already been embarrassed once that week in front of the Dudes. I wasn't going to let that happen again, so I agreed.

Andy clapped his hands together, and two of his friends set about dressing me in the pads. The leg pads were pieces of cardboard, and glued onto the back of them, were large pieces of soft foam, six inches thick. There was a breast plate consisting of random pieces of plastic, tied together with string. They slipped the awkward outfit over my head, securing the velcro catches at the back, allowing the configuration to cover my front with a strategically placed plate hanging down to cover my private area. Two more cardboard and foam pads were tied to my forearms, one being longer to cover my hand while the other was shorter allowing them to push a baseball glove on, even though it was huge and completely unusable for catching. Next, they forced a baseball catcher's mask over my head, Andy curled his fingers into the wire frame, tugging it back and forth to make sure it was tight. Finally, one of them thrust a wide goalie stick in my free hand and helped me waddle to the net by the portable.

The game was on, and after a slow start where I let in two quick goals, I got the hang of it. I didn't try to catch the ball, or control it in any way. As long as I threw an arm or leg in front of a shot, that was good enough. In any case, my confidence was building since the goalie opposite had let in five goals to my two. I was feeling good about myself, and had a proud smile under the catcher's mask.

That smile was about to be all but knocked off my face. A player from the other team ran down the wing. He made a clever move around my defenceman, then he was right in front of me. He took a wicked-hard wrist shot, and I dove to my left just trying to get any body part in front of the ball. Unfortunately, that body part was my ear. I screamed as I flung off the glove, my fingers reaching for my ear to see if it was still there. Lying on the pavement, face down, I was about to start wailing when hands grabbed under my arms and heaved me to my feet.

Andy, wide eyed, said, "You okay? That was a great save!"

His friend, the one who had taken the shot, held my other arm. There was a glint of admiration in his eyes. "Dude, that was awesome!"

My tears immediately dried up, after all, it was a great save. I picked up the glove I had discarded and the hockey stick, stating, "I'm okay. Game on!" I survived the rest of the game, and I could feel the new found admiration from Andy and his friends. Maybe it was a test of some type Andy had connived. It didn't matter.

My ear still stung as I was riding my Chopper home, but I felt great. I was about to cross Main Street, when I heard my name yelled from across the road. Glancing across, I saw Billy, sitting on his three-wheeler, waving his hand over his head.

I rode across to him and said, "Hey, Billy. What're you up to?"

Rather than answering, he tipped his head, glancing at the side of my head. "Never mind that. What the heck happened to your ear? It's swollen and as red as a pimple about to pop."

It was a joke I wouldn't fully understand until a few years later when puberty had set in. Still, I laughed. "Road hockey accident. I was playing goalie."

He nodded. No more explanation was needed, but now he did answer my question. "Have you ever met the mayor, Tom Winters?"

"Nope."

"Want to? I have a meeting with him. You could sit in, if you like."

When I became older, I realized being the mayor of a small town wasn't very important, but at ten-years-old, I felt like I was about to meet someone akin to royalty. So, wide-eyed, I replied, "Heck, yeah."

We rode up the hill along the far side of Main Street and parked our bikes in front of the small, one-story building that was the town offices. I locked my bike, but having no where to secure my hockey stick, I brought it inside with me.

Mrs. Rand, the secretary, receptionist and *do-anything-required* person at the front counter, greeted us. Billy indicated we were there for a meeting with the mayor, whereby she pointed to a door at the end of the counter. As I turned to follow Billy, I heard her say, "Ah, ah. That's not going in there." She snapped her fingers. "Give me that hockey stick, and you can pick it up on your way out."

Most things in Grand Valley looked old, but when we entered the office, it looked even older than that. On the floor was a thick dark-brown carpet while the walls were coated with beige paint, a colour where I couldn't tell if that was the original shade or a darker one due to years of accumulated grime. The questionable paint was on three walls, leaving the last wall covered with sheets of fake wood paneling, and I guessed it must have been left over material from someone else's basement reno since the grey colour didn't match the rest of the room. In the centre of the mayor's office was a green, metal desk, the kind that belonged in a factory, and behind it stood a large man with a pot belly hanging over his belt. He was dressed nice, but someone should have told him, if he tied his necktie longer, his big belly wouldn't be so obvious. There was a second man who rose from a chair as we entered. He greeted Billy before giving me a curious glance.

Billy, looking at the man behind the desk, said, "Mayor Winters, nice to see you again."

"Hi Billy," he replied before he glanced down at me. He was in thought for a moment before his eyes, under a sweaty, thick crop of brown hair, lit up. "You're Steve Kovacs kid, right?"

"Yes, Sir. My name's Joe."

Billy turned to the second man, then glanced down at me, "Joe, this is John Robie, an acquaintance of mine."

After the introductions, we sat down around the desk. Tom Winter's began the discussion. "Billy, tell me this crazy idea isn't true. John tells me the two of you are organizing this event up at the old pool grounds."

Billy took off his cap, then shrugged. "You're half right. John's organizing it. I'm just going to dive into the water."

Tom sat down in his chair and leaned over the desk. "But what on Earth for? John tells me the platform is going to be raised to 18 feet." The mayor tilted his head up and down, inspecting Billy's lean build. "When was the last time you jumped off a diving board?"

"That's a lot all at once," Billy replied. He took a breath before he answered. "First, I'm going to dive, not jump..."

Tom's cheeks darkened, and his eyes narrowed. "Okay, when was the last time you *dove* off a board!"

"When I was 12," Billy replied. "And I don't mean to be rude, but the reasons I have for doing this are my own business. We can leave it at that."

Leaning back in his chair, the mayor said, "If you get hurt, or god forbid, worse, the town can't be involved."

John interjected, "We've talked to Billy about this. He's agreed to sign a waiver, and we will obtain any required insurance."

Tom's eyes narrowed as he glared at John. "Who is, 'we?'"

"Roger and I..."

Rolling his eyes, Tom said, "I should have figured it was the two of you. You've been pulling pranks and stunts ever since we were in high school together. Things haven't changed, have they?"

I was surprised when Billy cut off that train of thought. "Tom, this is something I want to do. It's important to me. It's not about John and

Roger."

Tom intertwined his fingers together on his desk, and his voice lowered. "Billy, this is a quiet town. John told me he is going to try and sell 500 tickets to your jump…"

"Dive," Billy corrected.

"Right, your dive. Although the few businesses in town wouldn't mind some extra traffic, there's a significant faction of ultraconservative residents who have a mild tolerance to strangers at the best of times, so they certainly wouldn't appreciate the mass of people being proposed. This old-fashioned, hardcore group would hang me from the first tree they found if I agreed to this."

John and Roger had discussed this eventuality. They knew this approval would not be easy. Consequently, John came prepared to dangle a carrot. "I know the pool grounds have been a thorn in your side for many years. It's an eyesore and a reminder of a bad idea from the past. Roger has agreed, if the town allows our little event to proceed, Roger will tear down the facility after the event, and donate the land to the town of Grand Valley. He will absorb all the costs."

Tom paused, rubbing his chin. That was different. The land would be worth at least $100 thousand. "I can't make any promises, but I'll run it by our council. However, we're all going to have to work our butts off convincing the hard-core people in Grand Valley the one-day sacrifice will be worth it."

With the meeting over, I retrieved my hockey stick before Billy and I walked outside. We both got on our bikes, but I couldn't let Billy leave without telling him the concerns I kept in when I heard the adult discussion in Tom's office. "Eighteen feet is really high. You might hurt yourself. Why's this so important?" I asked.

Looking down at me, Billy's blue eyes were soft, but he sighed, something he most often did when he was irritated. "It's been a long day for me. I need some time on my own." He rose up and pushed down on the bike pedal. A moment later he was coasting down the hill towards Amaranth Street.

That shook me up. It was the first time since I had known Billy that we parted as anything but good friends and on good terms. I wasn't sure if he was angry at me, or was it something else about the meeting? In either case, I wasn't going to leave it at that, so when I saw Billy turn down Amaranth, I rode after him, keeping 50 yards between us. Two turns later, he was on Grant Street, then he turned north towards the old gravel pit. There were many dirt paths criss-crossing the pit, and I followed far enough behind

Billy so that he didn't see me. He bobbed up and down as he crossed the irregular terrain, and I tried to time myself so I moved forward when he disappeared over a rise. He was almost at the far end of the pit when I stopped on a berm, watching as he followed a hidden path into the forest— a path I never before realized was there.

After waiting a few minutes, I rode into the same opening made between two large spruce trees. A few yards ahead, I saw his three-wheeler parked beside a tree, and even further ahead, and only because of his bright green ballcap, I saw him walking a zigzag path through the forest of cedar and towering spruce trees.

I knew the river was on the other side of the woods, so he couldn't go too far. Following behind, I was still worried about the frustrated look he had on his face when he left me. I walked along close to his footsteps until I saw a break of sunlight ahead. Quietly, I snuck the last few yards and tucked myself behind a wide tree trunk. Shifting my head to the side, I saw a narrow clearing of short grass hugging the river. I heard a gurgling of rushing water which was odd because, this time of year, the river was typically slow and lazy. However, here, there was a line of rocks that had made a natural breakwall across the river. I assumed, over many years, rocks had been caught there, and that caused even more to be caught in the same manner. It created a partial dam, allowing the water to flow over it or through the cracks. Consequently, the water rushed through where it could find these paths and openings, and the fast-flowing water was what created the gurgling noise I heard.

On this side of the natural breakwall, there was a small, quiet cove where the water was motionless. It was ten yards across, and in the middle, sitting on a large flat rock, was Billy. He'd left his shoes and socks on the shoreline, now looking very relaxed with his bare feet dangling in the still water. Leaning back on his hands, his eyes were closed, but I was about to find out that didn't mean he wasn't aware of his surroundings.

"I heard you when you were half way across the forest," he said. "You might as well come out."

Having been caught, I rose up, dusted off my knees and walked to the edge of the river.

He turned his head. "Come in. The water will feel good on your feet."

I undid the laces on my running shoes before removing them, and the socks followed. After rolling up my jeans over my knees, with my hands held out from my sides for balance, I gingerly stepped one foot down in the water. The bottom was mainly small rocks, so it wasn't difficult to make my way to a spot beside Billy's rock even though the water level was over my knees, causing the bottom of my rolled-up jeans to get a good soaking.

He patted the rock beside him. "C'mon up."

Pushing down with both hands on the rock, I spun with my butt landing beside him. I scooted back and said, "This is a nice spot. I didn't know it was here."

"Not many people do. Not many like to walk through the forest, flies and mosquitoes being what they are. I think the bit of irritation is worth it."

"Do you come here a lot?" I asked.

"Only when I have a strong need to. This is my thinking spot. When I'm struggling with something, I come here to try and make peace with it."

I kicked the water, splashing droplets out in front of me. "Are you mad at me?"

He looked down, placing his hand on my shoulder. "Cripes, no. It's just not everyone's going to be happy with this diving event. Some'll even be mad at me."

"Then, why do it? Why is this so important?"

A long sigh came from his lips. "Joe, this is just something I have to do. It's hard to explain, and I'm not just saying that to avoid telling you. I don't understand all of it, but when I do this dive, I know it'll set some stuff in my mind straight."

Barely above a whisper, I said, "But you might get hurt. Is it that important?"

His hand hadn't left my shoulder as he continued. "This might help explain it. When I was a boy, I read a book called *The Black Knight*. I enjoyed it, but more important, I think I learned some things from it. It was important enough that, about ten years ago, I went looking for another copy, and I found one. It's in my apartment." He raised an eyebrow, speculatively. "If you'd like, I'm going to loan it to you. You're about the same age I was when I first read it. You might like it the same as I did."

"What's the book about?"

"Well, you know what a knight is, right?"

Sure," I answered. "A knight is from the olden days, saving people who need saving, and killing bad guys with their sword." With one hand clenched over the other and extended out in front of me, I moved my hands back and forth as if the imaginary sword was wreaking havoc on an imaginary dragon.

Billy laughed. "Yeah, that kind of knight."

"But why a black knight? Was he a bad guy?"

"All knights begin as good, Joe, otherwise their king wouldn't have made them a knight. They always try and do the right thing: helping those in need, especially the poor, helping women in distress, telling the truth, and above all, fighting evil. If they did that, they would be an honourable knight."

He continued, "It sounds simple, but it's not easy at all. There are many temptations that could cause a knight to lose their way. Pretty women and the lure of money were too much for the knight in this story. He did something very bad, and the king banished him from his kingdom even though they were best friends and the knight was his best warrior.

However, the knight didn't go far. He travelled across the kingdom, trying to stay close to the outlying castles and villages. He had removed the silver armour worn by the king's knights, replacing it with one of pitch black. Wherever he roamed, everyone feared the black knight, even though the black armour was his self-imposed mark of shame, not a sign of his behaviour. So he set about on a task. He redoubled his efforts for good, making every effort to set things right whenever he saw something was evil or just plain wrong. His hope was that, one day, the king would hear of his exploits and forgive him for the mistake he made."

By now, I was listening intently. "And did the king forgive him?"

He winked at me. I was happy the frustration I saw in his face earlier in the day was gone. He said, "For that, you'll need to read the book."

I groaned out an, "ah shucks," as I snapped my fingers. I kicked some more water with my foot, the droplets splashing out into the river. A thought came to me. Tilting my gaze up, squinting one eye since the sun was behind Billy's face, I whispered, "This need you have to dive into the water, is that your mission?"

He shrugged. "You might be right, but if I am a knight, every knight surely needs a good squire."

I bounced on the rock, clapping my hands together. "I could be your helper!"

"Exactly," he clarified. "But more of an assistant. You're young, so a squire is a good place to start."

"And, if I'm a good squire, then one day, I might be a knight as well."

"Yes, Joe, but you'll be a silver knight. I'm sure of it."

We didn't talk for a while after that. Sitting on the flat rock, side by side, we occasionally kicked at the water. I slid my hand across and held his, and his wrinkled fingers curled through mine. I heard a brief, discordant breath, one Billy tried to stop, so it was barely audible against the sound of the flowing river. I didn't look up even though I got the sense there were a few tears falling down Billy's cheeks.

Chapter 13: The Local News

The time was 6:20 p.m. As it was every Thursday in the CJHA television network building on Broadway Street in Orangeville, the evening news was concluded with a *Leisure Report*. Mandy Robertson was the young, newly-hired reporter who would find a local, noteworthy event or person that would receive the weekly spotlight. During the commercial break, she had scooted onto a stool beside Brad Sheppard, the long-time evening news anchor.

The light on the TV camera lit, and Brad, holding a sheaf of notes, hit the bottom edge against the table in front of them. "Welcome back, Folks. As we do every Thursday, we set aside time for our weekly Leisure Report. And with that, I'll turn it over to Mandy Robertson." He glanced to his left, and the camera panned in the same direction until Mandy's pretty face, framed by brown, curly, shoulder-length hair, was centred in the lens. "What do you have for us today, Mandy?"

Mandy had a great smile, one made for TV, and she used it to good effect now. "Thanks, Brad. We didn't have to go too far for our leisure feature this week. It was a short 15-minute drive west on highway 9, and we were in Grand Valley. That's the location of our story today."

Brad interjected, "For those of you who haven't been to Grand Valley, you should go visit. It's a quaint little town, and a great place to stop for a coffee if you're out for a drive in the country."

"That's a good point, Brad, but this piece isn't about the town. It's about a man who has lived in the town for over 30 years, a man who they call *Billy Fixit.*" Before Brad could interrupt again, she quickly added, "Before you ask, I asked the people in town if that was his real name. They didn't think so, but no one seemed to know his real last name, so he's been known as Billy Fixit because that's what he does—he fixes stuff around town."

Grinning, Brad said, "I feel you have more to share about Billy from Grand Valley. I'm sitting on the edge of my stool in anticipation, so fill us in."

At that point, a picture of Billy popped up on the left side of the viewer's TV screens. Billy wasn't an ugly man by any means, but, at the same time, he wasn't photogenic. Whoever took the picture must have asked him to push his ballcap back on his head, giving a *deer-in-the-headlights* look to his eyes. It was an adolescent appearance, confusing since his wrinkles were deep on his dark, baked skin. Finally, his beard and moustache were bleached almost white, contrasting the black overalls he wore.

"This is Billy. He wouldn't divulge his exact age, other than he was north of 50." Mandy leaned forward, closer to the camera. "Now, Billy has taken on a challenge that is being sponsored by two local businessmen, and supported by Tom Winters, mayor of Grand Valley." Slowing the pace of her words for dramatic effect, she said, "Billy is going to dive into the water at the old pool grounds from a height of 18 feet."

Brad was about to roll his eyes, but then had second thoughts. This must be one of those stories about senior citizens where they achieve something age-impressive, like running a five-mile marathon, or throwing three strikes in a row at the local bowling alley. So instead, he built on the drama. "Eighteen feet, that's like jumping off the roof of a two-story house. Wow! Has he done this kind of thing before?"

"No, and to be clear, he's diving, not jumping. That's what makes it interesting," Mandy added. "You see, Billy tells us he hasn't jumped, dove or swam in a pool or any body of water since he was 12, so it will be a monumental challenge for him."

Shuffling his note papers, Brad considered this for a second. His brows furrowed, partly because he was promoting an event that might have this old fool kill himself, partly because this was one of the stupidest leisure reports he had heard in all his years as news anchor. Still, he played along. "Mandy, are the town officials sure this is a good idea? He looks a bit frail, and—why exactly is he doing this?"

Mandy laughed. "He tells us, 'For no reason in particular.' It's just something he has always wanted to do, so he's going to do it, and the locals think it'll be popular enough that they'll sell 500 tickets to watch him dive in the pool. The big event is set for Labour Day Weekend."

Brad thought, *I'll have to add that to my calendar—NOT!* He shook his head, looking at the camera and with a twisted smirk, said, "There ya go, Folks. Another slow news day."

Mandy didn't like Brad's comment she thought was an insult, even though he might be right. Initially, she had questioned the assignment, but John Robie owned the TV station, so when she heard the request came from him, you didn't question it further. Nevertheless, they were on live

TV, therefore she laughed off Brad's comment and said, "If you are looking to buy a ticket, it's $10 a seat. Just phone the Grand Vally Civic Office, main contact number."

The TV camera zoomed in on Brad for his final word. In a sarcastic tone, he said, "Beat the rush and phone as soon as you can." For a moment, he did the mental math, remembering he had two more years before he could retire. "And with that, we'll call it an evening. Riley Mason will be here at 11 p.m. for the late report. Goodnite."

Chapter 14: The Town Council Meeting

"Can you cut open the top for me, Mr. O'Neil?" I asked.

"Sure, Joe." He reached under the counter, pulling out a pair of scissors. I held the pyramid shaped *lola* up to him, and he cut the top edge of the paper lining away.

I gave my thanks as Nik held his lola up for the same treatment. We walked out the door of his variety shop and almost ran headlong into the Tongue who just happened to be walking by the front of the shop. He veered out of our way, then turned, walking backward as he held his hands up, his splayed fingers vibrating. At the same time, he stuck his split tongue out at us, the two sides moving up and down in opposite directions. Nik and I stuck out our own tongues in response. Nik's was bright red while mine was purple. We laughed and the Tongue joined us as he slapped his hands together. I had learned by now that, although he looked a frightful sight, he was harmless enough.

We sat on the bench beside our parked bikes, our focus returning to the cold refreshments we just bought. Lolas were a great treat during the hot summer, consisting of a pyramid of flavoured ice. On that day, I asked for my favourite grape flavour while Nik preferred cherry red. The hard part of eating a lola was having the patience to wait. If you just rushed and kept sucking on the tip of ice protruding from the paper, soon it would turn into a white corner of flavourless ice. The trick was to wait for the heat of the day to melt some of the ice, the result being flavoured liquid pooling in the bottom. Then, with a bit of skill, you could tip the lola and have some of the liquid fall into your mouth while you sucked on the ice tip. And if you ate it slow enough, the ice would become soft enough to bite off chunks. That was the best!

Consequently, it wasn't a surprise that we both had a bit of syrupy splatter on the front of our shirts, but we didn't care. It was a worthy way of beating the heat of the day even though it wasn't as hot that afternoon as it had been the previous few days.

In all, we hadn't seen much rain, but the night before there had been a violent thunderstorm. Everyone in our house woke up from the cracks of thunder and the high winds pummeling the trees outside. It lasted an hour, and then, in the morning, another wave of light rain fell over the town. At that point, the excessive rain was a good thing since the town had dried out with almost every lawn parched yellow with only a few having a spattering of green, a sign those homeowners had more tenacious green thumbs than most. Once the sun came out, there was a cooler wind than we'd had in a week, and the standing water puddles evaporated.

It was earlier that morning when the kitchen phone rang. It was Nik, telling me to meet him down on Main Street. When we met, we were both sweating and needed something to cool us off.

Nik's mom worked as a clerk at the town office building while my mom worked at the bank for two days a week. During the summer, we had taken turns going to either location, putting on our saddest faces while begging for a couple of dollars so we could get an ice cream or a cold drink. On that day, it was my mom's turn, so we biked down to the bank. Knowing our odds of being successful were greatly increased if we lost the gangster look, we put our sunglasses in our pockets before we entered.

Clearly, we had been successful with the result being my head tilted back, holding the lola upside down over my open lips, letting the last few drops of flavour fall into my open mouth. After a satisfied sigh followed by a loud burp, I glanced over at Nik. He had a frown on his face as he held his lola in his hands on his lap. I was surprised to see there was still some ice in it.

"What's up?" I asked.

He said, "I think I ate too quick. I had a major brain freeze, and now I have a headache." He held the lola out towards me. "Do you want the rest of it?"

For a second, it was tempting, but even though he was my best friend, we weren't at a point where we were going to share spit. "I don't want your cooties, ya Commie," I said through a grin.

His lips turned into a snarl. "I shouldn't have even offered it. Hungarians don't deserve anything except a good Russian ass-kicking, something you should be used to."

A flash of light from the north end of town caught my eye. Chris, on his silver BMX, was flying down the hill at top speed. When he came close to a spot in front of the bench, he pressed the handle for the rear brake, and the bike did a six-foot brake slide before he came to a stop.

Out of breath, his words came between gasps. "You guys have to come with me! My dad is leading a group of 20 people on their way to the town council meeting. They're pissed, and it looks like there's going to be trouble!"

Without asking for more details, Nik and I hopped on our bikes and followed Chris to the town's office building. As we crested the hill, we saw the group of people, mainly men, led by Chris's dad, Viggo Eckland. He was setting a brisk pace as he rolled up the sleeves of his white shirt. The group passed the front door, heading towards the side of the town building where stairs led down to a lower entrance.

Once the last person was on the stairs, we tore across the road and parked our bikes beside the block wall protecting the stairwell opening. We skipped down the stairs and looked through the window in the metal door. Inside was the basement of the office building, comprised of a large room, twice as long as it was wide. Since the room was used by the town for various events, pushed up against a side wall were two folded ping-pong tables, folded tables and stacked chairs used for different game nights.

However, today was the day when the monthly town council meeting was held. At the far end of the room were two metal tables, and sitting behind them were Mayor Tom Winters and the three other councillors who held volunteer positions. Interestingly, Nik's mother, Mira Luzkin, in addition to her clerical duties, was also one of those volunteers.

Typically, the council meeting was lucky to see one or two visitors, but nevertheless, the volunteers always set out extra chairs in case of a surprise, like the one the mayor was seeing played out on that day. The majority of the group found seats, but Viggo along with a few other men stayed on their feet, facing Tom Winters.

"C'mon," Chris whispered as he cracked the door open.

Nik and I followed him in before we flattened our backs against the back wall, sliding towards the corner of the room. We were just in time to hear Chris's dad begin speaking.

Viggo had his arms crossed, and his hair was wet with perspiration from the midday walk from his house, under the scorching sun. "Tom, what is this news report we saw about some event that will be held in town up at the old pool grounds?"

The air conditioning unit for the building was old and didn't cool as well as it should. Even though we were in the basement, there were beads of sweat on the mayor's brow. He put his finger in his collar, loosening the knot of his necktie. "I was surprised by the news report coming out so quickly. My hope was I would have time to notify everyone before the story ran."

Viggo appeared to be the spokesman for the group. That wasn't a surprise because he held an odd seniority since his great, great, great grandfather was one of the town's founders in 1866. His descendants, at least enough of them to maintain a presence, continued to live in Grand Valley. There were other families who also had a long history in the town, but none as long as the Eckland clan.

Short-cropped light-blonde hair and a blonde moustache gave Viggo an appearance younger than his 40 years. I thought his nose was too large for his face with a noticeable curve to it, a trait, thankfully, not passed down to Chris. Viggo, standing in an aisle between chairs on either side of him, tilted his smoldering gaze down to the mayor. "What is this crazy story that Billy is going to jump into the old pool?"

"Dive, not jump," the mayor corrected.

Uncrossing his arms, Viggo waved a hand in the air. "That's not the point! Who has coerced Billy to do this?" There was a murmur supporting Viggo's question.

Tom wiped his brow with his sleeve. "Now, no one is coercing Billy. It was his idea, and Roger Thornhill and John Robie are providing the financial support—lots of it, in fact."

Viggo's eyes narrowed into sharp slits. "Roger and John? What right do they have to get their noses into this? This isn't what we want for our small community. We like it quiet and we expect it to be kept that way."

The mayor quipped, "I will remind you I am the mayor of the Township of East Luther Grand Valley, and although Roger and John don't live in the town proper, they do live in the township; and Roger owns the old pool grounds. That tells me they do have a right to have a say in this event."

The words flew back and forth with Chris's father's tone harsher and louder than the mayor's. With so many people in the basement, I noticed the musty scent, something that was normally at a barely noticeable level, was growing as tensions rose and tempers flared. In response, the air conditioning unit outside was rattling with its effort to fight the heat of the day.

I elbowed Chris in the ribs and was about to tell him his father was losing control when I heard a loud *smack!* Nik's mom had jolted to her feet and slapped her palm on the table. There was some irony to her action as Mira Luzkin was petite, no more than five feet in height, and she would not tip 100 lbs on a scale. Yet, she now had the complete attention of the room. Even though the Luzkin's and the Eckland's had been good friends for many years, it didn't mean they agreed on everything, and it did not mean she would let his sometimes-overbearing nature dominate the meeting.

"Viggo, I know you have influence with many people in the town, but there are others who also have an opinion." Mira took a deep breath in the hope it would calm her down. "Tom has told you that in exchange for allowing this event to proceed, Mr. Thornhill has agreed to demolish the eyesore of a decrepit pool, and donate the land to the town. To me, and to many others, that is worth one day where you would need to tolerate some added excitement."

I was surprised to see Nik's mother had a significant amount of influence over Viggo. He paused his tirade and fell back into a chair while wiping his fingers back through his short hair. When he looked up, his face was drawn and his eyes had lost their lustre. He asked, "How many visitors?"

Tom answered, "There will be 500 tickets for sale for the Sunday of the Labour Day Weekend. I imagine it'll be scheduled in the mid afternoon, so we can expect people to be here around noon, and they'll all be gone by 4 pm."

Viggo glanced at Mira for a moment before turning his gaze back to Tom Winters. He lifted a finger, pointing it at the mayor. His voice lowered in tone, but it still held the underlying menace that had been noticeable when he began the conversation. "Okay, Tom, I will back off and accept one day of city folk flooding our little town." Then, he rose to his feet and it seemed to reenergize his spirit. Pressing his finger closer to the mayor, his voice was quiet, the kind of quiet that could be more terrifying than if someone was screaming. "But there better not be any surprises, and things better not get out of control. As mayor, I'm holding you accountable."

Chapter 15: Higher Yet

Salami is one of three food items considered part of the culinary triad in a Hungarian home. Sour cream is the second staple, and paprika is the third although these two have qualifiers. Specifically, sour cream cannot be the low-fat variety, at least five percent fat being the only acceptable product. The paprika has to be the smoked variety, and it has to be fresh paprika. My father had told me many times that the rich flavour is lost much too quickly if it is left stagnating on the shelf.

I wasn't really sure why those thoughts were going through my head as I ate my lunch at the kitchen table. It was probably because I was half way through a salami and cheese sandwich on rye. That was another qualification; rye was the highly preferred bread type while Hungarian or German salami had the best flavour. My favourite used to be Yugoslavian salami, but my mother told me it was no longer available because the country was about to no longer exist. I scratched my head at that one. I was young, so oblivious to world affairs. My simpler view was, I just wanted good salami.

I glanced at the clock on the kitchen wall, and jolted up. I was going to be late. I took one last massive bite of the sandwich, leaving only a bit of crust which I placed back on my plate. I ran for the door and was on my Chopper, speeding up Grant Street a moment later. With one hand firmly on one monkey bar, my other hand retrieved my wrap-around sunglasses hanging from my pocket. I flicked them open before placing them on my face. A few minutes later, I cut across Main Street, continuing south towards Vicki's. I was half way down Main Street when I heard my name yelled out.

I should have seen it coming. Cindy and Karen, the twins, were standing on the sidewalk in front of the variety store. One of them had yelled out, and as much as I wanted to just keep on pedaling, I didn't have cause to be rude to them. I still didn't know which was which. They were both the same height, and from the neck up they were identical. One had black sneakers on matching her black, short-sleeved shirt. The other had red sneakers with a white shirt. They both wore identical cut off jeans that got me wondering how they could tell their clothes apart.

96

Now that my bike was stopped beside the curb, not knowing where to look, I picked a spot between them. "Hi Girls."

The twin with the white shirt said, "Where have you been hiding?"

Now, that had me wondering if she was the one who asked me to kiss her, but I saw her sister's cheeks darken when the question was asked. Maybe she was the one. I hadn't exactly been hiding, but considering the kiss, and then my embarrassment when I bolted after the ghost story centred on my house, well, I didn't go to their street as much as I used to, especially at nighttime.

"I haven't been hiding," I replied. "I just have a lot of things on the go."

We were interrupted by a loud, vibrating noise. In the distance, we could hear a worker using a jackhammer at the old pool grounds.

One of the sisters came closer, placing her hand on my monkey bar. With a raised voice, she asked, "Where are you going in such a hurry?"

"I have to meet Billy up at the pool grounds."

The same sister continued, "Why do you spend so much time with him?"

Pulling my glasses off, through a squint, I said, "Why are you so interested in my business?"

Now, the second sister came closer, her toes hanging over the edge of the curb. "No reason other than us being curious."

If they weren't so pretty, I would have ridden off. Heck, if they weren't so pretty, I never would have stopped. I really wished I knew which one kissed me because, even though the thought of it made me uncomfortable, I had enjoyed it; the soft lips had felt good. I wasn't about to admit it to them, or anyone else for that matter. But it meant I wasn't about to insult them, so I explained my relationship with Billy to them: how I liked learning new things as I worked with him, and now, I was helping him prepare for his dive into the pool. I finished by telling them I was his squire.

They giggled when I mentioned that. I put my glasses back on, then my ballcap that had been hanging on the monkey bar. "I have to go. He's waiting for me now," I said before riding away.

Behind me, I heard one of them yell, "Come up to our street and visit. You might get another kiss!"

I pressed the hand brake and twisted my head around, glaring at them, but I was too late. They were both giggling, and I couldn't tell which one had said it. Even if I had seen who did, it was immediately obvious they were in cahoots, and they were enjoying themselves at my expense. Things were weird, but now they just became a whole lot weirder, leaving me with a sudden urge to wash my tongue.

The best thing to do was just make my getaway, so that's what I did. Two turns later, I was riding towards Vicki's. The jackhammer had stopped, but there were still mingled construction noises: drills, saws, workers yelling and, every once in a while, the groan of gears from the crane parked near the back of the pool grounds. The day prior, the crane had appeared, and shortly thereafter, two long trucks came into Grand Valley, each carrying large sections of prefabricated bleachers.

The perimeter work had to be done before the bleachers could be installed, so ten days ago, the construction crew had arrived. The chain-link fence was quickly removed, and the berm was flattened with the extra dirt being piled in the field next to the back of the pool. Next, holes were dug for concrete pilons since the concrete had to cure before they were loaded with the weight of the bleacher sections. Then, just to keep the dirt down, a thin layer of asphalt paving was laid down in the area that would be under the bleachers. Since all of the build was temporary, the workers didn't bother with a gravel base or a thick layer of asphalt; a couple of inches was good enough. Today, two more trucks arrived with two more bleacher sections. When finished, there would be eight in all.

I rode my bike around to the High Point Apartments. On the far side, there was a gate through the temporary construction fence where I locked my Chopper before heading into the compound.

A security guard put his hand on my chest. "Hey, Joe. Don't forget your hardhat." He pointed to the wooden pigeon hole shelves that had been fabricated and installed against the back wall of the apartment building.

I skipped over to the shelves and pulled off my ballcap with one hand. With the other, I pulled out the plastic hardhat with my name stenciled across the front—*Little Joe.* Placing my ballcap in the pigeon hole, I pulled the hardhat down on my head. Even though it was the smallest one they could find, it was still huge, giving me the appearance of a Martian wearing an alien helmet. Unfortunately, anyone entering the worksite had to wear a hardhat, so I saw it as the cost of being Billy's squire.

Roger and John were standing together along the far side of the pool. Roger nodded and said, "There's that kid again."

John looked in the same direction. "That's Joe, Billy's friend."

"He's too young to be in here," Roger concluded.

"Don't worry. He's a smart kid, and we need him. For whatever reason, he and Billy have a close bond. When the kid is around, Billy seems to make more sense."

"Just make sure he doesn't fall in the hole," Roger quipped.

There were two workers in the pit, doing some final touch ups with vinyl sealer, the final repairs before the hole would be filled with water. Roger had arranged for the local volunteer fire department to bring truckloads of water. Then, they could check for leaks and make sure the new water pump they had installed, worked. Roger turned to John, "We're going to lose our shirt on this bet. The costs are higher than we forecasted."

It was as if the words passed right through John. There was no reaction. His jaw was held high while his eyes were narrow as they focused on Billy across the pool. "Actually, I think we're going to be just fine. In fact, we're going to be more than fine."

Roger tilted his gaze to his friend. "How are the ticket sales?" Since the smug look hadn't left John's face, he added, "You know something I don't?"

"There aren't many tickets left," John replied, a grin adding to his confident demeanour. "As you know, we fit in some extra seating, so we're looking at 580 spectators."

"That's still not enough to make up for our expenses," but even that didn't deter the smug look on John's face, so he added, "Out with it. What's going on?"

John's face changed as he tilted it towards his friend while both eyebrows rose unusually high. "Do you trust me, Roger?"

Roger snapped back, "You're a freaking salesman. Of course, I don't trust you!"

John laughed. "I get that, but you know, as a salesman, I can smell when something is going to be big." He turned, bouncing his finger against Roger's chest. "And I'm a newsman, so there isn't much that goes on in this province I don't know about."

"Care to translate that?"

"I'm just telling you this is going to be a heck of a lot bigger than either of us imagined when we made our wager. But don't worry about that. It's something I'm building, and speaking of building, are we on schedule to complete the construction work?"

"Bang on. I have my two best crews working here," Roger answered.

Turning to his friend, John put his hand on Roger's shoulder, and with a lowered voice, said, "I'm serious. This is going to blow up any time now." He leaned in, shifted his gaze from side to side, making sure no one was within earshot. "If things go as planned, we're going to expand out of the pool grounds. How many more work crews can you get up here on short notice?"

One eyebrow shot up. Roger was wondering what the heck his friend had in mind. "Four or five crews, 25 tradespeople in total."

"Make sure they're on call." John saw the look on Roger's face, his mouth open, about to ask another question. "Just leave it there for now. I'll let you know more when I have more details."

Roger knew better than to push it further, so he changed the line of questions. He pointed towards the diving platform. It had a metal frame, clad in white wood siding, and a worker was at the top exactly 18 feet to where the waterline would be. He was setting the last few bolts securing the aluminum side railings to the top of the platform.

Roger was pointing at Billy in his familiar black denim overalls and green ballcap. "Look at him, John. I can't help but think we're going to kill that old man. In that case, as the organizers of this event, we're screwed."

John shook his head. "No, I had Billy sign a waiver saying he is of sound mind...all the right legal stuff is included."

"But is he of sound mind?"

John replied, "I had Dr. Wilson give Billy a full physical at the little medical centre he has here in town. I was surprised, so you will be as well. Even though he looks frail and old in those overalls, the doctor told me, under that attire is a lean, well muscled man with a fat content low enough that it would put you and I to shame."

Roger tilted his face towards John. He didn't have to say anything since his face had a familiar, *you have to be kidding me*, look.

"The doctor says, Billy's overall health is as good as the average 30-year-old. His excellent physical condition is likely due to a few things: he's never smoked, never drunk alcohol to excess and he hasn't worked jobs with constant heavy labour, but at the same time, he has worked regularly for the past 30 years, keeping his joints limber and his muscles toned."

"But he's got to be crazy for doing this. There's no reason for him to jump into a pool from 18 feet."

"Dive, not jump," John corrected.

Slapping John on the shoulder, Roger said, "You know what I mean. The critical part is the old man is crazy!"

John pulled a folded paper from the inside pocket of his light jacket. He unfolded it and while reading it, he said, "No, Billy isn't crazy."

Roger asked, "What's that you have there?"

"Billy's cognitive evaluation. I had Dr. Wilson bring a therapist in to administer the test. He passed with flying colours."

"You seem to have all the bases covered," Roger admitted.

"I told you, Roger, you look after the construction and I'll look after the other pieces."

At that moment, there was a flash of light from the driveway into the apartment parking lot. It was caused by the sunlight reflecting off the side of a van pulling in. It was white, and in black and silver letters on the side, it read, *CTV NEWS*; CTV being the regional network out of Toronto.

Roger lifted his hard hat off his head and wiped his fingers through his hair. "I take it that's one of the pieces you're looking after."

John said, "They're here to interview Billy. We better go prep him."

When they arrived at the diving platform, the worker who had been securing the railing system was just climbing down the ladder. He said, "It's all set, Billy, if you want to have a look."

Billy moved towards the ladder when John stopped him. "Billy, give us a minute before you go up."

Standing beside Billy, I replied, "Sure Mr. Robie. Billy has a minute, but it needs to be quick. Places to go, things to do."

Roger's one eye shut while his jaw hung slack. He looked like the whole world, that had been teetering, finally turned upside down. The fact I answered for Billy was the final push.

"Sure, Joe. We'll be quick," John offered. He pointed towards the parking lot where a young lady and a man carrying a video camera were exiting the CTV van. Glancing at Billy, he continued, "Those people are here to interview you. Are you okay with that?"

Billy glanced at me, and I waved him down. We huddled for a moment, then, once we separated, I said, "Billy has time, but he was about to go and check the height. He'll do the interview when he comes down."

Billy didn't wait for a reply. He turned and started up the ladder. Roger watched closely as the old man literally skipped up the ladder; he thought, *I'll be damned.* Glancing towards the gate where the security guard was holding back the reporter and cameraman, he thought they looked odd in their red guest hardhats. He let out a whistle, catching the guard's attention, then waved his hand, indicating the news crew should be let through.

As the pair walked towards the platform, the cameraman, seeing Billy up on the platform, hoisted the camera on his shoulder and began filming. He kept at a distance where he could continue filming while the reporter introduced herself to John and Roger. Then, John took a moment to introduce me.

The reporter, Lori Dale, leaned down and shook my hand. "Who might you be?"

"I'm Billy's friend, and his squire."

She chuckled. "That sounds very noble."

"I keep Billy on track," I explained. "If you need something from Billy and you can't reach him, you can call me." I reached into my pocket, pulling out a small rectangle of white construction paper. Written on it, in marker, was my name and phone number. I placed it in her outstretched hand.

"I'll keep that in mind," she replied before looking up at the top of the platform. She lifted a hand to shield her eyes from the sun. "What's he doing?"

"He's verifying the height," I answered.

Now, everyone in the group was looking up, watching Billy. In fact, all the workers had also stopped, even the crane operator who was leaning out of his little cab. It had been decided, at that height, a diving board would not be appropriate. Rather, Billy would dive off the platform just as the Olympic platform divers did. Now, he was standing at the very front edge of the platform, again bringing the question of Billy's sanity to Roger's mind. Billy held his hand stretched out in front of him, then slowly look down from his hand to the deck of the pool. He did this several times.

"What's he doing?" the reporter asked. She was talking into the microphone she had just turned on.

"Who knows?" Roger quipped.

John interrupted, "It looks like he's doing some type of mental calculation."

After repeating the process a few more times, Billy clambered down the ladder. John was about to introduce the reporter, but Billy walked right past them and took a stance in front of Roger.

"It's not high enough," Billy said.

"You asked for 18 feet, and that platform is 18 feet from where the water level will be."

The cameraman had moved closer, and Lori Dale pressed the microphone between Billy and Roger.

"That might be, but it's not high enough," Billy insisted.

"How much higher do you want it?"

"Five feet higher."

Roger glanced at John who gave a barely perceptible nod of his head. He then turned his head until he spied his lead hand, Rick, on the other side of the pool. He lifted his hand, waving him over, and the lead hand jogged to them. Even though he had been out of earshot, by Billy's actions Rick already had a good idea what was happening.

Roger said to him, "Rick, the platform needs to be raised up about five feet."

Billy interjected, "There's no 'about.' It has to be *exactly* five feet higher."

The lead hand nodded. "I got it."

John and Roger managed to sneak away from the group, leaving Lori Dale to continue the interview.

Once they were out of earshot, Roger said, "Now it's a dive from 23 feet. Is that part of your plan?"

"It's a surprise, but it fits in very well," John replied. "I'm on a roll that is unstoppable."

"Then, I just need one thing from you," Roger said.

"What?"

"I need a copy of that waiver that's covering my ass."

Chapter 16: Rubber Duckies

There was a loud knock at my door, followed by muffled words. "Wake up! We're going out for breakfast."

I was on my side in bed, facing the wall. Without rolling over or opening my eyes, I answered, "Okay, I'm up."

I began to drift off as I often did when I wasn't in the mood to prioritize breakfast over extra sleep, but then I remembered—it was Rubber Duckie Day! That meant we were going down to the church for breakfast. I rubbed my fists into my eyes before prying them open. After a lengthy yawn, I rolled over before pulling on a pair of shorts. My t-shirt was lying across my chair. I picked it up, bringing it to my nose. Inhaling, I noticed a slight musty smell. Pulling it away, I then brought it to my nose for a second time. That was more than a little musty, I determined, throwing the shirt back on the chair. After retrieving a clean t-shirt from the cupboard, I also put on a pair of clean white socks.

A moment later, I opened my door and was skipping down the stairs. With my hand on the lower corner post, I spun around, redirecting myself towards the kitchen. However, my mom was framed in the doorway, and when she saw my disheveled hair, she held her hand over her head, rubbing her finger and thumb together: *Snap! Snap!* She then pointed her finger up the stairs. "Hair brush! Tooth brush!"

I rolled my eyes, but followed her direction. I had explained it to her many times how brushing your teeth before you ate was a waste of time. You were just going to get them coated in food after you ate. In any case, a little water sprayed on my hair helped the hair brush do its work. After brushing my teeth, I skipped back down the stairs for a second time.

My dad was already waiting in the car with Andy. My mom pointed to my shoes. "Hurry up. We're already late."

Every July there was a Rubber Duckie Race organized by the local Kiwanis Club. Nik had told me the details since he had attended the event every year since he was born. As he explained it, the rubber duckies were actually made of plastic, about four inches high. The Kiwanis Club provided at least 600 every year, and people could buy a duck for $10 each. The buyers were given a numbered ticket with the same number written on the duckie with black permanent marker, then, at exactly noon, the duckies were released into the river. That occurred at the far end of town in the campground situated near where Amaranth Street changed to a gravel sideroad.

Once the yellow duckies were set free, they moved with the current, floating down the river, under the bridge leading to Brooklin, then continued south. Just before the Edelweiss house, a metal sluice strategically placed in the river, pulled the army of duckies together until they were single file. The first ten winning number owners received prizes—and they were huge prizes. First prize was $500 cash! The rest of the prizes were gift certificates at different places like Canadian Tire and Foodland, but they also had big values with even lowly tenth place worth $50.

My mom had purchased two tickets. One was in my pocket, and the other was in Andy's. As we drove to the church on Main Street, I was already thinking how I would spend my money, all of it, even though if either of us won, our mom would make us share the prize between us. I could deal with that aspect of sharing and being fair, considering how much my mom had sacrificed in backing off on our dreaded equal treatment. That might sound awful, but it wasn't. My mom, up until the time Andy was ten, would dress us exactly the same. So when we went out, we would look like odd circus twins. Andy, being older, always led the way, complaining about this embarrassing aspect of our life. It was hard work for him. By the time he was eight, and I was three years younger and didn't know any better, he had convinced her to change the colours even though the clothes might be the same style. It wasn't until he was ten that he had claimed complete victory because our clothing was no longer synchronized.

Today, he was wearing long, faded jeans. He never wore shorts, and when, in the past, I had asked him about it, he gave me some silly story how he didn't want the girls seeing his hairy legs. It had me wondering if when I became his age, would I follow in those same, stupid footsteps?

As we left downtown behind, now on Water Street, I saw there were cars parked on the shoulder on both sides on the street. The church parking lot was full, so volunteers were directing cars to the grass field beside the church. On the other side of the church, the grass area was covered with rows of picnic tables, so many I couldn't count them. In the middle of the lines of tables was a cleared-out area where several barbecues were cooking food. As we moved closer, I could smell the bacon, and I saw the piles of pancakes on warming trays. *Yes,* I thought. *The added bonus of Rubber Duckie*

Day, was there was a pancake breakfast. Since the pancake event occurred twice a year at that location, the church garnered a nickname as the *Pancake Church.*

There was already a mass of people seated, filling their mouths, leaving only a short lineup for the pancakes. It moved quickly, so it didn't take long for the four of us to have our plates covered with food. My parents looked over the picnic tables, seeing there was barely a spot free. However, I saw an opening and pointed. "There's some room over there beside Billy and Ms. Stevens." We walked between the rows of picnic tables and sat beside them. There were greetings all around, and after that there wasn't much chit-chat since we were busy eating our pancakes. I had loaded mine up with maple syrup, and there was plenty to go around with a large bottle on every table.

We were fortunate to have two pancake breakfasts every year. The first had been in May during the Strawberry Festival, and since the strawberries were in season the difference was strawberry syrup on the tables and heaps of strawberries on the pancakes. I preferred the strawberries, but who was I to complain with a mouthful of maple syrup covered pancake in my mouth?

My mom noticed something that bothered her when we came over to the table, and it had been festering while we ate, but now that we were finished, she couldn't hold back the words any longer. "I have to apologize for some of the people of this town. They're so rude."

"What do you mean?" Ms. Stevens replied.

My mom sighed, then answered, "There was no one sitting with you when we arrived. It's like people intentionally made a space around the two of you."

Ms. Stevens laughed—in fact, it was more of a nervous cackle. "It seems more than a few townsfolk are upset with Billy because of this event that will take place in town." She turned her head almost right around, looking towards the far side of the picnic area where Viggo Eckland sat with his family and friends. She turned back to face my mother and continued, "Viggo, even though he has accepted the event, is still not happy. He has many friends holding the same sentiment, and they are all sitting over there sulking like children." She stared at my mother, one moment stone faced, the next, she burst out laughing, and my mother joined her.

My mother put a fist to her eye, feigning tears as she said, "Waa, waa, waa!"

My father was not impressed. He turned to Billy and asked, "How are things with you? Are people giving you problems?"

106

Billy shrugged. "I get the cold shoulder from a few, but most people treat me fine as they always have."

Nodding, my dad asked, "Are you sure you want to do this dive? I hear you moved the height up."

"I did, and this dive is something I have to do. I have my reasons, Steve. So let's just leave it at that."

"Fair enough," my dad said with a wink. "After all, we have tickets on the west side of the pool, front row."

Grinning, one eyebrow raised, Billy asked, "How'd you manage that?"

My dad put his hand on my shoulder. "Your business manager arranged it."

The adults all laughed even though I didn't catch on to what was so funny. My thoughts were interrupted by a familiar voice. Across the way, on the stairs leading up to the church's entrance, Pastor Fulton was standing behind a microphone stand and a large speaker. "Ladies, Gentlemen and Children, the duckies will be released in 15 minutes."

People ate their last few mouthfuls. Some hurried to the row of porta potties, to take care of last-minute business. For the rest, we rose, en masse, walking towards the river. I had to hold back my laughter, since the movement of such a mass of humanity in a small town, reminded me of a zombie horror movie I once saw. We moved like a herd of wildebeest, and by the time we arrived at Water Street, the families with children had squirmed their way to the front of the throng. Some people moved left, some to the right, all in an effort to find a spot on the other side of the road along the winding river. Children were pushed to the front, leaning into the yellow caution tape having previously been staked out along the river's edge.

We found a good spot with a great view of the sluice to our right, and the bridge from downtown to Brooklin on our left. Billy and Ms. Stevens were beside us when we heard a yell from the top of the bridge. "They're coming!"

There were mainly kids on the bridge, and they were facing away from us, bouncing up and down in their excitement. Suddenly, they ran from the far side of the bridge to the side facing us. They hung over the side, faces down. I could now see it as well. There was a mass of yellow from one shoreline to the other. The duckies bobbed up and down with the current, and although they moved slowly, they looked ominous, like an invading robot army.

They were coming closer when a group of about 50 duckies got caught behind some shoreline weeds. There was a collective groan from the crowd, but another battalion of yellow duckies pressed them from behind. The added weight overpowered the weeds, and the duckies burst through. A mighty roar went up from the shoreline even though the duckies on the other side of the river were now 15 yards ahead.

People strained their eyes in a futile effort to read the black numbers on the duckies. Chris told me, a few years ago, a group of participants decided to paint their duckies so they could distinguish them, and they were successful. However, the added weight of the paint gave the painted duckies an advantage as they bullnosed through the lighter ones. The next year, such modifications were outlawed. After all, Grand Valley duckie races were serious stuff!

The leading edge of the yellow mass was nearing the sluice gate, and when the first few hit the diverting plate, roars and whoops went up from the usually subdued people of Grand Valley. The duckies funnelled down to a single row, and Mayor Tom Winters pulled the first ten out. One at a time, he placed them in a special wooden duckie box, consisting of ten squares, each appropriately numbered.

During the time it took for the duckies to float from their release point to their capture, the microphone stand and speaker had been moved from the Pancake Church to a position beside the mayor. He said a few introductory words before he placed his fingers in the box, turning one of the duckies over. "In first place, number 323."

Everyone was looking down at their tickets, when off to our left we heard a woman yell out, "I won!"

The mayor lifted his hand above his eyes, peering towards the source of the words and said into the microphone, "Who is that down there?"

The woman yelled her name, but the mayor was too far away to hear it. A man beside us yelled her name out as did a woman far to our right. Now the mayor heard the name relayed to him.

"Congratulations to Helen Samson, the winner of $500, cash!"

The process was repeated five more times, and each time a winner was revealed in the same manner. The mayor called out the next winner. "Winner number six is 456."

My eyes opened wide as I looked at my ticket number, 455. My groan was interrupted by Andy.

"Fuck. I won," he mumbled.

My mom, quick as a whip, smacked Andy in the back of the head.

He flinched, then said, "I mean, heck, I won." With a wide smile on his face, he lifted a fist in the air. "I won! Andy Kovacs! I won!"

The name was relayed down to the mayor who announced, "Andy Kovacs from Grant Street, winner of a $150 gift certificate for Ace Hardware."

Andy's smile turned upside down. "Ace Hardware…"

My dad's eyes brightened while a crack of a smile formed on his lips. He said to Andy, "Don't worry. I'll give you $100 cash for that gift certificate."

Andy's eyebrows lowered down until they almost touched the bridge of his nose. "That's not fair!"

To my surprise, from beside my father, Billy said, "I'll give you $125."

Laughing, my dad turned to Billy. "So, that's the way it is."

Winking, Billy replied, "Yup."

The silly grin, no longer evident on my father's face had transferred to Andy. He held up the ticket, looking at our dad. "Any more offers?" he coyly asked.

"$150 it is," my dad grumbled as he snapped the ticket from Andy's fingers.

The last three numbers were called, then the remaining sea of yellow rubber duckies were fished out of the river. The event was over. My mom asked Andy and I if we were coming back home. At the same time, Ms. Stevens reminded Billy she was going to a friend's house for the afternoon.

Billy turned to me and asked, "Do you want to do a bit of reading?"

"Sure," but as I was saying goodbye to my parents, I heard a shrill whistle. I recognized the tone, and sure enough, when I looked across the road, I saw Chris peeking his face around the trunk of an old maple tree. He reached a hand out, waving me over. I told Billy I'd meet him at his van, then walked across to my friend. When I walked around the tree, I saw Nik was also there. "Why are you acting so weird?" I asked Chris.

"Can't you guess? You were with Billy, and if I came over and talked to you, and my dad saw me, there'd be hell to pay."

I rose up, pressing my chest out. "Your dad is being stupid. He's got this town torn apart."

Rolling his eyes, Chris replied, "Whatever. I don't really care. But we haven't seen as much of you lately. Are we okay?"

I exhaled, relaxing. "Sure, we're better than okay. We're bros." I held out my hand, and Chris fist bumped me, then Nik did the same.

"Good," Chris said. "Tomorrow, at noon, the Dudes and The Boys are having a dirt bike riding competition over at the gravel pit. You in?"

"You know it," I replied. I didn't care that we were on Water Street, declared neutral ground as I proudly pulled on my sunglasses. "See you there."

Billy was waiting in the van with the engine running, so I hopped onto the passenger seat. We agreed to go over to the Brooklin parkette across the river. For a couple of weeks, Billy and I had been spending some time reading books together. I did get his copy of *The Black Knight* and read it. At first I didn't enjoy it much, but after two chapters, just like that, I was fully immersed. The story dragged me in as if I *was* the black knight; I was hooked. From that point, every few days Billy and I would find a spot to do some reading together. Sometimes we'd read a chapter when on a break from a job he was working on; other times, we just arranged to meet at a quiet spot.

Billy drove over Brooklin Bridge, continuing down the Main Street extension to the parkette at the corner. After parking his van, we walked alongside the bushes to the end of the row, and just behind them was a picnic table, ten feet from the river's edge almost directly opposite from where we had been standing during the rubber duckie race. We sat on the same side of the table, facing the river. Billy had a small cooler with him as well as the book, *Robinson Crusoe*. He pulled out two cokes and placed the book on the table. We had been taking turns reading chapters, so he said, "Why don't you go first?"

I cracked open the coke and took a sip. Then, I opened to the bookmark at chapter four and began reading. He read chapter five. I read six, and he finished our reading for the day with chapter seven.

"I think I'd like living on a deserted island. It would be fun exploring all day every day," I said.

Billy tilted the coke over his lips, downing what was left. "It sounds like fun, but it'd be hard having no friends or family around."

His words brought a question I hadn't considered before. "Where's your family Billy? Don't you have kids?" When I saw his cheeks sag, I was sorry I asked. "You don't have to answer that."

He lifted his hand, wrapping my far shoulder. In a soft voice, he said, "That's okay, Joe. For a lot of people, I wouldn't answer, but you're special." He took in a deep breath. "I don't have any kids, and I've never even thought about getting married."

"Why?"

"I don't have a lot to offer a woman." He looked down at me, his blue eyes soft. "You see, I like the simple life I have in this town. I don't need money or a fancy car. Most women want that and more. They wouldn't be happy with me."

"What about Ms. Stevens? She seems to like you a lot."

"Oh, and I like her a lot. She thinks I should move in there and become a permanent friend." He tilted his head down, his eyes centered on a knot in the wood. "She might be happy for a while, but she'd find I have some issues that might bother her in time, because they bother me."

Taking off my cap, I scratched my head. "I don't understand. You seem swell to me."

He squeezed my far shoulder. "I think you'd have to be a bit older to understand. Let's just say, for now, Frances and I are great friends, and if we try too hard, we might not be friends at all. That scares the bejesus out of me because I don't have many people I consider my friend."

"But everyone is friendly with you!"

He shrugged, then said, "There's a big difference between being friends and being friendly. Being friendly is being nice to someone. Being friends is a whole lot more."

That got me thinking again. "Billy, when we were in the mayor's office, you introduced me to John Robie. You said he was your acquaint...acquaintan..."

"Acquaintance." Billy finished the word for me. "An acquaintance is someone you know and you're polite to. That would be an acquaintance. To be someone's friend is much more."

"Like what?"

"Think about your friends. What do you like about them?"

I thought for a moment, pressing a finger to my lip. "I like spending time with them, and they're nice to me," I said.

"You hit the nail on the head. You like spending time with a friend because they're nice to you, but more important, they're not mean to you. They don't do things to hurt you. They don't make fun of you, and they don't lie to you."

"Never, not even a white lie?" I wondered.

"If you have a really good friend, you don't even need little white lies." He saw I was confused, so he continued, "Let me explain with an example. You told me your best friend is Nik, right?"

I nodded my head.

"Let's say, one day, Nik was wearing a really ugly shirt, something green and purple. Would you tell him it was ugly?"

A laugh burst from my lips. "Damn right I would! He'd know it really quick!"

"Would he be mad?"

"No. He'd probably laugh right along with me," I answered. "And even if he got mad, in ten seconds he'd be over it."

"You also told me about the twins, Cindy and Karen. If one of those two had the same ugly shirt on, would you tell her?"

My eyes widened. "Heck, no!"

"Why not?"

I took another moment before I answered. "I wouldn't want to hurt their feelings."

"That would be very friendly of you."

I looked up at him and he winked at me. "I'm sorta getting it," I said.

Billy added, "Let me fill in the blanks. When you tell your friend he's wearing an ugly shirt. A good friend knows you're not saying it to make fun of him. You're trying to help him, even if it sounds funny. When It's an acquaintance, there's a good chance they won't understand that difference. They might think you're trying to make fun of them, and you're laughing at them, not with them."

For a while we just sat there. I took a few minutes to think about what Billy told me. We watched the road on the other side of the river. Fewer cars were passing by now that the Rubber Duckie Race had finished, so the town was once again quiet.

Billy had been thinking as well, and decided part of what he said needed clarifying. "You do have to be careful with white lies, though. I'm thinking of the example when you might be tempted to tell the twin with the ugly shirt that it was just fine. It seems innocent enough, but something like that can come back to bite you in the ass."

"How?"

"I'll give you another example," Billy said. "Quite a few years ago, I did some work for a woman up on Emma Street. I was there for a few days, replacing a section of bricks on her fireplace. The first day, with a huge smile on her face, she brought me a carrot muffin she had baked. I ate it, told her it was great and thanked her. Since I liked it, she brought me another carrot muffin the next day and another on the third day. Even after the job was done, if I happened to be walking by, she would run out her front door with a carrot muffin. You see, she got in the habit of keeping a couple in her bread cupboard for just such an instance."

"What's wrong with that?" I asked.

He leaned closer to me and whispered, "I hate carrot muffins."

I held my gut, I was laughing so hard.

"So, be careful when you say a white lie and who you say it to, even if it's a friend. It could snowball into something you can't control"

My voice lowered as I asked, "Billy, are we friends or acquaintances?"

Under his moustache, I could see the corners of his lips curl up. "My dear squire, we certainly are friends—good friends."

I turned my face down. I didn't want him to see my tears, or my trembling lips. "Then, I won't lie to you. I don't want you to make the dive because I don't want you to get hurt." I blurted the words out even though I knew they would not change his mind. I started to sob, pressing my face into his overalls. He didn't say anything, and I think that made sense. His arm holding me tight, his cheek pressed against the top of my head—that was all I needed.

Chapter 17: Blow After Blow

Charlie Huff, the caretaker at Bedford Private School, was shuffling backward as he worked the mop head back and forth across the white, tiled floor of the wide hallway. A movement from outside the window caught his eye.

Two of the older kids, Bart Kendall and Eddy Macneil, looked like they had stayed after class and were continuing to dally before going home. It surprised him since that day in March was unseasonably cold for the Halifax area. He knew the two youths, both 15-years-old, were the type who never found trouble. Today, in the late afternoon, they were horsing around at the edge of the playground where, all winter, a plow had moved the snow into a long, tall row. It had been much higher the week prior, before a warmer spell hit, shrinking it to half its original height.

During the melt, the kids had molded slides running down the other side of the remaining snow. The result was five runs in all, and now on this frigid day, each was covered in a layer of ice, making them perfect for sliding down their shallow angle over a ten-foot length. The younger kids, during recess and lunch breaks, slid down on their butts covered with snow pants or the length of their coats. The braver, older kids challenged the ice runs by sliding down while on their feet.

That's what Bart and Eddy were now doing, taking turns, their bodies at a right angle to the shallow decline of the run, holding their hands far out to the side to maintain their balance. They were both skillful, not falling once as they completed run after run. With so many kids sliding down the hill during the day, then climbing back to the top, there were steps that had been stomped into the snow, allowing the return trip to be completed more efficiently.

Charlie stopped his cleaning for a few minutes, resting his hand on top of the broom handle, his chin subsequently resting on his hand as he watched. After one of the return trips, Bart was waiting for Eddy to start down the hill again. He was standing on the flat surface of the paved playground, so it made sense Bart would not have been as cautious as when

114

he was accelerating down the short run. Consequently, when he shifted his foot and it hit a section of ice, his foot flew sideways. His arms flew outward, and he moved his other foot to catch his balance, but that foot also hit the ice, flying sideways. The movement was so immediate, he didn't have a chance to recover, and his body landed prone on the pavement with a thud. His face hit the hard surface before his hands could react. When he bent his neck backward, lifting his face, below him, he saw a pool of blood dripping from a cut above his right eye.

By the time Eddy was kneeling beside his friend, the double doors from the school were thrust open, and Charlie Huff was running towards them. A minute later, Eddy and Charlie were helping Bart to his feet, his head and the right side of his face covered in blood.

Ten years earlier, in 1945, Charlie had been a medic in World War Two, so he was familiar with blood and injuries. He narrowed his gaze, inspecting the gash above Bart's right eye and mumbled, "That's going to need a few stitches. Let's get you inside, and we'll call for some help."

Before Charlie had run outside, he had retrieved a clean, white rag from his cleaning cart. After folding it into a small square, he pressed it to the wound. He applied pressure as they walked into the school towards the main office. Once there, Charlie said, "I better call an ambulance."

Bart waved his hand. "No. My mom is at home. Just call her, and she'll come get me." He then told Charlie his home number.

After guiding Eddy and Bart to two chairs in the office waiting room, Charlie went through another door into the receptionist's area. A few minutes later, he returned and said, "Your mom is on her way."

Turning to his friend, Eddy said, "I better get out of here, Bart. If your mom finds me with you, she'll blame me for this."

Managing a feeble smile from under the blood covered rag, Bart replied, "You're right. I'll call you later and tell you what the damage is."

Eddy had been Bart's friend long enough to understand the hidden meaning. The cut would be sewn up, but the damage Bart was referring to was the mental cruelty Bart's father would inflict on him. It would add to the long list of incidents and events his father blamed Bart for. After placing his hand on Bart's shoulder, giving it a reassuring shake, Eddy left for his own home, a short 20-minute walk away.

Ten minutes later, there was a rattle from outside the office. Mary Kendall rattled the door handle a second time before Charlie opened the door for her. After a brief greeting, Charlie led her into the main office to her son. Once there, she glanced at Bart for only a fleeting moment, seeing his blood covered face, before saying to Charlie, "I will take it from here."

"Are you driving him to the hospital?" Charlie asked.

"No. I called Dr. Rogers before I came here. He is on his way to his office now, and we will meet him there."

Charlie nodded. He knew the people who sent their kids to this school were rich and privileged. It didn't surprise him that an unexpected call from Mrs. Kendall had the good doctor scurrying to his office.

Mary Kendall helped Bart to his feet, then to the Mercedes where she helped him onto the passenger seat. She didn't say a thing to Bart until the car was moving down the driveway leading from the school. In a pert tone, she quipped, "How could you do this to me? You know your father will find a way to blame me."

Bart's one eye was closed shut, but the other opened wide. "What I've done to you? I'm the one with blood all over my face!"

"Don't you yell at me, Bart! You know how your father is, but you don't know how he berates me when we're alone."

Bart knew exactly how his father berated his mother because his father performed the same kind of mental torture on him just, when he pushed his anger towards Bart, he had no qualms about doing so in public. And when he did, his mother always remained silent, so his sympathy for his mother was limited, at best. A twisted, sarcastic smile came across his face. "Well, at least you're old enough to get over it by having a drink, or taking one of those pills of yours."

Mary thought to slap her son. After all, it wouldn't have been the first time. But Bart already had an injury, so when her hand came up, it moved down, slapping the steering wheel instead. They didn't have any more words for each other for the remaining ten minutes it took them to arrive at Dr. Roger's office where he was already waiting inside, dressed in his white lab coat.

He had Bart sit on the edge of the examination table where he helped remove Bart's blood-spattered shirt. After, he gently removed the blood-covered rag. The bleeding had stopped, but much of the blood had dried making it difficult to see the extent of the cut. He filled a deep tray with clean, warm water before dropping a clean sterile cloth into it. It took quite a few swipes of the cloth to clean the wound, so he could determine the extent of the damage.

With his face close to Bart's, he peered down the bridge of his nose through his glasses. "I'll need to put in four stitches." After pulling away and turning to a cabinet to retrieve the suture materials, he added, "You're lucky. The wound is right on your eyebrow line. Once the cut heals, the scar will be well hidden." The doctor injected some lidocaine before applying the four stitches. He did a final cleaning before placing a gauze bandage over the wound. He turned to Mary Kendall, handing her a small bottle. "It might get sore. If it's excessive, give him one of these every four hours, but no more than four over 24 hours."

The drive home was quiet; both Bart and his mother were thinking about the interaction with Bart's father that was bound to occur. Their foreboding was proved accurate when Mitch Kendall arrived home from his typically long day at work. When he walked into the great room, he gave his wife his usual greeting with a kiss on her cheek. When he turned and saw Bart sitting on the couch, his eye purple, and just above it the thick bandage, he not only rolled his eyes; he swivelled his entire head on his neck. When his gaze came back down to his son, he spit out the words. "What happened this time?"

Bart, quickly and clinically, explained the circumstances ending with the cut over his eye.

Bart's father was pacing back and forth, his hands being thrown out to the side every time he emphasized a word. "How does that happen? How does someone—anyone—wipe out while just standing on a flat surface!"

"It was icy," Bart explained. He glanced at his mother, a second evening brandy in her hand. She wasn't about to help in his defence. She never helped him when his father was like this. Bart thought, *she's pathetic.*

His father turned, thrusting a finger at him. "You're just making excuses!"

"They're reasons, not excuses."

"Like your reasons why you didn't make the school basketball team?" Mr. Kendall added.

"I'm not interested in sports. I prefer to spend my time in Shop Classes. I like working with my hands," Bart replied.

Mitch Kendall's face, as the conversation continued, became flushed, but by now, his cheeks were a deep red. "Not interested in sports—just another excuse for failure."

Bart wanted the debate to end, and he knew what button to push for that to happen. "I'm sorry, but I'm not Malcolm."

Mitch Kendall froze. His eyes narrowed. His lips widened. "No, you'll never be your brother. Malcom would have made the basketball team, would have done just fine in Shop Classes, and I'm damn sure he wouldn't have slipped on ice, cracking his head open like some imbecile!" He took a breath and was about to continue when he saw the patronizing grin on his son's face. He didn't like when Bart taunted him almost to the point where he couldn't control himself. This time, he caught himself at the last moment—before he spilled out the words Bart knew were forever in the back of his mind.

It didn't matter that Mr. Kendall didn't say the words out loud; Bart knew them well. *His father wished Bart was no longer here, and his brother, Malcolm, was sitting here in Bart's place.*

Chapter 18: The Regional News Report

Lori Dale, the CTV news reporter, and her cameraman, sped back to their Toronto studio after interviewing Billy. It would take some time to process the video, but as long as they didn't hit a massive traffic jam, they should have their report ready for the 11:00 news. Lori hadn't been to Grand Valley, or anywhere near that part of rural Ontario, before. She was a city girl at heart, and couldn't understand how people could live in such peace and quiet. She needed the hustle and bustle of city life. Even when she went to bed at night, the honking of horns, nighttime voices and the vibration from the subway below her street, were the urban lullabies that rocked her to sleep.

Billy Fixit added to her confusion. She couldn't understand why the public were getting excited about an old man who was going to dive into a pool, albeit, it was from a height she wouldn't ever attempt. He was likely to kill himself, or at the least, cause some serious injury. Maybe that was the draw; people always wanted to watch a good train wreck.

They did get back in sufficient time to edit the video before they gave the tape to the news editor. It was queued up in the control room, and everything was ready with 30 minutes to spare. Lori's story was fourth in the queue, so she waited off stage until the commercial break. When the time came, she took a seat on the stool beside the night anchor. When they came back from the commercials and the red light above the main camera came on, Lori had a wide smile pasted on her face. Tony Mathews, the anchor, welcomed the audience back, then read off the teleprompter.

"Our next story comes to us from the little town of Grand Valley, 60 miles northwest of Toronto. We have learned of a story from the town that's gathering momentum. To tell you more, here's our street beat reporter, Lori Dale."

The TV camera rotated a few degrees until it was centered on Lori. "Thanks, Tony. Earlier today, we travelled to Grand Valley to visit a special man. Everyone in town knows him as Billy Fixit, and you might be wondering what makes him so special. Well, let's watch the interview, and you will see for yourself."

The production director in the control room pressed a button on the player, and the tape began to play. It was from earlier in the day when Lori was beside Billy who was facing head on to the camera.

"Billy, can you tell us what you're going to do that has people all over the province gaining interest?"

Billy tilted the bill of his green ballcap up. "I'm not sure why people are getting their knickers in a knot. It's simple." Billy pointed in the air behind him. "I'm going to dive into this pool of water from up there."

The camera panned upward, following the direction Billy pointed out until the top of the platform came into focus. After a few seconds, the scene changed to the earlier time when Lori and her cameraman arrived and filmed Billy up at the top of the platform. However, the present audio from the interview was overlaid.

"We saw you up on the platform when we arrived today. It seems too high for a safe jump," Lori said.

"Dive," Billy corrected.

"Pardon?"

"I'm going to dive, not jump."

"Right," Lori said. "Not to take anything away from you, but you're not the youngest man in Grand Valley. Aren't you afraid of getting hurt?"

Billy scratched behind his ear. "If I thought that was a big risk, I wouldn't be doing the dive."

"How high is it?" Lori asked. "I've never jumped or dove from such a height, and I would be scared."

"Eighteen feet."

"And I just heard you say you wanted it even higher. Is that correct."

"Yup. It's going up five feet to 23 feet."

"That's like diving off at almost the height of a three-story building," Lori clarified. "When was the last time you dove from such a height?"

"Ah—never."

For a moment, Lori was speechless. She was thinking, *this frail, old man is going to kill himself.* "When do you start to practice?"

"I never thought about that," Billy admitted. "But now that you've asked,

I don't plan on practicing. I'll just climb to the top when the time comes and dive in. Nothing like just getting it done."

Lori turned back to the camera, lifting her brows. "Billy, I'm hoping the best for you as I'm sure all our viewers are. Thanks for your time."

Billy walked out of camera shot, and John Robie strode in, taking his place.

"John, you're one of the organizers of this event," Lori said. "Aren't you afraid this dive could turn out badly? Billy isn't exactly a spring chicken."

"Billy is somewhere between 50 and 60 years old. He's lived in Grand Valley for over 30 years, so long that people aren't sure of his exact age. We had the same concerns as you've mentioned, so we had the doctors give him a thorough physical. He came through with flying colours, and Billy is adamant he wants to do this. To be clear, he's doing this of his own free will. Consequently, the day of the dive is confirmed for September 1st."

"There is more, right? Earlier, when we talked on the phone, you mentioned there might be some added events."

"Correct. We can't believe the massive positive response and support Billy is receiving from across Ontario, and also right across Canada. Billy's story is spreading like wildfire, and we're getting calls from coast to coast to coast. We can't figure it out, but all I can tell you is, every hotel and motel within 30 miles of Grand Valley is booked up for the long weekend. There's so much support, we're now in negotiations with the mayor to make this an all-weekend event, with a few more activities added."

"What activities, John?" Lori asked.

"There are a few farms west of town we are negotiating with to lease their fallow land. We are hoping to set up an outdoor country music concert for about 5,000 folks. We're ready to have an end-of-summer fair set up in the same area as well."

"Won't that be a problem with all the hotels and motels booked up?"

"Exactly, but we are planning to set up a large campground with an adjacent temporary RV park," John explained.

Turning to face the camera, Lori spoke to the viewers. "It seems Billy's story is spreading. Come out to Grand Valley over the Labour Day Weekend and support him. It sounds like there will be lots of activities, so if you need tickets or want more information, a hotline number has been set up."

A ten-digit phone number flashed in red across the bottom of the screen, then the scene was shifted back to the live feed from the studio.

"Excellent report," Tony said to Lori. "But I'm with you. I would worry about Billy's safety. He looks like he should be sitting in a rocking chair on a porch, not diving into a pool from 23 feet."

"You might be right," Lori said. "However, he has a quiet confidence that has convinced me he can do it, and CTV news will be there on September 1st to bring you the results." She reached onto the shelf under the high table she was sitting behind, retrieving a bright green ballcap. She fitted the cap over her head, and held her fist in the air. "Go Billy!"

Tony grinned as the camera panned back to him. "Folks, that's enough excitement for now. Time for a word from our sponsor."

The report from Grand Valley ended, but in reality, it wasn't an ending at all. *Billymania,* as it would soon come to be known, was just beginning.

Chapter 19: The Town Hall Meeting

It was a lazy Tuesday afternoon, and supper was almost ready. From the front patio, I could smell the macaroni and beef casserole cooking in the oven, causing my stomach to gurgle with anticipation. At the same time, my fingers were scratching the back of Phoebus's neck as he sat in front of me, his eyes closed, his tongue hanging out the side of his mouth.

I was surprised to see Billy ride up the driveway on his three-wheeler. He greeted me, playfully slapping down the bill of my ballcap over my eyes. "Is your father around?"

"Hey!" I exclaimed as I pulled my hat up. My eyes narrowed, and my lips parted about to let loose a sarcastic comment, but when I saw his grin, I couldn't help but laugh. I rose to my feet and asked, "My dad just got home from work. What do you want with him?"

"Adult stuff, so just go get him."

After rolling my eyes, I walked into the house. Phoebus shifted over to Billy where he continued scratching with the dog's approval. I walked back out a minute later, my dad right behind me.

"Hi Billy. What's up?" my dad asked.

"I won't take up much time, just a couple of minutes to clarify something."

"Sure. Want a beer?"

Rubbing his beard, Billy replied, "Sure. One won't hurt."

My dad left and returned with two ice-cold beers. He handed one bottle to Billy and took a long drink from the other before asking, "So, what's on your mind?"

Billy replied, "You know all about this dive I'm going to make into the pool up on the hill?"

"Billy, everyone in town knows all about it, and from what I'm hearing, half the people across Ontario know about it as well."

A couple of nods of his chin and Billy asked, "It's that bad, is it?"

"I'm not saying it's a bad thing, but it certainly is *a thing*. I work in Brampton, 40 miles away, and fellow workers who know I live in Grand Valley are asking me about the infamous Billy Fixit." My dad took another drink, then continued. "One of them told me he purchased two tickets and asked if he could sleep at my place overnight during the long weekend."

"I'm sorry it's causing you trouble. That's why I'm here."

"It's no trouble, Billy. I told him no, and that was the end of it, but it sounds like you have more on your mind."

I found it odd Billy was drinking beer. I hadn't seen him drink alcohol before, so I had assumed he didn't drink at all. I thought, maybe the pressure of this dive was getting to him. After all, even though outward appearances had him looking like the calmest person in Grand Valley, there must be tons of pressure. He took another drink from the bottle, adding to the relaxed, even subdued, look on his face.

"I do," Billy replied. "There's a portion of townsfolk that aren't happy about all the visitors being drawn to the event. Some people are blaming me, and to a point, they might be right. If I hadn't pushed to make the dive, none of these other added events would be snowballing into the long weekend."

"I watched the news. I hear there are events set over the entire three-day long weekend," my dad said.

"I can handle the negativity that's sent my way, but I spend time with Joe, and I don't want him to get caught up in this. It's three weeks to the long weekend, and I'm thinking it might be better for us to keep apart until the weekend is over with."

I saw my dad pause. He was actually thinking about agreeing to it. My voice rose to a high pitch as I interjected, "No one has bothered me about the dive, and if they do, I'm old enough to handle that just fine." Billy was sitting, and I moved closer, putting my arm around his neck. "Billy's taught me what it means to have real friends. Kids haven't made fun of me for being Billy's friend, but if they do, they ain't no friends of mine. I don't care if he's older. He likes me, and we do fun things together, especially reading books. I don't want that to stop."

Billy rose to his feet, sliding out of my arm. "Maybe I should leave that with you, Steve, and you can think about it."

Pointing to the seat, my dad replied, "Please sit, Billy. I don't need any time. When I heard about the divide that appears to be happening in this town, it doesn't make me happy because the small-town friendliness was one of the main reasons I moved my family here, one of the main reasons

I drive an hour back and forth every day to work. However, when I see the friendship you offer my son and the rest of my family, it reinforces those reasons I see others forgetting about. So I hope you don't stop a good thing, and that goes for Frances as well." He lifted a finger. "Just let me know if things get too awkward with people in town. I don't have a problem talking to anyone."

Billy had sat back down by the time my mom opened the screen door. She said, "Dinner's ready." Then, she saw Billy. "You have to stay!"

"I don't want to be a bother."

My mom waved her hand, shooing away Billy's response. "I insist!"

We had a nice meal together, one my mom ended with a tasty dessert. I had told my mom Billy's story about carrot muffins, just so she knew not to have carrot cake, carrot muffins, or any kind of carrot dessert when Billy was around, so apple pie was perfect.

It was a little after 6 p.m. when we finished eating. That gave enough time for us to clean up, so my mom could go to the town hall meeting set for 7 p.m. My father wasn't going since it was Blue Jays baseball night, and my dad asked Billy to stay for the game, to which he accepted.

I was going to spend some time up at Nik's house, but as I was going out the door, my father told me, "Don't you be going to the town hall meeting!"

I rode my Chopper up to Nik's where Chris and Mitch were also waiting. Chris said, "You got here just in time. We thought we'd be late for the town hall meeting."

I shrugged. "My dad told me not to go."

Nik laughed. "So did mine."

Mitch added, "It was my mom who gave me the same warning."

With a wide, wicked grin on his face, Chris said, "Let's go."

I hesitated for a moment. My dad told me not to go, but that's when I was walking out the door. I didn't answer him, so even after Billy's words about lying, I justified that, technically, I hadn't actually told a lie. If I got caught, I could always say I didn't hear him. In any case, the peer pressure was too great, so after a brief pause, I pedaled quickly to catch up to my three friends.

The special town hall, called by Mayor Tom Winters, was being held at the Pancake Church. There weren't quite as many people attending, or as many cars parked nearby, as there was for the pancake breakfast. This was because there were three types of people in Grand Valley. There were the angry people like Viggo Eckland and his followers, then, people who didn't care enough like my father who found a good sporting event more important, and, finally, there were people like my mother who were just curious about all the fuss.

When we arrived at the church on Water Street, people were just starting to enter the church. There were more people than could fit comfortably, but it didn't deter the people who continued to enter, forcing those in front of them down the centre and side aisles like cows entering a barn. Even then, a group of people were left outside, pressing against those squashed at the front door opening.

We knew we didn't have a chance of seeing or hearing the town hall from the front door, so Chris said, "follow me," and we did. He led us around the far side of the church to a small, add-on, wooden mudroom. This was the delivery entrance, and Chris knew the pastor, when the weather was hot, kept the wood door open, allowing fresh air to circulate through. Chris opened the screen door, and whispered, "Be quiet."

He led us down one short hallway, then a longer one that curled around behind the altar and podium area. I realized this must be how Pastor Fulton made his way to and from the podium on sermon day. The hallway ended, changing to a half wall with long flower pots sitting on top of it. On our hands and knees, we crawled forward and peered through the flowers towards the packed congregation.

Just in front of us was the pastor, standing beside a raised microphone, and seated beside him were Tom Winters, Roger Thornhill and John Robie. Fortunately, a cool breeze was blowing over the people at the open front doors, escaping through every open window and door on the back side of the church. Hopefully, it would cool the tempers likely to explode at the meeting. Everyone in the long room was standing in the rows of pews and in the aisles. Paperwork had been handed to those who entered, and many were fanning themselves with it now.

Pastor Fulton checked his watch and saw they were running a few minutes late. Since he provided a lengthy sermon every Sunday, I could attest based on the few I had attended, he was not a man short of words. So it surprised me when he remained silent, preferring to knock on the microphone with his knuckle. The chattering hum that had enveloped the church slowed, and when he rapped the microphone a second time, the chatter stopped completely. Not wanting to be more involved in the debate he knew was to come, he turned to Tom Winters and said, "Mayor."

The mayor had been sitting, listening to the chatter, looking out at the people of Grand Valley, especially towards those on his left. Viggo Eckland

and his wife stood in the front row, and around them stood many of Viggo's followers. Viggo stood as he often did, with his arms crossed in front of him, the flyer handed to him on the way in, crumpled in one fist. Tom was wondering if this was all worth it. The simple task of Billy Fixit diving into the pool had snowballed into a huge headache. It was out of control, something Viggo had warned him to avoid at all cost.

However, it wasn't only Viggo who had voted for him as mayor. He had a responsibility to all the people of East Luther Grand Valley. The event was exploding, and that meant a large amount of money was coming to town—much needed money. Even if the event survived the night, he wondered if he would run for mayor again. Maybe it was time for someone else to throw their hat in the ring. Then, he had a sarcastic thought. *Maybe Viggo deserved a shot at being mayor.*

Those were the thoughts going through the mayor's mind as he approached the microphone. He greeted everyone, then moved directly to the issue at hand. "Folks, we've known for a few weeks there would be an event on the Sunday of the Labour Day Weekend. It centres around Billy jumping into the water at the old pool grounds."

A yell came from the crowd. "Dive, not jump!"

Nervous laughter filled the room. The mayor was thankful for it as he continued. "The original estimate was for five to six hundred spectators, and for the inconvenience some might feel for the invasion of our little village, Roger Thornhill had agreed, when it was all done, to rip out the pool grounds and donate the land to the town."

There was another yell, but this time from within Viggo's following. "We know this! Get on with it!"

Tom cleared his throat. "You've seen the recent news reports. I don't know why, but there has been a massive amount of interest in this event, so much that before you, on the flyer is a proposal to expand the event to cover the entire three-day weekend." As he said the words, the mayor held up the flyer.

Viggo uncrumpled his copy, and while looking at it yelled out, "A three-day fair and a country music concert? What part of, 'this better not get out of control,' didn't you understand?"

There was a murmur of support from around Viggo, more than Tom had expected. Raising his hand, Tom said, "Settle down, Viggo. This is only a proposal, and it will be put to a vote tonight. It's up to the people here if we proceed or not." When the muttering complaints stopped, Tom added, "You've had a chance to read the proposal. Are there questions?"

From the back of the room, there was a yell. "How many people will be at the country music concert?"

Tom answered, "About 4,000."

"Where are they going to stay?"

"Many will come for the day, but we are setting up both a campground and an RV park on the Armstrong fallow land over on 26th sideroad. The fair and the concert grounds will be located just a little further north."

A man near Viggo asked, "How many visitors do we expect over the entire three-day weekend?"

The mayor turned to John Robie, who rose and moved to stand beside Tom. Leaning towards the microphone, he said, "Around 15,000, give or take."

There was a roar from the crowd, but still, Viggo, red with rage and as tight as a wound-up spring ready to pop, yelled over them. "We vote right now! Raise your hand if you are against this absurd proposal!" He turned to the throng, thrusting his hand in the air.

Those around him followed, and the raised hands were spreading quickly when John Robie yelled into the microphone. "Wait a minute! Hear us out!"

Viggo turned back to John. His pent-up energy was slowly releasing as he felt victory near, yet he rolled his eyes as he subsequently tilted his head. He stretched out his hands, bobbing them up and down, demanding quiet. With a confident sneer on his face, he said, "We should let the man at least finish his words before we yell no at him." Those around Viggo joined him in his laughter.

My jaw was hanging open as I watched the debate play out in front of me. I expected there would be some infighting between different groups of people, but it seemed more people were being convinced by Viggo.

John Robie spoke into the microphone. "We know the businesses in town will benefit greatly from such an influx of people, but there are fees for licences and permits that will bring money to the town as well. In addition, we have agreed to a percentage of the proceeds also going to the town."

"How much?" someone in the crowd asked.

"Our estimate is $100,000," John clarified.

Many in the crowd were shocked by the amount, and it showed by the silence in the room.

However, Viggo said, "It's not enough."

The quiet a moment before was broken by murmurs of agreement. Roger Thornhill, who had been quiet thus far, rose and strode to the microphone. The people knew Roger, just as they knew John, but Roger was known as the quiet worker type. Consequently, when he moved to speak, the crowd's curiosity resulted in silence.

Roger, in a hushed tone, said, "This town has been through some tough times. The general bad economic times should have been enough, but then the tornado came through town five years ago, and it has not been forgotten. Every time I drive through town, I see the grass covered lot where the library was. As much as the library was a benefit to the entire town, more than anything else it was a place for the children of Grand Valley."

For the people listening, they were confused since it seemed Roger had gone off on an unrelated tangent. Roger must have understood what they were thinking. "I see it on your faces. What's he going on about? I understand a three-day festival would be an inconvenience, but it's only three days." After pausing for a few seconds, he finally got to the point. "So if we vote to allow this event, John and I will pay to rebuild the library. It'll be double the size of the old one, and it'll be there for the kids of Grand Valley for the next hundred years!"

Citizens looked at those standing beside them, their jaws dropped in shock.

Roger added, "That's a value of about $800,000! So now that all the cards are on the table, let's vote. Hands up if you want a new library for the kids!"

Quickly, hands began to go up until almost half of the people raised their hands. Viggo, his arms crossed, held his ground, at least until his wife raised her hand. Her other elbow hit into her husband's ribs. "Think of the kids," she hissed through clenched teeth.

I never saw a look of sour defeat on anyone like I saw on Viggo's face at that moment. It was like his arm weighed 200 lbs when he finally lifted it over his head. His followers being followers did the same, and now it was easy to see a large majority of the citizens had their hands up.

John wrapped his arm around Roger's shoulders. Roger wasn't a natural salesman, but now John saw Roger had a survival killer instinct, knowing how and when to provide a winning blow. John never would have thought of it; use the kids to appeal to the sympathy of the parents.

Tom moved back in front of the microphone. "Folks, it looks like we're going to have a festival!"

Chapter 20: The National News

"Billy Fixit." Manny Saad, evening news anchor for the Canadian national news, said the name that had spread from rural Ontario, to its bigger cities and was now being showcased across Canada. "It's a name people in Ontario have been familiar with for the last few weeks, and his story has spread further across Canada. Some have said he is a six-foot-eight-inches tall, Paul Bunyon type character. Other's have said he does not even exist except in the eyes and pocketbooks of shady marketing specialists. Well, we're here to clarify the facts, and why this phenomenon, many are now calling *Billymania,* exists."

A picture of Billy in his black denim overalls and green ballcap appeared, covering half the viewers TV screens. At the same time, Manny Saad, appeared live on the opposite side. He gave a brief history about Billy, although there wasn't a whole lot to say. When his description shifted to the event, Billy's image was replaced by a video showing the newly renovated pool grounds. The deck ringing the pool, now filled with crystal-clear water, had been painted brilliant white. At one end of the pool was the raised platform Billy would dive off, and as the video camera zoomed out, the wider image showed the surrounding bleachers, ten rows deep.

As Manny Saad described the scene, he highlighted a significant change. "And we have a CBC exclusive, Folks. Those of you familiar with the event know the original height of the platform was 18 feet, then Billy requested the height be raised to 23 feet. We can verify now, at Billy's request, the height you are seeing is 27 feet from the water. He has checked the new height and accepted it as final."

Manny didn't even realize he was shaking his head as he announced the new height, thinking, *the old fool is going to kill himself.* He turned over the page on his table and continued. "The event is one aspect of what is occurring, but the other even more curious aspect is the spreading Billymania. To give you more answers about this, our reporter, Sam Andrews, was out on the streets of Ottawa this afternoon."

Manny Saad disappeared from the screen, replaced by a young, long-haired reporter holding a microphone while standing in the main aisle of the Rideau Centre shopping complex. He gave a brief introduction that was interrupted as a curious passerby stopped near him. Sam Andrews took the opportunity to ask the person about Billy Fixit, whereby a wide smile came across the woman's face. She voiced her encouragement for the man before waving at the camera. Three other people also stopped, each having knowledge of Billy, each showing their excitement and encouragement.

Sam was about to sign off when he said, "Wait." Walking past the cameraman who turned and followed him, Sam hurried towards a group of teenagers: two boys and two girls. They were similarly dressed, each of them wearing brown work boots, black denim overalls and green ballcaps. One of the girls had cleverly modified her overalls into cutoff shorts.

Sam said, "It's obvious you know about Billy Fixit. Give us your thoughts."

One of the girls leaned in towards the microphone. "I think Billy is great! He reminds me of my grandpa, and I just want to hug him!"

All four of the teenagers began bouncing up and down, whooping and cheering for Billy Fixit.

Sam Andrews said, "Hold on. Do the four of you have tickets for the event?"

One of the boys replied, "Nope, but we're going to Grand Valley for the long weekend, anyways. We'll figure things out when we get there!"

Sam turned, facing the camera as the four youths skipped away, continuing their boisterous support for Billy Fixit. Sam said, "It's hard to believe what is happening, but if you're looking for a pair of black overalls or a green ballcap, good luck! Across the country, they're in short supply, and in Ontario, they're completely sold out. Back to you, Manny."

The screen came back to Manny sitting behind his table, but now, beside him was an older woman dressed in a beige suit. She had short, grey hair and black eyeglasses with thick, round rims.

"Thanks, Sam," Manny said. Turning to the woman, he added, "This is well known clinical psychologist, Dr. Inga Tolenson, from the University of Toronto. "Inga—Billy Fixit, now a fashion icon—what is going on?"

Through a smile and a slight foreign accent, Inga replied, "Thank you, Manny." She pushed her glasses up the bridge of her nose before continuing, "What we are seeing should not be a surprise. There are two aspects to consider when we see a phenomenon like Billy Fixit. First, to understand, let's take a step back and look through a wider lens. All people have goals they try to achieve. Some are very big goals, but even the average layman has goals of some significance. For example, finishing a painting, completing a project at work, landing an account, or even something as simple as completing a week of work, are things our mind sees as accomplished goals. And we have all seen, when we complete these types of goals, we obtain a feeling of satisfaction, and it can be quite euphoric.

This is no accident. Our brain releases a chemical peptide called endorphins—what I refer to as *brain morphine*, because it is as powerful as morphine and acts in the same way. Endorphins are released when we feel pain, stress, anxiety, or when we encounter pleasurable activities. That's why, in a sporting event, when we score a goal, we get that rush of endorphins and the resulting high."

"Wow! I didn't realize it was so complicated," Manny interjected.

Dr. Tolenson laughed. "I have been studying this most of my life. Haven't you ever wondered why we cheer for a favorite sports team?" She didn't wait for a response. "For many who don't have great goals, they associate themselves with sports teams or sports figures. When those teams achieve their goals, we relate to them collectively and welcome that same rush of brain morphine.

The other fact coming into play, is during negative periods like the economic downturn we have been seeing for the last few years, there is less to cheer for and a general reduction in achievable goals, so when we see something as simple as Billy Fixit having a goal of diving into a pool of water, we latch onto it!"

"That's a fascinating perspective, Doctor," Manny Saad concluded. "Thank you."

The camera zoomed in on Manny, "To finish our report, the event, now named *Billyfest,* is scheduled over the three-day long weekend, beginning with activities Friday night. There will be a country music concert on Saturday, and a fair over the entire weekend. Of course, the highlight event when Billy will make his historic dive is on Sunday afternoon. Finally, CBC is working with the organizers to provide a live feed of the diving event, so Canada, prepare to have your brain morphine released." He spun his pencil in his fingers before tapping the tip on the table. "Goodnite."

Chapter 21: Eve Kendall

The sun was receding in the distance, leaving a purple line of clouds in the twilight. I was sitting on the grass with my back against the trunk of a tree in Chris's yard, the one with the fort just above me. Nik was sitting beside me while Mitch, and Ronnie were waiting beside Chris. Chet was late.

The day before, Chris called a meeting of the Dudes, something he didn't normally do unless something was bothering him. In those instances, he usually gave away hints as to what was on his mind, but this time he hadn't. He was determined to wait until everyone arrived before he revealed his concern.

A few minutes later, Chet arrived. He deftly slid off his bike while letting it fall to the grass. Chris slapped him on the back of the head while scolding him about his tardiness. Pointing to the ladder, Chris motioned Chet to lead the way. The rest of us followed him up, and we each found a cushion to sit on as we formed into a tight circle. Chris turned on a lantern and placed it in the open space between us.

Chris began, "I don't think we have anything serious to worry about, but I thought we should meet and make sure." He glanced around the circle, and not seeing any objections, he continued. "Billyfest is creating a problem for some people in town. My dad is one of them. He's agreed to the events, but he's far from happy."

"It's the same for my parents," Ronnie interjected.

I felt the need to defend Billy, so I chimed in, "My parents are fine with it."

Nik added, "My mom thinks a new library is worth it."

Chris laughed. "Adults always have different opinions, and they'll fight about dumb shit, but, I'm a kid, and even though my dad is against the festival, I think it'll be a hoot!" Again, he glanced at each of us in the circle. "I'm willing to bet each of you feel the same way."

Scrunching my nose, I asked, "What're you getting at?"

"I just want to make sure we're okay. We're the Dudes, and that means we gotta stick together, no matter what," Chris explained.

"Are you hearing any different?" Nik asked as he raised his shoulders and pushed out his chest.

"Settle down, Nik," Chris replied as he waved away his friend's feelings. "Hear me out. For example, my dad has been badmouthing a lot of people, including Nik's mom, and I'm sure Nik's mom has been spoutin bad words about my dad as well."

The grin on Nik's face indicated Chris's words were true.

"I don't care about any of that," Chris said. "What I'm telling you is to not give it a second thought, the same way I'm not. Leave that shit to the adults. For us, we're the Dudes! We need to stay tight, no matter what people are saying. Are we all good on that?"

Each of us said we were. I was surprised I actually felt better knowing my gang was behind me. I had been worried, being Billy's friend and spending time with him the way I did, that some of my friends might resent me. It was a relief to see they didn't.

We stayed in the tree fort for a while, just talking nonsense the way only a group of ten and eleven-year-olds could find entertaining. There was a receding, thin crack of twilight in the distance when we climbed down from the fort. Chris went into his house, and the rest of us biked away. Nik and I veered left onto Amaranth while Chet, Mitch and Ronnie continued straight, towards their homes.

When we arrived at Main Street we saw an unusual sight, one I hadn't seen in Grand Valley before. A long, black Lincoln limousine was creeping down Main Street. Both Nik and I pressed our brake handles, bringing us to a stop. We expected the limousine to pass by us, but the brake lights broke the darkness. The blacked-out rear window lowered, revealing an older woman with auburn hair tucked into a bun. She was pretty, and when she smiled, there was something familiar about her.

She said, "Hi, Boys."

I replied, "We're not supposed to talk to strangers." I was up off the banana seat, one foot on a raised pedal, ready to push all my weight down in case I needed to bolt away.

"Even if it's an old woman in a limo?" she asked.

I couldn't hold back my laugh. "Good one!" At that point, I should have left, but my curiosity got the better of me. "What are you doing in town?"

Her voice was smooth and the words flowed off her tongue. "I'm looking for Billy Fixit. Can you tell me where he might be?"

My eyes glanced from one end of the long limousine to the other, thinking she must be someone important. "It's Sunday, and Billy always has dinner at Ms. Stevens's house. You'll have to hurry to catch him, though. He'll likely be leaving soon."

"Thanks. Do you know the address?"

"Sure," I answered. "She lives a few houses away from me, and I'm on my way home. Just follow us, and I'll lead you there." She nodded before rolling her window up.

Nik and I led the way along Amaranth, before cutting over to Grant Street. We stopped at the end of Ms. Stevens's driveway where the limousine made a wide turn into it. The driver, in a crisp, black suit, exited and opened the rear door. The lady was wearing an expensive gold chain over a long-sleeved white blouse, a contrast to her black slacks. She walked over to Nik and I, asking, "This is the place?"

We both nodded our heads up and down, whereby she gave us each a five-dollar bill. "Wow! Thanks, Lady!" We were both ecstatic.

She didn't give us another thought as she turned towards the house. Nik whispered to me he had to get home since he was already late, and he suggested I do the same. I told him something big was happening, and I wasn't going anywhere—yet.

The lady instructed her driver to wait in the car, then walked towards the porch where Billy and Frances had been sitting, enjoying the stars even though it was a cool evening. However, when Billy saw the limousine pull in the driveway, he had risen to his feet.

When the smart-dressed lady arrived at the top of the stairs, her hand was shaking as it gripped the handrail to help keep her balance. She looked at Billy and in a low, trembling tone, said, "You're older."

Billy replied, "You're still pretty."

She cracked a smile. "You don't look as old as the picture of you I saw on TV."

Billy grinned back and shrugged. "That's something then, isn't it."

For the next few seconds, their obvious hesitation was awkward with neither of them knowing what to say next. They finally realized that was because it wasn't a time for more words, so they each took a step forward and embraced each other. I could hear them both crying—sobbing in fact.

Frances, not knowing where to look, fidgeted around in her chair, trying to find somewhere to hide, and it made me think I should leave. I had no idea what to do, so I just sat on my bike kicking at a few loose pieces of gravel, doing my best to hide in plain sight.

When they released each other from their embrace, Billy slid his arm around the woman's waist, turning her towards Frances. Billy said, "This is my sister, Eve Kendall."

I had never seen Ms. Stevens's face look quite the way it did right then. Her chin was so low because her mouth was gapped open, giving the appearance she didn't have a neck. Adding to that, her eyes were as wide as saucers. It was at that moment, I realized my own mouth was gapped open the same way, and I imagine I looked exactly as she did.

Billy must have noticed the look on my face, so he called me over. Months ago, when I first saw Billy, and Chris told me a tale where he was a monster who ate young kids, I never ran away from Billy, but I was thinking I just might make a run for it now. I lifted my foot to the pedal and was about to bolt when I heard him a second time. "It's okay, Joe. C'mon up."

Part of me said I was making a mistake, but Billy was insistent, waving his hand towards me. So I lay down the Chopper and took slow steps up onto the porch. I looked up at Billy and his sister, and now, with them side by side, I understood why she had looked familiar.

"Eve, this is a good friend of mine, Joe," Billy said.

Eve held her hand out to me. "Yes, I already met this fine young man downtown. Hi, Joe," she said in a soft voice.

I shook her hand, thinking it would make things less awkward, but it didn't. Billy and I had spent enough time together so that he understood the look on my face, and thankfully, he sent me on my way home. He said, "Joe, your mom will kill me if she finds out I'm the reason you're out after dark. Best you get home right now, and tomorrow you can get to know Eve a bit better."

"Yes, Sir," I stammered, even though I didn't remember ever calling him, *Sir*, before. I was nervous, and not wanting to say anything else dumb, I waved my goodbyes, then rode home.

Frances rose to her feet. "I'll invite your driver up onto the porch for a coffee. I'm sure you two have a lot to talk about, so why don't you go to the parlour."

Without waiting for a response, Frances walked by them towards the limousine while Billy and Eve entered the house. Once they were in the parlour, Billy closed the double doors behind them. Eve sat down on the couch, and Billy sat down beside her. He laid his hand to his side—hoping—and Eve placed her hand on top of his.

"When did Bart change to Billy?" Eve asked.

Billy wasn't dealing well with the shock that was settling into his system, so he looked forward, focusing on a spot on the far wall. "I decided to use my middle name even before I left. Bartholemew William Kendall was going to be no more."

"I understand," Eve replied. And she really did understand. She was three years older than Billy and had seen how their father had verbally abused Bart—now Billy—and how their mother had stood by and let it happen. She did not blame Billy for leaving, but she loved the Bart she knew, and it crushed her when he had disappeared.

"I'm surprised you recognized me. It's been a long, long time," he said.

Through a chuckle, she answered, "I saw you on TV, hiding behind your beard and moustache. You're older, but I still recognized your eyes. I never forgot that from when we were younger." She squeezed her brother's hand and whispered. "You're my brother, so there's some things we'll never forget." Her last word came through a sob as she was crying again.

Billy leaned into her as he wrapped her in his warm embrace. His hand moved to the back of her neck, drawing her cheek to his shoulder as tears flowed down his own face. They sat like that for some time until they were interrupted by a light knock on the door. Billy and Eve separated, each wiping their cheeks. Billy, his voice trembling, said, "Come in."

The door opened and Frances backed in, carrying a tray supporting a pot of tea, two cups and the relevant condiments. She placed the tray on the coffee table in front of them, offering, "I thought you could use some tea."

Billy was about to thank her, leaning forward towards one of the cups, when Eve put a hand on his shoulder. Eve looked warmly at Frances. "I appreciate your hospitality, but I have come into your home uninvited, and I think I have overstayed my welcome."

His face drooping, Billy said, "You're not leaving already?"

Rising to her feet, Eve quipped, "Bart—or Billy—I just found you, so, you won't be rid of me so quickly. I'll be back tomorrow, and we need to have a long talk about this ludicrous jump you're going to make."

"A dive, not a jump," Billy corrected.

"If I can talk any sense into you, it won't be a dive or a jump!" Eve was emphatic. "But right now, it's getting late, and I have to travel back to my hotel in Brampton. All the local hotels are booked up, so we have a bit of a drive ahead of us."

Placing her hands on her hips, Frances said with a firm voice, "Now, Eve Kendall, Billy is the closest friend I have in the world, and you are his sister. You are going no where. I have a spare room, and you are welcome to stay here as long as you need." She saw Eve about to object, so before she could do so, Frances interjected, "And if you even try and say no, I will take it as a personal insult."

Sheepishly, Billy was trying to crawl under the cushion when Eve let out a boisterous laugh. "Well, I can't say no then, can I?" Eve's eyes softened as she received an instant warm and comforting feeling about Frances. "It means a lot to me. Thank you."

The three of them went back outside onto the porch. Eve continued to the limousine where the driver was leaning back against the fender. "Jack, I'll be staying. I won't need you any further tonight, and likely not for the next few days. Head back to Brampton, but keep your phone on in case I need something."

"Of course, Miss Kendall." The driver pushed off the fender and retrieved a suitcase from the trunk before depositing it on the porch. With a tip of his hat, Jack left, leaving Eve Kendall to Billy and Frances and the coziness of Grand Valley for at least the next few days.

Billy carried the suitcase up to the spare room on the second floor, laying it on the bed, when Frances couldn't hold back a yawn. "My, my, it's only 11 p.m., but I think I've had it."

"If you don't mind, Eve and I will stay up for a little while. We have some catching up to do." Billy leaned towards Frances, kissing her on the cheek. "Thanks for everything." The interaction, resulting in Frances's eyes shifting in an instant from weariness to complete joy, told Eve much about their relationship. When she saw Billy's picture on TV, she wasn't sure he looked happy, but now, she was beginning to see perhaps he was.

Billy and Eve went back down to the parlour where Billy poured the still steaming tea into the two cups. Once again, he sat down beside his sister. She took a small drink from the cup before leaning back in the well cushioned couch.

"You know that Dad died, right?"

"Yes, it was in the papers. I heard about Mom as well, but I didn't find out until six months after she passed," Billy replied.

"Dad sent investigators out to try and find you after you disappeared, but he didn't seem overly interested. Mom felt bad, though. She took it hard."

"I don't want to talk about Mom and Dad, if you don't mind. I want to find out more about you. I heard the driver call you, "*Miss* Kendall.""

"That's correct, married, divorced after 20 years, and I have a son and two grandchildren—both girls."

Billy, whose face had been sagging when he heard the word, *divorced,* brightened when he heard he had new-found relatives. "I'm happy about your family. Maybe, just as we have become reacquainted, I could meet them at some point?"

"Of course," she replied. "How about you? I can see Frances cares for you, but have you ever married, and do you have children?"

The tea had cooled, allowing Billy to take a long drink before answering. "When I left Halifax, I wandered around for a year before I found Grand Valley. It was the type of quiet town where I could easily remain hidden, lost in obscurity. Having a father such as we had, in a marriage such as we saw, did not inspire me to follow in his footsteps. So the answer to your question is, no, I have never even been in a long-term relationship or contemplated being responsible for raising children."

Eve's one eyebrow perked up. She took note of the odd manner in which her brother described having children. It was a peculiarity she thought better to leave alone, at least for the moment. In a soft voice, she asked, "Are you happy?"

The response, however, was too quick for Eve's liking. "I think I'm content." Billy replied. He saw the confusion beginning to come into his sister's face. It was a good time to change the topic. "Are you still working for father's company?"

"Yes, but it is not his company, Billy. It is yours and mine. Collectively, we own 60 per cent of Kendall Enterprises." She hesitated for a moment, unsure if this was the right time to reveal more critical details, but her impulsive side pushed her to. "I am the Chief Financial Officer of the company and I own 35 per cent of the shares. You have 25 per cent in a trust fund I administer, and it has a value of a little over $20 million." She watched Billy closely, expecting surprise. She had always assumed Billy would think his father would have left him nothing.

"That'll buy a lot of pizza," he dryly replied.

Eve threw her hands in the air. "You're rich! You can live wherever you like. You don't have to stay in Grand Valley! You don't have to be *Mister*

Billy Fixit any longer, and you don't have to prove anything to anybody by diving into a pool of water, likely a feat that will leave you with a broken neck!"

Chuckling, Billy patted his sister's knee. "I appreciate the concern, but I've been here for 35 years. This is my home, and I don't see that changing." His gaze penetrated Eve. He wanted her to feel his passion. "This town has made me a survivor while allowing me to keep my sanity, and in some small part, I feel I've helped this town as well. Keep the money in the trust fund, or I'm more than happy signing it over to you."

She placed her hand on top of his. "And I know exactly what you are doing with this dive into the pool. When I heard on TV that the height was exactly 27 feet, an odd number to most, it hit a nerve with me right away." She squeezed Billy's hand. "The accident wasn't your fault, so you have nothing to prove to anyone."

Pulling back his hand, Billy shot to his feet. The beard and moustache couldn't hide the flush on his face. "Don't ever mention the accident! You don't know me, or what I've gone through!"

Slowly, Eve rose to her feet, her lips trembling.

Seeing this, Billy's shoulders sagged. He felt a need to explain the tumbling emotions he was feeling. "When siblings are young, it's always too awkward for one to tell the other their feelings towards each other. At some point, they realize how important that acknowledgment is. Some time in the last 35 years, I think that time passed me by, Eve, but nevertheless, better late than never, know that I love you."

Eve's lips stopped quivering, cracking into a smile. "And I love you, Brother."

The tender moment was interrupted by creaking from the stairs. A moment later, Frances, pulling a thick housecoat tight against her thin frame, appeared in the doorway. Her eyebrows were angled in. "Are you two okay? I heard shouting."

Billy replied, "I think we're fine, but I'm bushed. It's time for me to head home."

Normally, Frances would have tried to convince Billy to stay the night, even though he always refused, but tonight, she sensed both he and his sister needed some space. "I'm sure Eve's had a long day as well, so let her sleep in, in the morning."

"I was hoping to take the two of you up to Vicki's for breakfast."

"I won't hear of it," Frances answered. "I'm going to make Eve a late breakfast here. Besides, I think we need a talk of our own."

Instantly, the blood drained from Billy's face as his eyes darted from side to side, but his appearance quickly reverted back to normal as he chuckled. Then he shrugged—a comical shrug of surrender. It was inevitable the two women would eventually have some alone time to gossip in any case. "Very well. I'll come by a bit later, and I'll take both of you up to Vicki's for dinner instead."

Without waiting for a response, Billy walked towards Eve, kissing her cheek, then he shifted towards Frances, kissing her cheek as well, although it lasted longer while he lingered a comforting touch on her arm.

He left the house now not minding that in the early afternoon, he had walked to Frances's house instead of riding or driving. It was a cool night for late August, but the brisk breeze he felt was a welcome cold slap to his emotions and something he needed to maintain his sanity. In a matter of a few hours, his life had changed. He once again had a sister and family. She would do everything in her power to deter him from making the dive, but in this, he would be adamant and focused. His sister had been correct when she mentioned her suspicions about the accident, but she was wrong about a significant part of it. After more than 30 years, Billy was still obsessed with the accident, and he had *everything* to prove.

Chapter 22: A Bad Memory

July was the hottest month in Halifax, but even in that month, there were only a few scalding days where the air hung heavy, suffocating the city. Those were the days when people went shopping just so they could find a store with air conditioning, or they headed to the shoreline, hopeful the ocean breeze would bring relief from the heat.

For Malcolm and Bart, there was only one option, and that was the quarry, half a mile west of their Bedford subdivision. The old, open pit quarry had been mined out many years before the Kendall family moved to Bedford, but thankfully, at least for the teenagers of the community, the pit had filled with crystal-clear water.

Malcolm and Bart were twins, only 12-years-old, and they had been to the quarry several times through the summer. They were both good swimmers, so they felt comfortable visiting the quarry where, typically, only older teenagers ventured. Today, they were walking the half mile to the site, Malcolm leading while Bart had to skip every ten yards or so to keep up to his brother.

Even though they were twins, Malcolm was the better athlete. He could run faster, walk further and hold his breath underwater longer than Bart. In fact, the difference between the brothers was evident in almost everything they did including academics. Bart was smart, but it always seemed when Bart brought home an A on a test, Malcolm would achieve an $A+$. It would have bothered Bart, except Malcolm was a good brother. He encouraged and helped Bart in everything they did, and he never diminished Bart's efforts by boasting of his own superior prowess.

When they reached the entrance to the quarry grounds, they followed the curved, gravel-covered road down to the edge of the small lake. Trees, a mix of white pine, spruce and paper birch, had grown in the area surrounding the lake wherever sufficient soil had endured, and as they followed the shoreline in the shade of the branches, they came to the grass-covered clearing they had visited before.

There was a group of older boys and girls sitting on the far side of the clearing. They glanced over when they saw the twins, but they had seen them before, so they gave Malcolm and Bart no further thought. The twins kicked off their shoes and pulled off their sweat-spotted t-shirts before running to the edge of the water. They stopped abruptly before they came to the edge since the last five feet was covered with large, irregular stones. Holding their hands out for balance, they crossed carefully, like soldiers crossing a minefield, but it didn't take them long before they were knee-deep in the cool water. Having entered there before, they knew there was a sudden drop off, therefore they walked out slowly until Malcolm took a step forward and was abruptly up to his neck in the water. From there, the two boys swam out 20 yards to the raft the older boys had constructed earlier in the summer.

For most of the next hour they jumped into the water, then climbed up the ladder attached to the raft, repeating the process over and over; sometimes they dove, sometimes they jumped in cannonball style, sometimes the more difficult can opener was their choice.

They were interrupted by screeching from further along the shoreline. The older group of teenagers had climbed up the rocky hillside to a high plateau. On the side facing the water was a ten-yard-wide promontory, jutting out into the lake. Several times now, Malcolm and Bart had seen older teenagers up there, jumping into the water far below—a distance of at least three stories. They performed their jumps many times, doing the same cannonballs the twins were doing, but with more astounding results with skyrocketing splashes shooting 20 feet into the air. The screeches, however, did not come from those jumping. Several species of birds nested in the rocky cliffside under the tip of the promontory, and if a jumper came too close to their perch, they would shriek out their dissatisfaction.

Malcolm and Bart watched the action from the raft. The older kids would have continued for longer, but the trek returning up the hillside was tiring in the stifling temperature of the afternoon. After their last jump, they turned and began to swim for the raft. Although they didn't mind the younger twins sharing the quarry grounds since, after all—they were Kendall's—they weren't about to share the raft with them. Malcolm and Bart knew their place in the pecking order, so they dove off the raft for the last time, heading for shore.

Once they were there, they dried themselves with large beach towels they had brought with them. Malcolm looked up at the plateau, then brought his gaze back down to his brother. "We should go up there and do a couple of jumps."

Grinning, Bart replied, "I'll jump, but I think you'll chicken out!"

Since they were extremely competitive, Malcolm had no choice but to defend his honour and answer the challenge. He said, "We'll see. Let's go."

They put on their shirts and running shoes, while slinging their moist towels around their necks. They ran to the bottom of the hillside, using handholds to help them zigzag their way up to the plateau. At first, they paused, looking across the landscape from the highest point in the area. They could see their subdivision in the distance, and even further, the city of Halifax proper.

"C'mon, let's have some fun," Malcolm said as he slapped Bart on the shoulder.

The two boys walked to the edge of the cliff, Malcolm just ahead—he was always just ahead. Looking down, they saw the side of the rocky cliff slanted outwards toward the water. Bart stood a little further away from the edge. When he looked down to the water, he never thought it would look so much higher than what it did from the waterline.

Malcolm took off his shoes and shirt, his twin brother following his lead. "We'll need to make a running jump to get as far out into the water as we can," Malcolm concluded. He glanced at Bart. "I'll go first."

Bart's brows furrowed. Malcolm went first in everything, and he *came* first in everything. Impulsively, Bart replied, "No, I'm going first."

Glancing down at the water again, Bart was sorry the words came so quickly. Malcolm walked back a few feet, giving his brother room for his jump, but he stayed close enough to the edge to see the water below. Hearing a shrill whistle, Bart looked across to the group of teenagers. They were standing on the raft, one of them waving his hands over his head. Malcolm saw them as well.

"They look worried," Malcolm said. "Let's get this done before they chase us off."

Nodding, Bart walked backward until he was ten yards from the edge. He took a starter's position, but he hesitated. He jogged to the edge, looking down again after which he backed up for a second time, leaning over while once again taking a starter's stance. A few seconds later, he brought himself upright, placing his hands on his hips. Another few seconds went by before he glanced at Malcolm, shaking his head.

Malcolm walked over to stand beside him. "What's up, Brother?"

"It's...too high. I can't...do it," Bart stammered.

Giving his brother a wide, reassuring smile, Malcolm said, "Sure you can. Just watch me, and do what I do."

Before Bart could object, Malcolm was running towards the cliff's edge. Bart followed at a slower pace, stopping at the edge, watching Malcolm fall downward, his speed reminding Bart of a predatory bird focused on a tasty fish. The thought lasted only a moment before Malcolm hit the water feet first. His hands were perfectly placed at his sides, but his angle was not true vertical. Yet, there was barely a splash as he broke through the water.

Two of the older teenagers really were worried, so they had already swum over near the landing site. When Malcolm did not surface, their worry turned to all out fear. With rapid strokes they rushed to the point of impact. They dove down, their feet angling up out of the water before they disappeared. They were gone for a good minute before returning to break the surface, gasping for air. For a second time, they dove under. Again, one minute went by, then a second. This time, when they broke the surface, they were supporting Malcolm between them. He was unconscious, blue in the face, and his neck was at an odd angle, one that shouldn't be possible.

The two boys swam to the shoreline with Malcolm where the two girls were letting out frantic screams. One of the boys yelled back at her to go get help. She ran for the car they had left at the end of the roadway leading to the pit. The other boy began doing CPR, but since Malcolm and Bart were twins and had a unique connection, Bart knew the effort was in vain. Malcolm was dead.

Bart turned, looking down at the exact spot Malcolm hit the water. He thought, *if only he would have jumped.* Bart was frozen in shock until his guilt was interrupted by a screech, followed by a burst of white and grey. The osprey had flown up the side of the cliff, appearing as a blur not two feet in front of Bart. It was as if the bird knew what he was thinking, vehemently showing its objection.

The osprey turned, circling above him. It was a juvenile, not long in the world, with a pure white chest surrounded by grey feathers. It shrieked at Bart again as it circled for a second time. Then, its yellow eyes looked at him one last time before it swept away.

One life ends. A new life begins.

Chapter 23: Hectic Preparations

My eyes cracked open as the first signs of the sunrise cast shadows across my bedroom. It was Saturday morning, exactly eight days before Billy's dive into the water at the pool grounds, a facility once an eyesore of abandonment, but now renovated, cleaned and polished. I rolled on my back, placing my hands under my head as I stared at a point on the ceiling, thinking of the experiences the summer in Grand Valley had brought me, and the added ones likely to continue over the next week.

I thought about Billy's sister, appearing out of nowhere. He never mentioned a sister in all our discussions at job sites or during our reading sessions. She seemed like a nice person, carrying herself with elegance, and she couldn't be all bad. After all, she gave Nik and I five dollars each just for showing her where Billy was.

Letting out a sigh, I realized I enjoyed living in Grand Valley. I was still in the habit of locking my bike everywhere I went even though I didn't have to. Everyone in Grand Valley knew everyone else, consequently, all the townsfolk, be it adults or kids, knew my red Chopper. If anyone saw someone else riding it, they wouldn't get far. Everyone had a routine, everything had a place and a purpose. The Tongue always walked down the sidewalk on only one side of the street, and the Worm always sat on the same bench downtown. Viggo's dad was the guy to go to if you wanted metal work done, Nik's dad was the go-to-guy for woodworking projects, just as Billy was the guy to see if you needed general repairs or simple modifications.

That's why people in town were having difficulty with the concept of Billyfest. It was a change to the quiet routine of small-town life. It had been voted on, and passed, but that didn't mean people weren't irritated by the added visitors coming through town. Many came just as part of a drive through, while others came for lunch, dinner or just a coffee. They browsed the shops on Main Street, especially the Stained-Glass Shop. The owners of the businesses and restaurants were thrilled with the added patronage, but not so much the citizens. The only grocery store was downtown, and on most days, parking was at a premium at Foodland or anywhere on Main

Street. The only solace taken was knowing after the long weekend it would all be over.

The sun had crept higher in the sky, its rays breaking through my window and assaulting my eyes. I propped myself up, yawning before rotating my legs off the side of the bed. In my pajama bottoms, eyes half closed, I made my way to the bathroom, taking care of my morning activities before I returned to my room. White sports socks, one of my many pairs of summer shorts, and for today, a gray t-shirt were my preferred choices. My blue ballcap given to me by Billy was on my chair. Beside the chair, on my bookcase was a stack of eight comics Billy had also given me, and beside them were three books; these were the books we had read together over the summer. Each time we closed the back cover on a story, Billy offered me the book, and each time, initially, I refused. But after Billy told me how many times he had read each book, along with the fact they were kid's books that should belong to a kid, I relented.

However, it wasn't the things Billy gave me that were most important. He treated me with respect, something I didn't understand until he explained it to me in terms I could comprehend. He wasn't afraid to share his thoughts, and he listened to mine with interest. Billy cared for me. In fact, I knew he loved me. It's something he would never tell me, just as I would never tell him I loved him as if he was part of our family. He was like a beloved uncle to me. I knew as I grew older, the relationship I had with him would grow—that is if he didn't kill himself with that stunt diving into the water from a height of 27 feet!

Placing the hat on my head, I skipped down the stairs and turned the corner towards the kitchen. My mom and dad were already awake having started their busy Saturday. As soon as she saw me, my mom put two pieces of toast on a plate beside a mound of scrambled eggs. I was at that age where I was growing in great spurts, so I made short work of the food. I asked where my father was, and my mom pointed out the back window.

I knew exactly what that meant. After putting my running shoes on, I stepped out the back door and walked towards the side yard. My dad was busy attending to a chore common in every Hungarian household, and also common to many other gardens in any small country town. That chore was tending to a vegetable garden.

Early in the spring, my father had expanded the small garden alongside the wooden side fence to a 30 yard long by three-yard-wide area, representative of a person interested in extensive vegetable yields. Against the fence were the cucumber vines, now filled with fat specimens ready to be picked. The next row was tomato plants: smaller cherry varieties as well as the big beefsteak ones. The third row was a mix of sweet yellow peppers, green bell peppers, broccoli and a few vegetables he would change, year to year. That was his experimentation area. Last, across the front of the garden, to deter animals from stealing his vegetables, was a variety of hot peppers. Rodents, squirrels, skunks and rabbits would enter the Kovacs vegetable patch at their own peril.

In the distance, I heard lawn mowers at work, just as I knew my father would cut our grass after tending to the vegetable garden. I took in a deep breath as I walked towards my father, smelling the scent of cut grass. All these things reminded me why I never thought back to my suburban life with any regrets. I loved this little country town.

I snuck up on my dad, giving him a hello and a hug. We had a few words about what I would be doing during the day, and it always ended with him telling me to be careful. Typically, as it was today, I was already running to the garage to retrieve my bike when the last few words faded away behind me.

Nik had told me he would be up early, and I should meet him at the Brooklin Bridge since his father would be doing some work there. I took the typical path making my way towards Amaranth Street, then down to Main Street. Once I arrived at the Foodland corner, I saw Main Street was blocked off with orange and yellow street barricades. That's when I remembered the downtown core would be blocked off for the entire weekend, not allowing any vehicular traffic. It was a dry run since the same barricades would be set up in an identical manner for the long weekend. Anyone travelling through town would have to divert up to Emma Street, then come back down to Main Street on the other side of the downtown block.

I stopped my bike at the barricades. Mounted across the top, supported by added wooden posts, was a massive green, vinyl sign. It stretched across the entire roadway, and on it in two-foot-high letters was one word: *Billyfest*. I was not surprised when I glanced down to the other end of the block to see workers were installing an identical sign above the barricades there. What did surprise me was the scene between the barricades. Since there would be no vehicular traffic, the two downtown restaurants and the coffee shop had a mass of tables and chairs under wide umbrellas out on the street. In total, there had to be at least 20 tables. In addition, at the far end, a food truck was parked along the curb with many more tables in front of it. People were already seated at some of the tables with most being the nosy Grand Valley variety who wanted to experience the pop-up venue before the expected mass of visitors showed up during the following weekend.

I rode my Chopper along the sidewalk, now noticing the large white and green ribbons hanging from the street light poles. I was amazed at the transformation, but after checking the time on my watch, I didn't dally. It was just past 10 a.m., the time I agreed to meet Nik. Consequently, I increased my pace as I left the downtown area until I reached Brooklin Bridge. I looked around since Nik and his father were not there.

The Pancake Church parking lot was across the road where I saw a flurry of activity. Three large propane barbecues and an even larger smoker were being moved to the edge of the pavement. The women of the Kiwanis Club were not about to be outdone by the festivities downtown. They also had a Billyfest cloth sign, albeit hand-painted. Beside it was a large two-sided chalkboard revealing the menu: burgers, hotdogs and fries at a reasonable price and smoked brisket or roast chicken for those willing to pay a premium.

I heard a whistle drawing my attention back to the near side of the road. There was a wide "Welcome to Grand Valley" sign a few yards from the bridge, and I now saw Nik's face peeking out from behind it. When I made my way to him, I saw his father bent over painting letters at the bottom of the wooden sign mounted to the top of a short, stone wall. The background on the sign was white with a forest green border, the same colour as the lettering.

What was new was a second smaller wooden sign Mayor Winters had contracted Nik's father to make. The added three-foot-wide sign was made of cedar, primed and painted the same shade of white as the larger sign, and there were raised letter across it, reading, *The Home of Billy Fixit*. Nik's father had a can of green paint beside him as he was deftly painting the raised lettering.

"I thought you'd like to see the added sign," Nik said.

"It looks great," I replied. Then, I looked at Nik's dad. "You did a great job—" In my mind, I thought the added words, —*for a Russian.*

I heard a familiar voice behind me. "Hi guys," Billy said. He came closer, inspecting the sign. "Great job, Rudy."

"I still have a protective coating to paint on top once the lettering dries," Rudy replied. "It should last for a long time after that."

Billy didn't say the words he was thinking. After the long weekend, he wanted everything to be back to normal where Grand Valley would once again be a boring country town, one free of city folk visitors. That meant the added sign would only have a purpose for a short time. It would be removed and never see the winter; he preferred it that way.

In the distance, winding down Water Street towards them, was a short yellow school bus, one of the half size variety. I saw it coming and said,

"That's weird. Why is there a school bus out on Saturday and on summer break to boot?"

Nik answered, "My mom says they're asking visitors to park at the water plant at the top of the hill. This weekend, they're not expecting too many visitors, so, they're using one short bus. Next weekend they're going to have five full size buses taking people back and forth to the downtown area and the pool grounds."

"It's going to be crazy," I muttered. It was at that moment when I realized Billy looked different. He was wearing dark-green work pants and a short-sleeved, grey, button-downed shirt, but the biggest change to his appearance was the hat he was wearing. Where, normally, we would have seen his green ballcap, a red one had replaced it. I pointed at the hat. "What's up?"

He rolled his eyes. "For the last week, I can't walk more than ten yards in town without some newcomer stopping me and asking me for an autograph. One woman was wearing black overalls just like mine. She pulled the side of the material down and back, asking me to sign the top of her butt. So I had to lose the overalls and the green hat. This is my disguise," Billy added with a snicker.

Billy and I were walking across the road, back towards the downtown, when two vehicles slowed as they were driving by. Both were filled with teenagers, and the vehicles were barely moving when they saw us. Two people in the first car and one in the pickup, stuck their heads out the windows while waving their hands over their heads. They yelled, "Hi Billy! Good luck next weekend!" The girl hanging out the window asked, "Can I have a kiss?"

Billy gave them a humble wave and a grin but kept walking past the barricades as the vehicles veered up towards Emma Street. However, even there in the pop-up courtyard, as the people seated at the temporary tables heard his name, all eyes turned towards Billy.

"So much for your disguise," I said through a grin.

"Do you think your dad would mind if I hid out at your house for a bit? I have to meet my sister at noon at Frances's house, so I have some time to kill, hopefully somewhere people won't bother me."

I told Billy it wouldn't be a problem whereby he put his hand on my shoulder, directing me towards O'Neil's Variety. Once inside, we picked out two sodas and two ice cream bars. Since I was with him, Billy pulled a five-dollar bill from his pocket, but Mr. O'Neil waved him away. "I won't hear of it," he said.

We were finished the ice cream bars by the time we were half way down

Amaranth Street. We were going to wait, but by the time we hit the top of Grant Street, we cracked open the drinks. As we walked by Frances's house, Billy thought to go say hi, but he remembered Frances wanted to have some time alone with Eve, so we continued past her house.

Phoebus was lying on the grass in the shade of a large maple tree across the road, but when he saw us, he rose to his feet and plodded over. As he walked beside me, my fingers scratched behind his ear. When I took my fingers away, he pushed his nose under my hand, a clear sign he didn't want me to stop.

Since I obliged his desire, he followed me up our driveway. I told Phoebus to stay with Billy until I talked to my dad who had just finished cutting the grass. Explaining the situation, I asked if we could use his man cave in the garage for a bit, to which he gladly gave his approval. I cut a path across the grass to the garage as I waved at Billy, indicating he should head in the same direction. Billy nodded his understanding, and when he began walking towards the garage, Phoebus plodded along behind him.

Both garage doors had been open all morning, so we entered on the right side where my father had his man cave. Billy sat on the couch under the side window while I diverted to the well-stocked minifridge against the back wall. I pulled out two ice-cold cokes, handing one to Billy as I sat beside him on the couch. "My dad said to make sure you get a cold drink."

Billy twisted off the cap and took a long drink. He let out an, "ahh," then added, "Your dad's a good man."

Phoebus had found a cold spot of concrete floor to lie on. It didn't take long for him to be fast asleep. We listened to his snoring for a few minutes before I asked Billy, "Will you tell me about your sister?"

"Sure, Joe." He lifted his hand up to his face, his finger and thumb spreading to stroke along the two sides of his moustache. I had noticed in the past it was something he did when he was carefully thinking about what words he would say. "Eve is three years older than I am. She lives in Halifax, and that's the place I also lived before I moved here."

"Halifax!" I exclaimed. "That's far away!"

Chuckling, Billy agreed. "It certainly is." He gave me a sideways look. "I haven't seen my sister for 33 years."

I put my cap down beside me and whistled. "Wow! Why so long? I mean, Andy and I don't get along sometimes, and we might not talk for a few days, but I couldn't ignore him for longer than that."

"And that's the right way of thinking, but sometimes things happen that don't give you many options—something bad can make you do things you couldn't have imagined doing."

"What could be that bad?"

"I had a brother as well, Joe," Billy revealed. His voice cracked every few words as he explained, "There was an accident, and he died when he was 12, not much older than you are now."

"That's terrible." My eyes were as big as saucers. "What happened?"

Billy shrugged. "It was a long time ago. The exact details didn't matter then, and they still don't matter now." He lifted a finger in the air, and his voice grew stronger. "But even when there's an accident, people involved think if they did something different, it might have changed the result. It's something I struggle with."

"Is Eve here to help you with that?"

"I'm sure she thinks she is. It's tough to know for sure because we haven't seen each other for so long; she doesn't know me very well, and I don't know her."

"Then, why is she here?" I asked.

Billy reminded me, "Remember when we talked about what it means to be friends? She wants us to be friends, again, like we were before I left Halifax."

"Friends like you and I are friends?"

He smiled. "Yeah, something like that. I'm glad we became friends, Joe." He leaned over close to me. "Since we don't lie to each other, I'll tell you, I'm not afraid to dive in the water, but all these people trying to make some kind of celebrity out of me, well, that scares the bejesus out of me."

"I'm your squire," I reminded him. "I'm here to help you any way I can."

His smile grew wider. "You help me more than you think. I forget about all the fuss and bother when I'm with you, whether we're reading or just having a coke like we are now." He paused for a few seconds, again wiping the corners of his moustache. "Don't take this wrong, but when I spend time with you, it reminds me of my childhood when I spent a lot of time with my brother."

At the innocent age I was at then, I didn't understand the negative implications he was tip-toeing around. I never would have thought he was spending time with me because of anything but the fact he liked spending time with me. It was one of the important factors that had to be there for two people to be friends—at least that's what Billy taught me.

"Next Sunday, when I go out to the diving platform, will you walk out with me?" Billy asked. "It would mean a lot to me if you said yes."

My eyes lit up. "Sure!"

"Are you really sure? There'll be a lot of people there," Billy warned.

"Oh, yeah. It'll be a hoot!"

Chapter 24: Heck of a Dinner

Eve Kendall had always been a driven person, never being idle for long and managing with an average of four hours sleep a night. When she saw a picture of Billy Fixit on TV earlier in the week, she didn't think much of it, other than it was a curious story in curious times. However, when she saw the interview, heard the voice and saw a close up of his face, her jaw dropped. Her instinct was, *That's Bart!*

The interview only lasted a few minutes, leaving her questioning herself. That in itself was not a surprise. Often, when people see or hear something they think is unbelievable, their mind tries to convince themselves what they saw made no sense, so it must be wrong. Eve went through that phase when she saw Bart, second-guessing herself, but there is always a time when you have to go with your instincts—the good old gut feel. So that's what she did, calling her executive assistant at home, telling him to book the company jet for a flight to Toronto the very next day. After all, even if she had some reluctance to believe what she saw, having not seen her brother in 33 years, she was not going to let another week go by without verifying if Billy Fixit was indeed, Bart Kendall. Either way, she needed to know.

The following day, Friday, her assistant picked her up in the morning from her home in Halifax. It was a short drive to Halifax airport's business class terminal and adjoining hanger. On the way there, she asked her assistant for the information she asked him to retrieve. He handed her a folder, and as she opened it, he gave a commentary about what she had in front of her.

"You asked for a rundown on Grand Valley, Ontario," he said. "It's a small town, what some would call a village, having a population of 1,500 people. The mayor is Tom Winters. His profile is on page two, and there are pictures of the town on pages three, four and five."

Eve flipped through the pages as her assistant provided the update. She flipped to page six to see another profile. "Who's this?"

"You asked about Billyfest, and specifically, who is organizing it. The organizers are John Robie and Roger Thornhill. You're looking at the profile of Mr. Robie, and if you flip to page seven, that is Roger."

Flipping back and forth between pages six and seven, Eve examined the content for a few minutes. Then, she muttered, "Shame really."

"What is?"

"Mr. Robie owns a media company, and Mr. Thornhill is in construction. That means Robie is a salesman and likely the person responsible for marketing. He's the one we need to focus on."

"Why is that a shame?" her assistant asked.

"Well, Mr. Thornhill is the good looking one."

Before they had finished laughing, their car had arrived at the business terminal building. As soon as Eve and her assistant went inside, she said to him, "Get John Robie on the phone—" she pointed to one of the many complimentary offices and added "—in there."

A few minutes later, her assistant was on the phone with John Robie's assistant in his Toronto office. They had been arguing for several minutes, long enough for Eve to tire of it. She snatched the phone from him and said to Robie's assistant, "This is Eve Kendall. It's urgent I speak with Mr. Robie immediately. It's about Billyfest."

"That's what I've been trying to explain to your assistant. There are so many things Mr. Robie needs to finalize for the festival; therefore, he told me not to interrupt him at all today."

"Tell him this, and he will change his mind," Eve replied, the words spoken through clenched teeth as she tried to control her temper. "Tell him Billy Fixit's sister wants to speak to him."

There was a long pause from the other end of the phone connection, and even after that there were only two words. "One moment."

It took more than "a moment." After two minutes, a man's voice came over the phone. "Hello, this is John Robie."

Her voice now changed to one of sweetness. Eve said, "I'm sorry to bother you Mr. Robie, but I live out of province, so just heard about Billy Fixit. Well, I'll get right to the point. I'm his sister, Eve Kendall, and I..."

John interrupted, "Billy has never mentioned a sister."

"I'll be in Grand Valley, tomorrow," Eve continued. "It would be a good idea for us to meet, just to ensure there are no road blocks for Billyfest."

"Road blocks?"

"Let's say 11:00 a.m.? I'll call you with the address in the morning."

There was another awkward pause. John was confused by the sudden appearance of a sister, and a sister with implied threats. A part of him was telling him to just hang up, but more than anything, he was curious to see if Billy really did have a sister. Consequently, his response was, "I'll look forward to hearing from you in the morning."

"Wonderful! And, Mr. Robie..."

"Yes?"

"Bring Roger to the meeting."

John heard a click as Eve hung up the connection. He scratched his head, wondering how in God's name she knew about Roger.

That was yesterday. Now, Eve was sitting on Frances's porch chair, with Frances sitting beside her after having a great morning together. Frances read people well, so she was right in the thought Eve would prefer a lighter breakfast of fruit and homemade muffins, although she did fry up some bacon to tempt Eve's discipline.

Just before making an early morning phone call, Eve asked Frances if she could use the parlour for an important meeting at 11 a.m. Since Frances had agreed, the result of that call was a black Cadillac pulling into Frances's driveway. She recognized John Robie and Roger Thornhill when they exited the vehicle. Frances didn't know either of them well. In fact, she didn't know either of them at all until Billyfest came about. Now, she at least knew them by sight.

Frances welcomed them when they came up the porch, introducing Eve. They shook hands, but when John was close enough, he said to Eve, "You look familiar. Have we met before?"

Providing a practiced smile, Eve replied, "No, I would have remembered." She then turned to Frances. "As we discussed, I'd like to use your parlour for a short time. Is that okay?"

"Of course...Eve." She replied with hesitation because the odd nature of the meeting was just dawning on her. It was unlikely Eve had heard of John or Roger until recently, and that meant the connection between them was Billy. Although her morning with Eve had been pleasant, she suspected she was seeing the business side of Billy's sister, one she might not appreciate near as much. Frances turned to face Eve, her eyes a darker shade Eve was seeing for the first time, the darker colouring meant as a warning for Eve to tread carefully.

Eve noticed Frances's concern, answering with a reassuring wink. It satisfied Frances to the point her manners returned. She asked the two men, "Coffee or tea?"

Both men said they preferred coffee, and Eve declined after which she led them into the parlour. Once they were seated, Eve began the discussion. "I'm not going to go into a detailed history of our family, but I will say the man you know as Billy Fixit is my brother, Bartholemew William Kendall. Our family is from the east coast. Bart—sorry, Billy—left our family when he was 18. Let's just say he wanted to spread his wings, and he never came back."

Something was still bothering John Robie about Eve. There was something about her he was missing. He said, "Okay, if we take you at face value, why did you want to meet?"

"Why, I want you to cancel this preposterous event. My brother is likely to kill himself!"

John chose his words carefully. "Eve, that's impossible. As well as the diving event, there is a fair, a country concert, camping and RV rental spaces fully booked."

She crossed one leg over the other, a casual pose, yet her face was firm, her eyes narrow. "I didn't come here all the way from Halifax to take *no* for an answer."

Frances interrupted as she brought in the tray with two mugs of coffee, cream and sugar. She left just as quickly, leaving the three of them to their discussion.

Roger thought it best to drink his coffee and let John deal with her, and John was doing just that. His mind was hard at work. *Halifax…Kendall.* Then he had it, his eyes opening wide. "Now, I know where I have seen you before—at least your picture. You're Eve Kendall of Kendall Enterprises out of Halifax!"

Roger wasn't as connected as John was, but even he was well informed about Kendall Enterprises, the largest shipping conglomerate on the east coast. He knew, just as John did, Eve Kendall, as the majority owner of the company, was ten times as wealthy as both he and John put together!

Thinking the same thoughts, John took it one step further. He just realized it was likely Billy Fixit was worth more than he and Roger were. He had to be careful dealing with Eve. "We would both lose our shirts if we cancel the events now with it being less than a week away, but even more important are our reputations. We could never recover that hit if we cancel now."

Grinning, Eve said, "I've done my research, John. Your salesmanship skills don't take a second seat to anyone. You could recover very well, especially if I cover all your financial losses. Just send me the bill, and I will make you whole for the amount."

Beads of sweat appeared on John's brow. "Even if we agreed, the issue would still be Billy. He is the one driving this event. He would never agree to cancel the dive since he's obsessed with it."

They debated the positive and negative implication of the event, or canceling it, for most of the next hour. So consumed were they with their conversation, they hadn't heard the knock on the front door or the creak of footsteps down the hallway.

As such, they were surprised when Billy stood framed in the doorway. "I was passing by and saw Roger's vehicle in the driveway, thinking, *that can't be good.*" Bobbing his head from side to side, his eyes wide and bright, he clapped his hands together. "And I was right." Short one seat, Frances brought one from the dining room. Billy sat down as Frances scurried away, satisfied he was here to participate while not wanting any part of the debate herself. Billy continued, "It sounds like my sister is trying to pay you for canceling the events." He shifted his gaze to Eve, his eyes twinkling. "Is that about right?"

"I'm just trying to look after your best interests," she confessed.

Now, he pushed aside his playful demeanour. Staying calm, his voice low, his words slow paced, he replied to his sister. "We haven't seen each other for 33 years. This is my affair, so don't mettle in it, or our reunion might be short-lived."

"Bart!" she exclaimed, reverting to the name she was familiar with.

"It's Billy. From here on, I'll always be Billy." His words might have been hurtful to his sister, so he lessened the blow with the soft look he now gave her. "I love you, but you need to stay out of this, other than supporting me. Okay?"

With her lips set in a tight line, she gave a barely perceptible nod of her head.

It had been an awkward exchange for John and Roger to sit through. Now, since it appeared over, they rose to their feet. However, Billy pointed to the couch and said, "We're not quite done."

The two men sat, wondering, since the issue seemed resolved, what else could be on Billy's mind. They were about to find out Billy's mind was not as simple as they thought. In fact, the Kendall family acumen for business and finance was about to materialize.

"I am committed to my diving event," Billy began. "But we've never talked about my fee."

"Fee?" John asked.

"Yes, a fee. It's my name being used for Billyfest. I should get a fee, don't you think?"

Leaning back in the armchair, Eve's eyes lit up. It would be interesting to see how her brother would do against the two businessmen. She would jump in, if need be, but her gut told her that would not be necessary.

"I thought your goal was to make the dive?" Roger said.

"It is, but you should think about it," Billy added. "How would the people right across Canada feel about the two of you if they knew I was receiving nothing while you were making bucketfuls of money? From what I hear, above everything else, you have a TV contract to live feed the event. That's why you hastily built that scaffold frame in the corner of the pool grounds."

John chimed in. "How about two per cent?"

"It's a start," Billy replied. "I've seen advertising going up. I bet you have a healthy contract or two."

John upped the offer. "Five per cent."

Billy looked at his sister, who nodded her chin. "I can accept that," Billy said.

Glancing at Eve, knowing her financial background, John added. "I'll have my lawyer draw up the papers indicating Billy will get five per cent of the total profits."

"That's not quite right," Billy interjected.

With a sly sideways smirk on her face, Eve was enjoying the interchange immensely. Roger and John were both squirming on the couch cushions, and both had broken out in a sweat.

"Five per cent of the *gross revenue*, not of the profit," Billy clarified. "I don't want Eve to have to deal with your accounting *mumbo jumbo*, expensing this, that and the next thing. I want it simple, so five per cent of the gross."

The mention of Eve Kendall reviewing the expenses had John's blood pressure rising such that his face was bright red. Yet, the percentage proposed would still give he and Roger a sizeable profit. "Agreed, five per cent of the gross revenue. I'll have my accountant and lawyer here with the papers tomorrow morning. Will that do?"

"Perfect," Eve interjected. "I'll be here to help and make sure nothing is omitted."

Frances had impeccable timing. She came into the doorway, asking if anyone required more coffee or tea. It gave Roger and John an opportunity to offer their thanks for Frances's hospitality, and to make their escape.

Once they were gone, Eve congratulated Billy on his negotiating skills. Eve's effort to coerce the two men into cancelling Billy's event were forgotten, and Eve, Billy and Frances had an enjoyable afternoon together. Billy and Eve learned more about each other. Since they hadn't talked in 33 years, there were many holes to fill in.

They had been sitting on the front porch for most of the afternoon. It was typical for people to be out walking on a Saturday afternoon, and in typical small-town courtesy, greetings between people sitting out and those walking by were normal. However, today, it was odd. As the afternoon went by, the number of people walking by Frances's house grew, until Billy said, "This is getting downright strange."

Then, he let out a burst of laughter. When the two women asked what that was about, he explained, "Before I left the Kovacs house this morning, I made a call to Vicki at the restaurant and told her to save us a window table for 6 p.m., for dinner."

"So?" Frances asked.

"I told Vicki I would be bringing my sister for dinner," Billy offered. "She must have told someone, and when that happened the news must have travelled like wildfire."

It was Eve's turn to laugh. "They're passing by to see me, the mysterious sister of Billy Fixit, a man mysterious in his own right!"

Clapping her hands together, Frances squealed, "The people around town must be going crazy!"

"Speaking of dinner, I better head home for a shower and fresh clothes. I'll be back in an hour," Billy said.

As he was about to rise from the chair, Frances put her hand on his arm. "That's nonsense. You keep a fresh outfit here for your Sunday dinners, and you can shower here."

Rising to her feet, Eve said, "I'm going to shower first. I've found going into the bathroom after a man can have disastrous results."

Billy's lips angled, showing the confusion on his face, and it was exasperated when Frances started laughing, holding her hand over her mouth, failing in her effort to hold it back. With her other hand, she pointed at Eve while vehemently nodding her head up and down.

Eve finished her shower, then Billy followed, finally meeting the two women back on the porch. He was wearing black work pants and a short-sleeved, yellow polo shirt, and of course, the green ballcap. He saw Eve looked great in an ankle-length summer dress, tie dyed two shades of blue, but Frances wasn't changed.

"Why aren't you dressed?" Billy asked.

"I realized I haven't given you and your sister any time alone. I'm going to sit dinner out, and I'll catch up with you when you bring Eve home later," Frances explained.

Billy protested Frances's decision, but she would have none of it, therefore, at 5:30 p.m., it was only Billy and his sister who were walking up Grant Street towards Main. It was the first time Eve had seen Grand Valley in the light of day. As they walked up Amaranth Street, he stopped them for a minute, so he could explain the tornado that caused massive damage and two deaths. He pointed at the lots where houses were rebuilt, and finally, the empty lot where the library once stood.

As they turned the corner, Eve had her hand holding her brother's arm as they walked along the sidewalk through the cordoned off downtown block. Eve took note of the "Billyfest" signs. "You're quite famous," she said through a snicker.

Billy leaned close to her and whispered, "The news of your arrival in town has spread fast. There's lots of people seated in the make shift courtyard who I know very well; they're the well known nosy contingent here to see you, not me."

They walked up Mill Street to Vicki's. Billy was surprised when he pulled on the door handle finding the door locked. That's when he noticed the sign, *Closed*. He lifted his ballcap and scratched his head when, thankfully, he saw Vicki's face appear on the other side of the glass. She unlocked the door, shooing them in. Billy introduced his sister, then asked, "Why was the door locked?" It didn't take long for him to realize something odd was happening. "Why is the restaurant empty? Saturday is your best night."

Vicki reached behind Billy and relocked the front door, then she turned to face him. Her face was white, emphasizing the few creases she had. "I'm sorry Billy, but when you told me your sister was coming down for dinner, Melanie Vortman was sitting right there on that stool. She asked me, 'Who was that on the phone?' I told her Billy and her sister are coming for dinner before I even thought about what was coming out of my stupid mouth. She said she didn't know Billy had a sister, and that's when I realized, I didn't know you had a sister either. So, right then…"

Billy put his hand on Vicki's shoulder. "It's okay, but why's the place empty?"

She slapped her hand down the apron she wore. "It wasn't like this an hour ago. The place was full up, and I had a lineup outside. I never have a lineup," Vicki mumbled. Her eyes came up to Billy's and she gave him a sinister smile. "I kicked them all out! Told them I was closed for the night! Nosy, good for nothing people."

Eve laughed and said, "I like you already."

Vicki turned, waving her hand across the restaurant. "Sit wherever you like!"

Considering Vicki's words, Billy thought it advisable to sit at a booth near the middle of the room, mainly because it kept them further away from the windows and prying eyes. They ordered drinks, and Eve agreed with Billy's recommendation for Vicki's fish and chips specialty. Being from Halifax, she was preferential towards seafood in any case. While they ate, they continued to have quiet conversation while Vicki kept out of the way, keeping to the kitchen and backroom area. They were having coffee, when Eve broached a difficult topic.

Eve said, "After Malcolm died, I should have paid you more attention. At the time, I was a teenager, preoccupied with anything but family. I didn't realize father's attitude towards you was having such a large impact."

"I appreciate that," Billy replied. "But it wasn't about you. It was mainly Dad, and to a degree, Mom as well."

"It probably won't help, but I think Dad was sorry you left. He didn't show it often, but he was upset."

The words of empathy for their father hit a nerve. Billy's nostrils flared, and his voice rose. "He was upset! He was the problem, not me!"

Placing her hand on top of his, she tried to calm his anger. "You're right. It wasn't your fault."

It didn't help. Little blood vessels at Billy's temple began to bulge. He clenched his teeth, trying to hold back emotions he had held back for 39 years. Then, his shoulders sagged like a balloon with a hole in it. His gaze dropped to the table. Barely above a whisper, he groaned, "It was my fault."

Eve realized Billy was no longer talking about their father. He was talking about their brother, Malcolm. "God, no, Billy! Malcolm dying wasn't your fault. He jumped. He was always the one testing the limits. You didn't force him to jump."

His eyes narrowed as his penetrating gaze rose just as his tone did. He repeated the words, spitting them out as if there was a bad taste in his mouth. "It was my fault!"

In the kitchen, Vicki heard Billy yelling, and Billy never yelled. She felt like a rabbit hiding from a coyote under a car. It didn't take long for her to throw her apron on the counter and make a break for it. As she scurried out from the kitchen, she placed a fresh pot of coffee on the heater behind the counter. Passing the booth she said, "Don't mind me. I think I'm going to go for a walk downtown. See what all the fuss is down there. I'll be back in about half an hour." Without waiting for a reply, she left, making sure she adjusted the *Closed* sign on her way out.

Once she left, Billy intertwined his fingers together on the table. His knuckles were white, and his lips were trembling.

Eve was worried. Billy looked like he was about to melt into a puddle of raw emotions. She placed her hand on his. "Billy, Malcolm's death was not your fault, no matter what Dad said or thought."

His head hung limp from his neck as he replied. "I'm not talking about Dad. I'm saying it was my fault because I was there." He lifted his head. Tears were streaming down his cheeks. He whispered, "I was supposed to jump first."

"What?"

"No one knows this," Billy explained. "I told Malcolm I would jump first, but I chickened out, so he jumped off the cliff before me to show me it would be okay." A sob racked through Billy as he put his forehead down on the table. Muffled words came up to her. "But it wasn't okay."

Rising quickly, Eve moved onto the bench beside her brother. She wrapped her arms around him, letting him release the guilt he had felt for so many years. There was nothing more she could say to help him completely release the feelings he felt, but now, at least, she understood the reason he felt the need to dive off the platform at 27 feet. When the police investigated the scene of Malcolm's death at the quarry, they took numerous pictures and recorded every detail possible.

The math from the investigation added up. The height from the cliff to the water had been measured to be exactly 27 feet.

Chapter 25: Labour Day Weekend

It was finally here: the Labour Day Weekend; three days when the entire country would be in holiday mode. It was seen as the last summer opportunity for escape from responsibility. All you needed was a cottage, a tent or an RV, along with a two-four of beer and a charcoal barbecue. However, it was expected that between 10 and 15 thousand Canadians would forgo the typical long weekend escapades, preferring to visit Grand Valley and Billyfest instead.

By 10 a.m., Friday, I was already out the front door, riding my bike towards Main Street. There, I saw the downtown core had been cordoned off in the same manner as the weekend before. There was only a slight breeze fluttering the long, green and white Billyfest signs at either end of the makeshift courtyard. The cool breeze was a good sign for the days to come. The forecast was for no rain, and temperatures between 70 and 75 degrees. The heavy rains had come earlier in the week, consisting of a drizzle lasting a good ten hours. It was the kind of rain that coaxed the grass out of its yellow dormancy, the growing splotches of dark-green a welcome change.

I heard a sharp whistle from behind me. Turning my head, I lifted my sunglasses and saw Nik riding his BMX bike towards me. "How's things, you Hungarian slimeball?" he asked with a sarcastic grin.

Quick as a whip, I replied, "Better than a Commie on my worst day!"

The quick interaction reminded me, only true best friends could share such insults on a regular basis, then put the disparaging remarks behind them a moment later. That was the case today when Nik glanced around the courtyard. "Any action yet?"

There were only a few people in the courtyard, most making their way in and out of Foodland or Ace Hardware. These were townsfolk making last minute purchases since they knew access to the stores would be near impossible after visitors began to arrive in volume. Whether the people of Grand Valley welcomed the visitors, or were firmly against them, all knew the three-day long weekend would be a challenge for the town, likely flexing it to its breaking point. That was the case even though the mayor and the town council had passed some last-minute bylaws. The first was there would be no on street parking allowed within Grand Valley town limits, unless the vehicle had an official parking pass provided by the town. Even then, to make it easy to enforce, citizens were encouraged to bring all their vehicles into their garages or driveways. The mayor also made it known that citizens were not allowed to charge money for visitor parking on their properties. Parking on the grass was deemed illegal, and the townsfolk were warned, even visitor's cars parked in their private driveways would be dealt with severely. All this effort was to keep the town proper free of excessive vehicular traffic. These bylaws were to be effective as of 4 p.m. Friday. In addition, security personnel would be stationed at the four main access points to town. They would stop each vehicle and hand them a flyer, describing the weekend schedule, a map, and the town rules, now including parking restrictions.

It was still too early to expect a mass of visitors, but there were a few vehicles turning up the Mill Street detour. One had a storage container strapped down to the roof. Another was pulling a short tarp-covered trailer. They were obviously campers, heading for the temporary campground up on 26th sideroad. A few minutes later, a large RV followed the path of the cars, making a wide turn onto Mill Street. They would travel further north on the same sideroad to the RV grounds.

In the distance, cross corner from the bank where we were situated, was the Pancake Church. It was hard to believe, but there were seven churches in our small town. They represented different religious denominations or sub denominations. At my young age, at the time, I couldn't make sense of it, nor did I care to.

I let out a guffaw.

"What's so funny?" Nik asked.

"I was just thinking we might have to reconsider the nickname for the church," I replied.

"No, it's the Pancake Church," he clarified.

I pointed to the church where three people were dragging barbecues out to the edge of the parking lot. "Those aren't for pancakes," I said.

Nik laughed. "They're going to have lots of competition," he added. "There's going to be food trucks all over town all weekend."

He was right. One lucky truck vendor rented the one available spot in the downtown courtyard. There were two more food trucks up the hill at the makeshift parking area at the south end of town. At the north end, in the arena parking lot, three more would be located. These were in addition to two at the campgrounds, one at the RV park and four in front of the huge field being used for the country music concert.

Nik slapped me on the shoulder and said, "Let's ride up to the 26th and see for ourselves."

I agreed. We rode up Mill Street, then across Emma to Amaranth. From there, it was three quarters of a mile further to the 26th sideroad. To our left was a late corn crop, while right in front of us was a fallow field, the grass having been cut short. Individual camp sites were identified with numbers on top of stakes. One food truck was already parked there, and beside it was a running generator. Other than that, there wasn't an electrical supply in sight. The campers would need to rough it, or bring battery or propane powered devices with them. To complete the campground, off in the distance, was a line of light-blue porta potties.

We veered right on the 26th until we reached the Armstrong farmhouse set back a half mile from the road. The Armstrongs had been offered a large sum of money to allow two temporary underground electrical lines to be run from the generator station across the road, then up the length of their property. The result, looking at it now, were two lines of wooden posts with 120V weather resistant outlets on the top of them. Since one RV could park on either side of each outlet stand, there was room for 80 RVs, all told.

We biked quite a distance, and our legs were tired, so we stopped for a few minutes. Far in the distance, to the northwest, we could see the massive aluminum framework that had been erected at the back of a raised platform. That was the site of the country music concert scheduled for Saturday.

Billy and I were scheduled to be at the concert at 4 p.m. on that day, one of many such Billy Fixit celebrity appearances. John Robie and Roger Thornhill had drawn up the contract allowing for Billy's payment of five per cent of the revenue, but they insisted an appearance clause must be added. Since Billy was being paid from revenue outside of the scope of just the diving event, he needed to work for it. On Saturday, he was expected to split his time between the downtown courtyard and the country music concert with a brief autograph signing at the campground. On Monday, he was expected to be at the fair, providing a public appearance there.

At each location there were specific times when he would be available for autographs and pictures. John Robie also insisted he revert back to his signature, black denim overalls and green ballcap. After all, that's what the people wanted to see. Billy wasn't happy with the added terms, but he realized he brought the situation onto himself by asking for the payment, so begrudgingly, he signed the contract with the added tasks.

Two large trucks were driving along the gravel sideroad towards us, throwing up a cloud of dust. Nik and I pulled off through the ditch and onto the grass on the other side. The two trucks were bright red, and each carried a collapsed fair ride on the back platform. They were travelling north, past the country music stage to Old Man Wilson's farm just beyond it, the temporary location of the fair.

Nik and I biked around town for most of the rest of the day, doing the same things we would normally do. It was Nik's turn to ask his mom for a few dollars at the town office. From there we bought ice creams and sat at one of the tables in the courtyard watching the line of campers and RV's coming down Water Street. They were turning up Mill Street towards the campgrounds more frequently. Yellow school buses were mixed in, stopping in front of the courtyard, letting off visitors. As a result, the courtyard was filling with people. It was beginning. We both decided it was a good idea to leave the downtown area to the visitors. We had one last look before we put on our sunglasses and biked back to our homes.

Previously, Frances and Billy had asked me to come to Frances's house for dinner Friday evening. I had seen Ms. Kendall from time to time through the week, but I hadn't had a chance to spend time with her. After eating, we sat on the back deck where she sat beside me. She was clever and subtle, asking me many questions without seeming to pry. After her initial efforts to cancel Billy's diving event, she became vocally supportive of him as a good sister should. I liked her from the time she rolled down the window of her limousine, but her visible support for her brother settled my final verdict; I liked her a lot!

Before I left for home, Billy told me his first appearance the next day was at 11 a.m. He said he would appreciate it if I could be there with him. So the next morning, I set out, but I only made it as far as Foodland on my Chopper. I couldn't make it any further since the entire courtyard was filled with a mass of humanity. Even the sidewalks were congested, so I locked my bike to a metal bollard along the north wall of the supermarket. I wound my way through groups of people, pushing against them to the central area in front of the glass shop. Once there, a huge black man in a black suit put his hand on my chest. "That's close enough!" he bellowed.

From behind him, sitting in a chair behind a table, Billy yelled, "It's okay, Cordell! Let Joe through."

Cordell took a step back, once again taking up an alert position beside the table, his massive hands at his side, ready to manhandle any overambitious fans.

There was a long line up of visitors waiting to see Billy up close. As each person stood in front of the table, Billy politely asked them their name and where they were from. Each one of the fans placed something on the table in front of Billy: a photo, a green hat or their visitor's flyer. Each time, Billy would sign his name on the object. Even though some asked specifically for his last name on the autograph, Billy only signed his first name. He would not reveal *Kendall,* and *Fixit* was a name people in the town gave him, but it was one he never used himself.

In between the fans cycling through, Billy greeted me, then looked up at the behemoth of a man beside him. "Cordell, this is Joe. He's with me."

Cordell glanced at me and smiled, an action that made him look no older than a teenager. It was odd because it certainly was the body of a well-built man, his muscles pressing out on the confines of his clothes. I sat down beside Billy as people passed through, more than a few of them wearing black overalls, even more wearing green ballcaps. I couldn't understand it. Billy was one of my best friends, but I never thought to dress like him, or Nik, or anyone else for that matter. These people were obsessed!

Cordell looked at his watch constantly. At exactly noon, he lifted his fingers to his mouth and let out a piercing whistle, after which he bellowed, "That's it for now, Folks! Billy will be back here at 2 p.m. and at the country music concert at 4 p.m.!"

There were grumbles from the lineup, but none were about to challenge Cordell.

As Billy and I left the courtyard, Cordell followed close behind. He had been given orders to shadow Billy for the entire weekend, no matter where he went. After retrieving my bike, we walked back to Frances's house. We sat on the porch, except for Cordell who stood at attention at the bottom of the stairs. Once Frances saw this, she strode down, taking up a position facing him, her arms crossed. "Young man, I won't have you standing in front of my house like this. My neighbours will think I'm a horrible host." Cordell only managed to get his mouth half open before Frances cut him off. "Stop while you're ahead, and don't say a word. Now, get into that chair over there right away." On her last word, she lifted her hands pushing her fingers towards the big man, shooing him along.

Having no apparent choice, Cordell shuffled up the stairs only to see both Billy and I snickering. We understood his plight, both of us having been in his shoes more than once. He took a seat in the chair as Frances, her voice now exuding sweetness, said to him, "Lemonade?"

Wide-eyed, he could only nod his head, sending Frances on her way into the house. When she returned, she had a large pitcher of ice-cold lemonade and four glasses. We finished the refreshments just in time to walk back to the downtown area and the next meet-and-greet session. It was at 3:30 p.m. when Cordell pulled a small walkie talkie from his inside jacket pocket. He said a few words into it before directing us to the north end of the downtown courtyard. As soon as we arrived there, a black SUV with heavily tinted windows screeched to a halt in front of us. After Cordell held the back door open, I entered, followed by Billy. Then, the big security guard walked around the vehicle and entered the front passenger seat area.

It was only a ten-minute drive to the site of the country concert. It should have taken only five minutes, but there was heavy traffic up on the 26 sideroad. As we came closer, we could hear the music. There were ten acts booked through from mid-morning to 9 p.m. with the feature act being Brad Burton, the newest heartthrob country star out of Calgary, who would perform for the last hour.

When we arrived at the site, we took the second entry, the gravel roadway curling around behind the stage. After a security check, we arrived at the end of the driveway where ten large trailers were parked. It was obvious to me each trailer was being used by the people from each act. Still, it surprised me when I saw a smaller, white trailer near the stairs leading to the back of the stage with a sign on the front, *Private – Billy Fixit*.

Cordell led us towards the trailer, but when we were about to step inside, a man with headphones on, skipped down the stairs from backstage. "Mr. Fixit," he said. "We're running a little late. I'll come get you in 30 minutes." He seemed busy, so he didn't wait for a reply before he moved back up the stairs and out of sight into the backstage area.

Billy and I entered the trailer, but this time Cordell was insistent he wait outside the door. He whispered to Billy, "There's lots of security people around, including my boss. I need to look like I'm doing my job."

Inside the trailer was a small, comfortable living room. Curious as I was, I searched around the room and found the full-size fridge stocked with every kind of drink imaginable. I pulled out two cokes and sat down beside Billy. We enjoyed our drinks while listening to the music coming from outside the trailer.

Billy chuckled and said, "I can't believe people are making all this fuss."

"You're a celebrity now, Billy. These people are all here to see you."

"Hell, no!" Billy waved away the comment. "All these people are here for the music stars, or to have fun at the fair, or just to drink beer over at the campground."

"But it's all about Billyfest," I offered.

"Let me explain how it works. Have you ever heard the story of stone soup?"

"Nope."

He leaned back in the couch, took another drink of coke, then began.

"Back in the medieval days…"

"med...medieval?" I stammered.

"Back in the day when the *Black Knight* lived." He saw my eyes light up with understanding, so he continued once again.

"There was a peddler, what today we would call a travelling salesman, who would go from village to village trying to buy and sell anything he thought had value. People who knew him were wary because he had what they called a silver tongue. It meant he could be very convincing.

One day, he was leading his horse, through the countryside. He hadn't eaten for two days, so when he saw a thatch-roofed house in a meadow behind some trees, he walked towards it. The house was run down with broken shutters and spots of mold on the thatch. Nevertheless, he was hungry, so he knocked on the door.

A middle-aged woman, skinnier than he was, answered the door. When the peddler saw her, he asked, 'I've travelled far with no rest. Could I stay here for the night?'

The woman frowned. 'We don't like strangers here.' With that clear, she was in the process of closing the door when the man made her stop.

'I can make you some nice soup!' he suggested.

She turned back, looking him up and down. 'You don't have any food with you to make soup!'

Now, he provided his best slippery, peddler smile as he reached into the inside pocket of his tattered coat. He pulled out a shiny, pink stone with streaks of glittering silver through it. 'This is a magical stone, and with it I can make the most wonderful soup.'

'You can't make soup from a stone,' she hissed.

'But I can—since it's a magical stone,' he offered, his smile widening.

The woman thought, well I have nothing to lose, so she let the man into her house. She filled a large pot with water and set it on the hearth of the fireplace where a fire had been burning all day long. There was a short-legged chair beside the fireplace, and the peddler lowered himself onto it. The woman sat in a larger rocking chair a little further away, her arms crossed in front of her.

Once the water began a slow boil, the man retrieved the magic stone. He let it fall in the water and wrung his hands in anticipation. After a few minutes, he lifted a spoon and scooped out some of the liquid. He let it slide between his lips, and his eyes opened wide. 'This is one of the best soups I've ever tasted!'

The woman shot to her feet and said, 'I don't believe you. Let me taste it.'

The peddler shook his head. 'No, not until it cooks for longer. Then, it will taste even better.'"

I shook my head. "It's just hot water!"

Billy lifted his hand. "Shhh! Let me finish the story."

"As the stone soup continued to simmer, the man was whistling a tune, but he stopped for a moment. Barely audible, he mumbled, 'I wish I had a carrot. The soup would be even better.'

The woman was getting hungry, so she rose to her feet again. 'I have one.' She walked to a side cupboard and pulled a long carrot from it. Moving to the peddler, she handed it to him. He placed it in the soup, then tasted it again before he returned to his whistling.

Another few minutes went by, and he tasted it once more. He said, 'This soup is even better! If only I had an onion.'

The woman's stomach was now grumbling with hunger. She retrieved an onion from the same cupboard and took it to the man who immediately dropped it into the stone soup. The process repeated several more times, and each time the man said the soup would be even better if he had another ingredient. Soon, the pot was almost overflowing with vegetables including two potatoes, celery, cabbage and a parsnip. After that, it was not difficult for the peddler to convince the woman to add salt and pepper.

He took another taste, stating, "The stone soup is now ready!"

The scent of the wonderful soup had been wafting through the room, making her hunger unbearable. She jumped to her feet, retrieving two bowls, spoons and a ladle. She handed them to the man, whispering, 'I can't wait to try it.'

The peddler filled the two bowls to the rim, each one having a generous portion of vegetables. She took her bowl to her chair, where she sat, blowing on the hot soup. She lifted a spoonful of liquid, rolling it in her mouth before swallowing. She nodded her head, her wide eyes showing her amazement at the first wonderful bite. A portion of carrot and potato was captured on the second spoonful. She enjoyed that even more.

By now, with the ladle, the man had retrieved the magic stone from the bottom of the pot. The woman's pace slowed as her stomach filled. Between two bites she confessed, 'I never would have thought it. How could a pretty stone make such a wonderful soup!'

I couldn't hold back my laughter any longer. "Oh, c'mon, Billy! It was all the vegetables that made the soup taste good!"

"Of course, but the man convinced the woman the stone was the star of the soup."

Scratching my head, I asked, "I forgot. Why did you tell me this?"

"Because the soup is like Billyfest, and I am like the stone."

On one side of my face, the corner of my lips scrunched up, showing my confusion.

Billy explained, "Billyfest might have begun with just me, but it has grown much bigger. All the people are here for the concert, the fair and the fun times that come with camping. They're not here to see me. I am the stone in the soup."

I shook my head. "There'd be no Billyfest without Billy."

Our discussion was interrupted by a knock on the trailer door. The man with the headphones popped his head in and said, "It's time, Mr. Fixit."

Billy and I rose and left the trailer, following the man up the stairs into the backstage area where we watched two sisters with guitars finishing their set. There was a roar from the crowd when they waved goodbye, and as they left the stage, they slowed while walking by us. One of them gave Billy a cute smile and said, "Good luck tomorrow, Handsome."

Cordell was beside us, and I slapped his arm as I laughed; I even let out an unexpected snort.

A man who had been MC'ing the event walked to the centre of the stage with a microphone. He asked for quiet and the crowd complied. He said, "Folks, it's that time. It's time to meet the man of the hour." There was a roar of voices and whistling that interrupted him. He yelled, "Without further delay, here he is, Billy Fixit and his friend Joe!"

Billy shuffled towards the centre of the stage, and I followed beside him. As the MC handed Billy the microphone, I stood a bit behind Billy, finding a spot where I could hide but still peek around him.

The crowd was whooping and whistling cat-calls to show their approval. I think Billy just wanted to get it over with, so he raised his voice, "Hi. I'm Billy!" The roars grew louder, then subsided because they saw Billy wanted to say a few words. Billy said, "I won't take a lot of your time because there are more great acts waiting to come out and perform, and they're more interesting than I am."

From the mass of faces, a woman's voice yelled out, "We love you, Billy!"

Billy shuffled back and put his hand on my shoulder. I whispered to him, "You're doing great."

It gave him the strength to finish his last few words. "Thanks for all your support, and I'll see you tomorrow for the big dive. Enjoy your night!"

There was another roar from the crowd. At least for that weekend, Billy was their hero. I gazed out over the crowd, somewhere between four and five thousand people, and all I saw was a mix of Billy's colours. Many wore black overalls. Even more wore bright green ball caps, but no matter what the form of their attire was, it was a sea of black and green, like a massive field of tall grass waving in a soft breeze.

Billy lifted his hand and waved as the people began to chant, "Billy! Billy! Billy," each time their collective voices roaring louder. I had a wide smile on my face as I realized, Billy was wrong about his comparison to stone soup. Billy was the heart and soul of Billyfest; without him, it was nothing.

Chapter 26: The Big Dive

I thought the past few weeks in Grand Valley had been crazy, but after experiencing the masses of visitors on Saturday, I knew it was only a prelude to the insanity yet to come. Today was the day Billy would make his dive, the event people across Canada were supporting in full force. Consequently, more people would be in and around town today. Now that the country music concert was over, overnight, a large fabric screen had been erected on the stage, and a packed crowd of five thousand people was expected to watch the event from that location.

Several smaller screens were set up at the campground and the makeshift RV park, but, of course, since they had electricity available, those having televisions could watch from the comfort of their vehicles. At the last moment, CBC decided Sunday was going to be a slow news day, so they moved the *Big Dive,* as it was now nicknamed, to national coverage. Additionally, to allow the viewing to be available in all time zones, the event time was shifted back to 4 p.m.

Billy called me in the morning and told me he would be spending the morning with Eve. As we were talking, he poked his face through the curtains at the window of his apartment. Even that small movement was seen by a group of 50 fans across the road. They were all dressed in black and green, with many wearing overalls and ballcaps. Some held signs supporting Billy, and when they saw his face framed in the window, they jumped up and down, screaming as if John Lennon had just been resurrected and reunited with the Beatles.

Billy pulled away from the window, and told me, "Don't come here until after 2:30 p.m. It's already getting weird up here."

Consequently, I spent the morning at home. playing a few card games with Andy until I tired of it. Then, I watched television with my dad, while constantly glancing at the clock on the wall, the hands moving at a painfully slow pace. My impatience was interrupted by a knock on our screen door at 2 p.m. I jumped up, running for the hallway, sliding across it in my stocking feet. My mom happened to be coming down the stairs at the time, so she beat me to the door. I stood behind her as she said, "Can I help you?"

A tall man in all black, suit, shirt and tie, as well as dark sunglasses, stood on the other side of the door. His words were crisp, military style, matching his short, military haircut. "Joe Kovacs please."

I pulled at my mom's shirt. "Billy told me a car would come for me."

My mother stretched her neck and saw the black SUV in the driveway behind the man. She turned while shaking her head before taking a few steps down the hallway where my dad, sitting in the living room, could see her. "This weekend is getting stranger by the minute," she told him. "Do you believe it? They sent a car for Joe—our son, Joe!"

Without removing his gaze from the television, my dad mumbled, unenthusiastically, "Yes, very strange."

Seeing my mom clench her fists, I thought it was a good time to leave. I slid my feet into my running shoes and yelled out, "See ya later!" I was already out the door, the crack of the screen door on the frame drowning out any response my parents might have made.

It was a short drive to the High Point Apartments, but it seemed to take forever. Despite the mayor's best efforts to pre-emptively alleviate traffic congestion, the roads were packed with vehicles, and visitors paid them no heed as they walked between cars and across traffic, oblivious to the risks those actions created.

Once at the small apartment building which was attached to the pool grounds, there were security personnel and local police everywhere. Even though the flyers handed out to those entering Grand Valley clearly stated there was no parking at the pool grounds, stupid people still had to drive up and check for themselves. Also, other visitors who were destined for the fair or the concert venue, couldn't resist a drive by at the pool grounds. And, of course, they had to do so at a snail's pace, snapping pictures as they crawled by.

There was a metal fence around the entire pool ground complex with two primary entrances. The first was a main gate where buses were already deboarding fans, and the second entrance, one used for VIP's, was the one we turned into. A guard in a yellow and orange vest recognized the driver and waved us through. The vehicle was parked in front of the apartment building where I exited. I straightened my blue ballcap and pulled my sunglasses from my pocket, lifting them over my eyes as I walked along the row of doors.

Cordell saw me walking towards him and smiled wide. "Hey, Little Man. Ready for the big event?"

I lifted my hand, and Cordell gave me a solid fist bump. "I'm good, but how about Billy?"

"He seems cool. He's just chilling out inside."

I knocked on Billy's apartment door. A moment later, the door cracked open where I recognized Eve peeking through. When she saw me, she opened the door, grabbed my arm and yanked me inside. She slammed the door behind me, the entire process taking no more than three seconds.

When she first opened the door, she looked worried, but now she smiled and welcomed me. Billy had a large studio apartment, and he was sitting in his favorite chair with his feet up on a footstool. I couldn't help it as I burst out laughing. Billy was wrapped in a new black bathrobe, wearing flip flops on his feet, and his old, faded green ballcap was angled on his head. His favorite chair was a matched set, so I sat in the twin chair beside him. He greeted me as he always did, but after that, there were a few moments of awkward silence. Finally, I said, "You ready?"

"Sure," he replied as he straightened up in the chair. He reached onto the table between the two chairs, retrieving a book. He threw it in my lap and said, "*Gulliver's Travels*. It's the next book we'll read."

Billy had a digital clock in his room. I saw we still had over an hour to kill, and he seemed to be struggling for conversation, so I said, "Why don't we start now! We have some time."

Before he could object, I opened the book and began reading chapter one. He read chapter two, and we went back and forth as we always did. While Billy was reading, I noticed Eve, sitting at the small kitchen table on the opposite side of the room. She was leaning forward, her chin resting on her hand as her elbow rested on the table. She had a satisfied smile on her face, and her face was relaxed, allowing her eyes to settle half-closed. More than once I saw her sigh, and I got the distinct impression she was envious of the relationship Billy and I had, one that brought back memories of her youth. I could see it made her happy that Billy and I were friends.

At 3:30 p.m., there was a knock on the door. It seemed Eve had taken up the responsibility of controlling access to Billy, so she once again cracked the door open. A moment later, John Robie entered the apartment. "The place is full up, Billy," he said. "Are you all set?"

Billy nodded, but that alone did not convince John. Billy saw the concern in John's face, so he added, "It's all good. How much longer do I have?"

"I'll be back for you in 15 minutes."

As John was about to leave, Billy added, "John, I won't be doing any interviews before the dive, only after."

Running his fingers back through his hair, John replied, "The people are going to want to know how you're feeling going into it."

"No interview before," Billy repeated.

I saw they were at an impasse, an awkward one, so I blurted out, "I can speak to them about Billy."

At first, John just shook his head, but he realized he needed something. "Okay kid. We'll give it a go, but make sure you do a good job. Your parents are sitting in the front row."

John left. Billy bookmarked the page before he rose to his feet. He did a series of stretching exercises that surprised me. I thought, *for an old guy, he's pretty limber.* Not only could he touch his toes, but he could put his palms down flat on the ground.

John came back and told us, "It's time."

Billy led us out where Cordell wished him luck. Once Billy passed through the gate, there was a loud roar from the fans in the packed bleachers. Billy gave a sheepish grin and provided a feeble wave. Eve saw Frances sitting on a lower bench, and she waved Eve over to a spot beside her. There was a chair beside the gate, and on it was a large, folded, white beach towel. I lifted it, supporting it in front of me as I followed Billy towards the diving platform.

I began to worry. Billy was typically a fast walker with a determined gait, but today, he looked different. Something changed once he entered the pool grounds. His steps were still determined, but they were slow, like he was labouring with a bag of cement on his shoulders. Billy lowered himself onto another chair by the platform's ladder while I continued past him to the far side of the pool. Beside the pool ladder was a third chair where I deposited the towel.

Many within the crowd were yelling out words of encouragement. On one side of the bleachers, a large group began *the wave*, standing up while raising their arms in a sequential motion. It spread to the other bleachers, and soon the wave was travelling around the pool grounds.

John Robie had told the news commentator I would be coming over, and the man was impatiently waiting in a covered booth near the back wall of the apartments. I strode over and said hello to John and Roger who were with him. The newsman came around the front of the booth with his microphone. "Folks, we're almost ready to begin," he said, the words echoing around the raised bleachers.

It took a minute, but the crowd went silent. The newsman was tall, so he leaned down and said, "You're Billy Fixit's friend?"

"Ya, I'm Joe Kovacs."

"I was told you were with Billy before he came out. How's he feeling?"

I wasn't sure I was telling the truth, but I pointed at Billy sitting in the chair beside the platform. "You can see he's pretty chill, and he's ready."

There was a whoop from the crowd. When it subsided, the newsman asked, "Is Billy worried about the dive, or are you worried?"

As I walked into the pool grounds, I had seen the two EMT's trying to be inconspicuous, just as I saw the orange and white ambulance on the other side of the fence. There were also two frogmen, one on either side of the pool, but none of these safety measures deterred my confidence in my friend. "Heck, I'm not worried because Billy isn't worried. He thinks it's going to be fun, and he says he'll come talk to you when it's all done."

The tall man rose to his full height. "There you have it! It sounds like Billy is as ready as he will ever be."

I walked away from the interview towards Billy. I told him, "It's time." He didn't rise right away, but his eyes lifted with a questioning gaze. "You can do this," I told him. Putting my one arm around him, I pointed at the crowd and whispered, "All these people are your fans, but I'm your biggest fan."

His hand flashed up, his fingers gripping my forearm. Some of the fogginess I saw in his eyes cleared, and the corners of his mouth lifted in a quivering smile. Rising out of the chair, he slipped out of the flip flops and passed me his hat. He pulled the bathrobe off his shoulders and handed it to me. I was surprised at what I saw, but not as surprised as the people in the crowd. There was a murmur from the spectators when they saw Billy was as fit as a 30-year-old athlete in their prime. His body was ripped and lean with an insanely low fat content, something I had a glimpse of before when I saw him working. If Las Vegas was providing odds of Billy's success, they would have just risen significantly.

Still, it was an odd look, as if his head didn't belong on his body, a wrinkled face behind a scraggly beard under flowing shoulder length grey hair, on top of an athlete's body. To make matters more comical, Billy had an extreme farmer's tan. His arms, face and neck were golden-brown, but half way up his biceps his skin turned lily-white, and the pale appearance continued down the rest of his body.

He turned and put his hand on my shoulder, and I wished him luck. A moment later, his gaze was searching skyward. Billy heard a screech, and now he saw a large bird in the distance. As it came closer, Billy saw it was a white and grey osprey, a huge adult! High above, it circled over the pool and landed on the top rung of the TV tower above the cameraman's cubby hole.

Billy pointed. "Do you see it, Joe—the osprey!"

I tilted my gaze up, searching. "I don't see anything, Billy."

The crowd had been buzzing in anticipation of the dive, so they didn't hear the conversation, and as a result, only a few looked, following where Billy pointed, but their search only confused them.

The announcer said into the microphone, "This is it, everyone. It's time for the big event."

The words snapped Billy out of the glossy-eyed look he had, but as he climbed the ladder, his eyes remained fixed on the top of the TV tower. Once again, his pace was slow, like the bag of cement was still weighing him down. Eventually, he arrived at the top where he waved at the crowd while continuing to gaze at a spot just above the cameraman. Billy walked out to the front edge of the platform and looked down at the crystal-clear water. For the most part, the crowd had quietened, but there were a few shouts of encouragement. They reminded Billy of the teenagers who shouted at him from the raft at the quarry. Backing away, he grasped the side railing with both hands and closed his eyes tight. He was frozen there until he heard another screech from the TV tower, bringing him back to the present.

Ten feet away from the front edge of the diving platform, he took a starter's stance. There was complete silence in the bleachers, and likely the same silence pervaded Grand Valley and much of Canada as people were holding their breaths in front of their TV sets. But Billy rose up and took a deep breath before walking to the edge of the platform, looking down for a second time.

There were a few more yells of encouragement that coaxed Billy back into the starter's position, ten feet back. From my position on the deck, I could see Billy as his head swivelled, bringing his gaze to bear on me. I had my hat in my hand, but when he looked down, I put it on my head and gave him a thumb's up along with a wide smile.

The tense silence continued, so I could hear Billy when he told me, "I got this."

His eyes opened wide, and a savage, wild look came over his face as he began a slow run down the platform. This time he didn't hesitate as his toes curled over the edge, and he leaned forward. He was falling over the void, but when his body came to a 45-degree angle, he bent his knees, and thrust himself outward. From that moment, Billy appeared to be in control, but then his chin fell to his chest and he began to tumble forward. There was a collective gasp from those watching, but they were all to be proven wrong. Billy had made this dive thousands of times. In his dreams, every night for 39 years, he had made this dive from 27 feet. He had tried cannonballs and jack knifes, but he chose to dream this more complicated dive because he didn't need to just conquer his demons; he needed to crush them.

Billy continued the roll, keeping his legs straight as he pulled his arms down, his hands sliding down the sides of his legs, forming a perfect pike position. He continued to somersault forward, a uniform roll until five feet above the water. When his head was pointed downward, he flashed his hands forward and his feet up in a synchronized motion. As his fists broke through the water, he was perfectly perpendicular to the surface. There was barely a splash as his body continued until his feet disappeared below the water.

During the few seconds it took to complete the dive, there were mixed emotions in the bleachers and likely with the people watching across Canada. Most had expected Billy to just fall forward and manage to enter the water without killing himself. Others were watching in the same manner they would view a horror movie, anxiously waiting to see him break a limb, or worse. But now that he had completed a complicated dive, a third group arose: the conspiracy theorists. These were the people who instantly thought the entire buildup and event were a scam. Billy was really a young, professional diver in disguise, and they had all been duped!

However, no matter which group the spectators were in, their emotional experience resulted in a mass, collective rush of endorphins and the euphoria that followed. The same rush hit Billy as he burst up through the water, his body clearing the surface to his waist. His head snapped to the side with a spray of water flying off his hair and beard. At the same time, he lifted one fist in the air, while bellowing, "Yes!"

The two frogmen, at first worried because Billy did not surface right away, relaxed once they saw him. I'm sure Frances and Eve felt the same relief for the same reason. Billy was okay!

Billy swam to the ladder as the crowd cheered. He danced up the rungs onto the concrete deck where I waited for him, towel in hand. I told him, "You did it!"

His eyes were bright, and he had a different kind of smile on his face. Usually, Billy's smile was seen by the corners of his lips being upturned, but right now, his lips were parted wide, and I could see huge dimples at the corners of his mouth. He looked ecstatic!

He dried himself off while I held his hat for him. He was about to put it on his head, then he paused. He lifted it, the brim facing him. He kissed the front of it before pulling back his arm. Snapping his hand forward, he sent the hat spinning into the crowd.

Billy slid his feet into the flip flops before he paused for a second time. This time, he looked up at the top of the TV tower, having heard a shriek for a third time that afternoon. He pointed while shaking my shoulder with his other hand. "Do you see it—the osprey!"

I tried my best to see what he did. "I don't see anything."

He saw the proud bird release the top rung of the tower as it unfurled its wide wings. It swooped down before powerful movements of its wings carried it angled upward and off into the distance.

"Look! It's leaving!" he exclaimed.

Spectators who saw Billy's excitement searched skyward, to no avail. They didn't see it, and I didn't either. It wasn't important. I realized, all that mattered was Billy saw it.

Earlier in the summer, he had warned me about little white lies, but nevertheless, I slapped his arm, then pointed up in the sky. "I see it now! It's beautiful!"

Chapter 27: After

By Monday of the long weekend, most visitors had left Grand Valley. With the *Big Dive* completed successfully, most people wanted to beat the traffic back to their homes. Only the fair remained in operation, so those who stayed found their way there. Some of the hardliners at the campgrounds or the RV park, lingered as well; at least those having enough alcohol to sustain them to the end of the weekend.

On Tuesday morning, the Billyfest signs, ribbons and barricades were removed, and once again, the downtown core looked as it had before the mass of fans descended on Grand Valley. Billymania had abruptly come to an end. The rest of the Dudes and I rode up to the 26th sideroad. The grass had been chewed up by the vehicles, so now a tractor was snaking its way back and forth across the field, the plow behind it turning over the soil and any memory of the campground.

Further up the sideroad, the workers at the fair were in the final stages of packing up their rides and gaming stalls. Soon, they would be on their way to their next booking, but they would be back in mid-October for our official fall fair.

Eve stayed at Frances's house for a few days after the long weekend. She tried to entice Billy back to Halifax to become part of the family business before she left, but Billy swept away any thought of leaving Grand Valley, making it clear the small town would always be his home. Before leaving, she also explained there were a few legal matters to take care of. First, now that he had been found, he would need to sign papers giving her his proxy vote on the company's board, if that was what he wanted. Billy readily agreed. As well as the shares in Kendall Enterprises Billy owned, there were miscellaneous cash and securities in the amount of $5 million which needed to be transferred to him. Eve told him her lawyer would visit Billy in the next two weeks with the required forms. She added, she would also be back to visit on a regular basis.

Billy had been occupied with Eve for most of the week following the long weekend. I knew her departure would be difficult for both of them, so

I didn't interrupt their time together. However, I was sitting in the kitchen having lunch, one day, when I heard a knock on the screen door. I rose and when I arrived at the door, I saw a thin man on the other side of the screen. He was wearing white running shoes, blue jeans and a bright-green polo shirt. Through the screen, I asked, "Can I help you?"

The man said, "Joe, it's me."

"Holy…" I made a point not to swear around adults, but the situation had me losing all control, so a really bad word burst forth. The man was Billy! He was clean shaven and his grey hair was cut short, neatly parted at the side. I opened the screen door and let him in.

At first, I thought his smile looked silly because it was missing the surrounding face hair, but it didn't take long for me to realize Billy was having difficulty coming to terms with his new appearance just as much as I was. Once I thought about it, it wasn't hard to see the awkward smile was him overcompensating. "What do you think?"

I didn't tell him what I really thought because he might take offence. The Billy I knew who had been hiding behind his beard and moustache for all his life looked much older than the Billy who stood in front of me. Now, with the cheeky smile, he looked much younger than his 51 years.

That was the first of many changes those of us close to Billy saw in him. A week after the reveal of his new appearance, he asked Frances Stevens to marry him, to which she immediately agreed. The *Big Dive* had changed Billy. Whatever demons he had carried were gone, and you could see in his now purposeful gait, the brightness in his eyes and his new found confidence, the man we knew as Billy Fixit was gone. A new man, Billy Kendall, had emerged.

It took a few more weeks for the finances of Billyfest to be consolidated. Once that process was completed, Roger Thornhill came to visit Billy at Frances's house. He told Billy he had just left a cheque with Tom Winters along with two contracts: one was for the new library and the other for the demolition of the pool grounds. Both contracts were fully paid for out of the proceeds from Billyfest, but the contracts were still required to meet zoning and legal obligations.

He then handed Billy his cheque for five per cent of the gross revenue. Billy looked at it, seeing it was a huge amount of money. He handed it back to Roger and told him to use it at the pool grounds. Once the present, old facility was demolished, Billy told him to build a kid's waterpark on the site.

Roger was visibly taken aback. He was a businessman and loved profits and money as much as the next person, but the show of kindness by Billy was another in a long line of similar actions Roger had seen over that summer. Billy's kindness and charity finally got to Roger, and it changed him. Billy was a selfless man, caring for others more than he cared for himself. From that moment when Billy handed the cheque back, Roger made a vow to himself; he would strive to do better. He would become a better man, one worthy of being Billy Kendall's friend.

For most of the following year, Billy continued to repair things around town, but it was only previous commitments that were undertaken; no new jobs were added to his list. So in September of the following year, Billy and Frances were married at the Pancake Church. Although, I was just under 12 years old, Billy asked me to be his best man, and the entire town of Grand Valley came out to the wedding.

During Billyfest and the time leading up to it, there was a faction in town that thought, if Billy had never come to Grand Valley, all the disruptive commotion would not have occurred. However, now that construction of both the expansive new library and the impressive kid's waterpark were well underway, they conveniently forgot about the long weekend of chaos. In fact, the entire country forgot about Billyfest and Grand Valley. Some visitors still came through town on Sunday drives for a few months after the event, gawking at the pool grounds, but it wasn't the same. There was no sign of an old man wearing black overalls and a green ballcap. Billy Fixit was gone.

The day after Billy's wedding, he officially retired from repair work. Of course, he still helped with neighbourhood projects, and helped neighbours generally, but he was never again the *go to fixit guy*. He decided, he would enjoy his retirement with his new wife, making up for the time he lost before his reawakening.

In the years following, I grew into my teenage years, during which I still spent much of my time with Billy. He moved into Frances's house, and I went to their house every Sunday for dinner, often with my parents. We still read regularly, but the books were now more complicated literary works, and we often had long discussions about them well into the early morning hours.

Over Billy's time in Grand Valley, he had rarely left the confines of the town limits. Now, he felt the need to expand his experiences. He knew he would never fly on a plane, or go too far from home, but we did travel to other local towns more often, Orangeville and Fergus being his favourites: Orangeville for his new found love of the cinema and movies, and Fergus for their country market.

Eve did visit every few months. Her relationship with her brother grew, healing old wounds until it was as if the gap in their history never existed. A few times, she brought her son, Martin Kendall, the doctor, and Martin's daughter, Vanessa, who showed a keen interest in her long-lost grand uncle and the small town he lived in. I saw what Eve had originally professed in that Martin didn't have any interest in being part of Kendall Enterprises. He preferred to work helping people.

Eventually, life caught up with me. I was accepted to a university on the other side of Ontario, and soon, only my summers and holidays were spent in Grand Valley. I was in my final year and home for Christmas break when my mother asked me to run an errand to the supermarket for her. When I was coming out of Foodland, I literally ran into another person on their way in. I lifted my gaze, seeing the most attractive young woman with long blonde hair and blue eyes.

"I'm…I'm sorry," I stuttered, a bit taken aback by her beauty.

One of the oranges had fallen from my bag. She leaned over, picked it up, then handed it to me. At the same time, her face tilted before a sudden recognition came to her eyes. "Joe. Joe Kovacs!"

Now that I heard her voice, I knew who she was—almost. She was one of the twins from Emma Street, all grown up. Avoiding a name, I said, "Wow! It's been forever since I've seen you."

She laughed. "I get back home more often than Cindy does since she's in the military."

What a relief, I thought. She was Karen. We talked for a few minutes before we decided to continue our reunion at the coffeeshop. It didn't take long before we began dating, and a year after I received my business degree, we were married.

On the rehearsal night, just before our wedding day, I was determined to solve a long-standing mystery that bothered me since I was ten, but now that Karen and I were about to be married, my curiosity was at an all-time peak. During a break in the rehearsal, I pulled Karen and Cindy aside. Thankfully, Karen had long hair, while Cindy's was short, otherwise I would still have difficulty telling them apart.

Making sure no one was within ear shot, I explained to them, "Something has been bothering me since I was ten, and I need an answer before we get married."

The two sisters looked at each other, perplexed.

"When I was ten, we often played kick the can. One night, one of you

185

two kissed me behind a flowerbox. Which one of you was it?"

Both of them began to laugh.

I held a finger to my lips. "Shhh! I need to know."

After winking at her sister, Cindy lifted her hand. "That was me. I had a crush on you when I was young."

Oh, God, I thought. *I was marrying the other one. Life was never easy.*

However, in reality, life wasn't bad at all. I began a successful career in business for a financial company in Mississauga, a larger city an hour from Grand Valley. My career, and Karen's, as a nurse, kept us busy, but somehow we managed to have three children in record time. They loved Grand Valley, and since my parents and Karen's had remained there, we visited often. In fact, every year, our three kids spent their summers in Grand Valley, a custom made more enticing by the fact my parents now had an in-ground swimming pool in the backyard.

Billy and Frances were very much part of our extended family, my children calling them Uncle Billy and Aunt Fran. When my oldest son was seven, I saw Billy pull him aside. They didn't know I was watching, and it was a good thing, because when I saw Billy hand him his first comic book, it brought back fond memories and tears to my eyes.

Chapter 28: Much Later

Twenty-five years after Billyfest, I received an upsetting call from Billy. His sister, Eve, had died. Her son, Martin, had called Billy and told him his mother had a massive stroke and died instantly. I gave my condolences after which Billy asked, "I know it might be asking a lot, but I could use your help for a week or so."

I immediately told him I would help in any way I could. As it was, I had some vacation time owed me, so I told him I would be up to Grand Valley the following morning. When I arrived at Billy and Frances's house, my parents were already there. After a few minutes of greeting, Billy and I made our way to the parlour for a private discussion.

Billy, now 76 years old, said, "I have to go to the funeral in Halifax this coming weekend. Frances's health would make that long a trip difficult for her. I was hoping you would come with me."

At first, I was taken a bit aback. It was a lot to ask, but then that thought quickly passed. Billy had been there every single time I needed support, and there were even more instances where he was there to help Karen and our kids. I replied, "Of course. Do you want me to book a flight?"

He laughed. "No, I'm not getting on a plane. There's a train leaving from Union Station the day after tomorrow. We'll be in Halifax two days later."

"The train?"

"Yup. Frances booked us a sleeping berth this morning."

Rolling my eyes, I offered, "Am I that predictable?"

"Reliable, not predictable," he answered with a grin.

Two days later, we were on a train leaving Toronto. Although, I initially would have preferred a quick plane ride, once I sat in a comfortable seat in the observation car, and we were speeding across the countryside towards Montreal, I felt my whole body relax. I realized this was the first time I had been away from my wife and the kids for an extended length of time, other than through work. It made for a tranquil time, reminding me of my youth when I would spend time with Billy with our conversations leaving nothing off limits. As a result, the two-day trip across Eastern Canada was enjoyable, but the time passed quickly.

When we departed the train, Billy put his hand on my arm. I thought maybe he stumbled, but when I saw his face was pale with beads of sweat across his brow, I realized he was shaky because this was the first time he had set foot in Halifax in the past 58 years.

Outside the main entrance to Halifax Station, Martin was waiting for us with a car. It was only a 20-minute drive to his home, one I found to be humble, but elegant at the same time. Martin's family met us there, but the person who came running to Billy first was Martin's daughter, Vanessa. She, having visited Billy often in Grand Valley, had become very fond of the man she called *Uncle*. She threw her arms around Billy, sobbing, unabashed in showing her emotions even though she was 30 years old.

Although Eve Kendell was a popular and famous citizen of the city, and many people would have preferred a large funeral, Eve's desires were for a small, private funeral for family only. After the humble ceremony, I asked Billy when he would like to return to Ontario.

He told me, "Tomorrow afternoon, I have to meet with George Kaplan, the chief operating officer of Kendall Enterprises before we go. Martin will be there as well, and I'd like you to come along. I might be able to make use of your business sense. Once that's done, we can go home."

So, the following day, Martin, Billy and I drove out to the Kendall Enterprises Global head office, near the Halifax dockyards. It was a huge building, and behind it, I could see the length of the shipping docks filled with stacked sea containers. Two large ocean-going vessels were being loaded, both having the red insignia of Kendall Enterprises on their exhaust stacks. It was surreal, sitting in the car with Billy and Martin, the two men who owned the majority share of all of this.

It didn't take us long to park the car and be whisked up to the top floor of the building, then to the primary conference room. There, the nine members of the board were seated at a large maple conference table. Conspicuous by Eve's absence, one chair was empty. Billy and I were introduced to the board members. Of course, Eve had made the board members familiar with Billy, but I was a new face that surprised them.

After the introductions, George Kaplan released the other board members, leaving only Martin, Billy and I there with him. George offered his condolences before we sat, and he got right down to it. "I'm not good at being delicate," George said. "So, forgive me for getting right down to business." He glanced at Martin. "Your mother owned 35 per cent of

Kendall Enterprises. In her will, she has left this to you." He then turned to Billy. "You retain 25 per cent of the company, but what remains at issue are your plans now since your sister is no longer holding your proxy."

Martin knew George well, just as George knew of Martin's aversion to anything business related. Martin said, "You know I do not wish to be on the board, so the issue is, who do I trust with my proxy vote?"

George turned to Billy. "What are your views?"

"My view is that after this week, I will likely never be in Halifax again," Billy replied.

"Martin told me you would say that," George confessed.

Martin added, "The question then is, who will vote for us since we won't be here, and who will be the CFO of the company replacing my mother?"

George's eyes lit up. "The CFO should not be a problem. I have four candidates waiting to meet you. They are in the next room."

"That won't be necessary," Billy replied. "Martin and I had a previous discussion about this, and we have a selection for our proxy votes."

"Who?"

Martin answered, "The same person who will be the next CFO of Kendall Enterprises."

"That's impossible!" George blurted. "Candidates must be interviewed, and the board has to vote."

Martin pointed to himself, then Billy. "Between us, we own 60 per cent of the company, and we have already voted."

There was a pause. George didn't like the loss of control. "Who is this person?"

Both Martin and Billy looked at me at the same time. Billy said, "Joe Kovacs."

I had been drinking a glass of water and almost spit a mouthful of it from my mouth. "Hold on a minute!"

"I agree," Martin added through a smile.

I thought to argue, but that wouldn't have looked good in front of George. I chose to just nod an acknowledgment, and argue the point later. *Later* was in the car on the way back to Martin's house where I vehemently explained why I was not ready, and then gave a list of reasons why I was not prepared to move to Halifax.

Billy countered with the reasons he thought the job made perfect sense. "You have a business degree, and you just finished your Master's. You've worked at a financial institution for many years and are one step away from being a full partner. And you don't have to live in Halifax since we have a satellite office in Toronto. You can work out of that location, and they have this thing now—what do they call it?

"Facetime," Martin interjected.

There was no use arguing. Both Martin and Billy told me they didn't have a backup plan, at least one that provided a person they trusted. Their next best candidate was Martin's daughter, Vanessa. She was five years my junior, but she was inexperienced, having just begun her business career. I had no choice but to accept, at least until Vanessa gained some experience working her way up the ladder within the company.

I was voted in as the new CFO, and George Kaplan was actually thrilled with the selection once he saw my resume. I was also put in charge of an additional subsidiary of Kendall Enterprises. After Billyfest, Billy and Eve, through Kendall Enterprises, had begun The Kendall Foundation. It was a not-for-profit charity created to help kids across Canada. For the last 25 years, the foundation had been financing three or four projects a year. Typically, these were pools, waterparks, arenas and libraries, funded for the kids of needy communities.

When I decided to write down the story of Billy Fixit, I was 55 years old. Both Billy and Frances had left us long ago. I had difficulty with Billy's death, and I thought writing down his story would be therapeutic for me.

When Billy died, I retired from Kendall Enterprises, handing over the CFO reigns to Vanessa Kendall. Billy left half of his interest in the company to Martin and half to Vanessa, leaving control of the company with the Kendall family. I retained the position as director of the Kendall Foundation, and to this day I continue the work helping kids across the country in needy communities, many of them small ones just like Grand Valley.

Since Billy had no children, he left me his assets outside the company shares. It was enough money that I would never have to work again, nor would Karen. Some would say the money made us wealthy, but the day I met Billy was the day I became rich with Billy's friendship and love. He taught me that was something money could not compare to, and it was a concept I imparted to my children at every opportunity.

Having time on my hands, I visited Grand Valley more often than when

I was focused on my career. However, in the third weekend of May every year, I always make a special trip, and the trip had two purposes.

First, that was the time of the strawberry festival and the pancake breakfast at the Pancake Church. I was not alone at the event. Between the growing Kendall clan and my wife's extended family, we took up three entire tables outside the church.

I recall, only last year, Viggo Eckland had been sitting at the table across from us with his own impressive extended family. He had aged: bent over, bald except for a few long wisps of hair that blew in the breeze. He was telling his grandkids the story of Billy Fixit, the Billyfest Weekend and the 15 thousand visitors that descended on Grand Valley. His hands moved emphatically as he described the events, and finally he rose on unsteady feet, holding his hands together in front of him, imitating Billy completing the *Big Dive*. After he fell back into his chair, he said, "You know, Billy Fixit was a great man."

Viggo was what I would call a hardliner, a person from an age being left behind by the progressive world. It was then I realized I was also becoming a hardliner. I didn't want Grand Valley to be swamped with the internet, streaming cable or video games. I wanted Grand Valley to be stuck in the time I knew, one where you didn't have to lock your bike or be afraid of a neighbourhood dog—a town where your kids would be safe playing in front of their house after dark.

At that moment, I knew our family home on Grant Street would always be a Kovacs family home. If not me, then someone in my family would always love Grand Valley as much as I do and live in the home I grew up in.

After the strawberry festival, the next morning would find me up early with a second task I took care of every year. I gathered my small toolbox and walked towards the downtown area, preferring to walk because Billy had always preferred to walk. He said it gave him the opportunity to be sociable with the townsfolk, and today was no different as many others were out tending to their gardens or just having a morning coffee on their porches, but no matter what they were doing, they always had a wave or a few words of greeting.

When I arrived at Amaranth Street, I made another realization. The trees that Nik Luzkin had first described to me as small, having replaced the century trees uprooted by the 1985 tornado, were now massive sentinels, towering over the houses. The town was only as resilient as the people who lived in it, and the tornado had challenged Grand Valley's character, but the people had won.

Then, I walked by the library, the one built from the Billyfest proceeds. After Billy retired from *fixin*, every weekend he volunteered some time reading to young children, many of the books being the same ones we had read together when he was alive. The mayor wanted to name the library after Billy, but he would have no part of that. Even though, for many years, Billy had millions of dollars in his bank account, he remained humble and downright frugal when spending on himself.

I continued across the downtown core, passing the place on the sidewalk where Billy sat beside me, signing autographs for the people suffering from Billymania. Stopping for a moment, I glanced around the town block. It had not changed much at all. The variety store was still there, run by Mr. O'Neil's son. The Ace Hardware was now a Home Hardware, and the Mac's Milk was now a Circle K. I took in a deep breath, enjoying the country air. Long ago, I realized it wasn't about a specific scent being there; rather, it was about what wasn't there. Missing was the smell from cars stuck in a traffic jam. Missing was the smell from a factory's discharge, or just the smell of sweat from people packed in lineups or in an overcrowded mall. It was much different from the smell of sweat from an honest day of working outside.

A few moments later, I walked to Brooklin Bridge and just beyond it to the *"Welcome to Grand Valley"* Sign. I moved to the far side that faced the traffic coming into town. The sign had remained white with green lettering over the years, and below the large letters was a smaller sign, likely not even big enough for people to read unless the cars stopped in front of it.

I knelt, and as I did every spring, inspected the smaller sign for wear: chips, rot and flaking paint. I would sand or chisel the defects out, filling with wood putty if need be. The original lower sign placed there by Nik Luzkin's dad had been made of cedar, lasting many years. But eventually time was too much for it, and I had the original sign replaced by an identical one. Since this sign was fairly new, there were only a few spots to fix. After those repairs were complete, I removed the small can of white paint from my toolbox. With a narrow brush I painted over the repaired areas on the smaller sign's primary surface. Then, I pulled out a similar sized can of green paint and painted over all the embossed letters on the wide sign.

Billy had always showed himself to be humble. Only the hardliners remembered him for what he did for the town. We told Billy's stories to our kids and grandkids, hoping they would continue to spread the word of Billy's exploits, explaining how one doesn't have to have superpowers to be a superhero.

I made it my goal to make sure, even in a small way, that my friend, Billy Kendall, would not be forgotten. I rose to my feet, paintbrush in hand, and took five backward steps. Just below the line, *Welcome to Grand Valley*, I read the words I had just freshly painted in green.

The Home of Billy Fixit.

A wide smile came across my face.

It was perfect.

Dear Reader:

Reviews are important to every author. We are thankful that many readers take a few moments to return to the purchasing website, in this case, Amazon, and leave a rating and a review.

If you could do so for this story, it would be much appreciated. Keep in mind, a Hollywood style review is not needed. Even a few simple words would be great.

Thanks again, and I hope you enjoyed the story.

About The Author

Zach Sheridan is a pen name I use for my literary fiction work. Under my real name, Peter Sandor, I have written eight other books, and they are listed on the next page if you are interested in science fiction. There's also a hilarious fictional comedy I had to get out of my system, so that is on the list as well.

All my books are available at Amazon in all markets, and at the second-tier sellers Amazon uses around the world.

With that out of the way, here's an intro and a little more about me.

Biography

Reading books, to many, has become a lost art. To those of us who do read avidly, we understand the draw of a good story. We understand how a well written tale makes you part of the book. As a writer of six books to date, I can tell you when I write it has the same effect, but it is greatly multiplied.

That's why I write. I enjoy being in the story, just as I write so my readers can be drawn in, in the same manner. With this as my somewhat selfish goal, I do not write stories to make money. In fact, with the publishing business being what it is today, it's a mind settling goal, allowing me to only worry about the quality of what I put to paper.

I live in Barrie Ontario, a midsize city an hour north of Toronto. My wife, Jane, is my helpful editor and partner in crime. She is the inspiration that has me coming back to my desk for the next chapter, along with my two daughters and two stepdaughters.

I believe a popular writer must be excellent in many skills required for a good book, but most excel in a minority of them. Personally, my strengths are in the plot. I take a lot of time to develop a web of interlinked threads. I enjoy leaving the reader a little baffled, at times, only to have a "holy shit" moment when the threads are pulled together. With that said, my books might not be for the very simple reader, but if you are a thinker and enjoy the challenge, give one of my books a try.

Other Books by Peter Sandor

The Wyld Wynd Trilogy

Book 1 – Wyld Wynd The Rising

Book 2 – Wyld Wynd The Unrest

Book 3 – Wyld Wynd Unleashed

The Wall Plug Boys – a hilarious adult comedy

The Talus 3 Series

Book 1 – Arctic EMP

Book 2 – Galactic Illusions

Book 3 – Forsaken Drifter

Book 4 – Time Undone

If you are interested in purchasing any of these paperbacks or ebooks you can copy the links below into your browser.

In America   www.amazon.com/stores/author/B08DMDC8TQ

In Canada   www.amazon.ca/stores/author/B08DMDC8TQ

In the U.K.   www.amazon.co.uk/stores/author/B08DMDC8TQ

In Australia   www.amazon.com.au/stores/author/B08DMDC8TQ

www.ingramcontent.com/pod-product-compliance
Lightning Source LLC
Chambersburg PA
CBHW020446270626
47155CB00022B/1687